A VAMPIRE BEWITCHED

DEATHLESS NIGHT #1

L.E. WILSON

EVERBLOOD
PUBLISHING

NOTE FROM THE AUTHOR

This is the very first book I ever wrote. I've run it through a few editors and tweaked it a bit here and there over the years, but I've never changed the story even though my writing has matured and improved because Nik and Emma will always have a special place in my heart. They were my first, and I hope you love them as much as I do. <3

This book was previously published with the title "Blood Hunger" and with a different cover.

ALSO BY L.E. WILSON

Deathless Night Series (The Vampires)

A Vampire Bewitched

A Vampire's Vengeance

A Vampire Possessed

A Vampire Betrayed

A Vampire's Submission

A Vampire's Choice

Deathless Night-Into the Dark Series (The Vampires)

Night of the Vampire

Secret of the Vampire

Forsworn by the Vampire

The Kincaid Werewolves (The Werewolves)

Lone Wolf's Claim

A Wolf's Honor

The Alpha's Redemption

A Wolf's Promise

A Wolf's Treasure

The Alpha's Surrender

Southern Dragons (Dragon Shifters & Vampires)

Dance for the Dragon

Burn for the Dragon

Snow Ridge Shifters (Novellas)

A Second Chance on Snow Ridge

A Fake Fiancé on Snow Ridge

Copyright © 2014 by Everblood Publishing, LLC

All rights reserved. No part of this publication may be reproduced, distributed, or transmitted in any form or by any means, including photocopying, recording, or other electronic or mechanical methods, without the prior written permission of the publisher, except in the case of brief quotations embodied in critical reviews and certain other noncommercial uses permitted by copyright law. For permission requests, email the publisher, addressed "Attention: Permissions Coordinator," at the address below.

All characters and events in this book are fictitious. Any resemblance to actual persons – living or dead – is purely coincidental.

le@lewilsonauthor.com

ISBN: 978-1-945499-40-1
Paperback Edition
Cover Design by Coffee and Characters

This book is dedicated to my family and their ability to fend for themselves while Mom is writing. But especially to my husband, Joe, whose love, support, encouragement, and knowledge of websites and marketing has saved me from a lot of hair pulling. I love you all!

PROLOGUE

SEVEN YEARS EARLIER

SEATTLE, WASHINGTON

"I have a bad feeling about this, Luuk."

Nikulas Kreek touched his brother's arm as he strode past on his way to the elevator, the one that would take him down to the garage under their apartment building. "I don't think you should go."

Luukas shrugged off his brother's hand. "I have to, Nik. The bitch is never going to give it up until I deal with her once and for all. Now, please, stop with all the melodrama. It's not like you to be so serious. You're freaking me out."

Nik clenched his jaw, a sure sign of his frustration. Blood brothers from before they'd been reborn, they often knocked heads out of nothing but plain old stubbornness.

But this time was different.

He tried again to convince his older brother that this was a bad idea. "You can't trust her Luuk. You *know* this. Why would you want to risk yourself this way?"

His brother ignored him, as usual, and walked toward the door.

Following right on his heels, Nik grabbed his arm again as he reached for the doorknob. "I'm telling you, now is not the time to confront her. She's up to something, Luuk!" Forcibly spinning Luukas around, he shoved his face all up into his brother's personal space, gritting out, "You are our Master. As in, the guy we need to lead us. What if it's a fucking trap?"

Luukas bared his fangs with a hiss, eyes glowing an eerie green, a warning Nik did not take lightly. He immediately backed off and lowered his eyes, breathing hard as the threat of a fight had adrenalin flooding his system.

He tried one last thing. "At least take Christian with you. As your Guardian, it's his job to protect you. Or take me. I'll go with you."

Luuk grabbed his brother by the shoulders, his aggression gone as quickly as it had come on. He gave him a slight shake. "Nothing is going to happen, and I need Christian *here* right now. And you, too. Besides, Guardian's are an outdated tradition. I don't need a fucking bodyguard."

Then he sighed. "Even if it is a trap, Nik, so what? She can't contain me and you know it. I am a Master Vampire. As in 'one with which you do not fuck.' No one can make me do anything I don't want to do. Especially not that dried-up old whore."

Nik would've laughed at that description of the forever young and stunningly gorgeous Leeha, if not for the fact that she was also extremely dangerous. More so, he thought, then Luukas liked to believe.

She'd also been after Luukas for most of her immortal life.

The two brothers stared each other down, Nik's baby blues testing Luukas' aquamarines, until Nik, knowing he wouldn't win this one, finally nodded in defeat and gave his brother a reluctant smile. "You're right. I'm probably worrying over nothing. I've just had this weird feeling in my gut all day. Must've had some bad blood or something."

"I keep telling you, bro, bagged blood is risky. You need to find yourself a nice, juicy, live vein. Preferably one belonging to a curvy little female." Luukas grinned at his younger brother, showing strong, white teeth. Smacking him hard on top of both shoulders, he turned to leave. "I'll be back in a few hours. Lock up when you leave."

Nik clenched his fists at his sides and watched his older brother saunter out the door of his Seattle apartment, casually waving in his direction.

He had a really bad fucking feeling about this.

1

Nikulas pushed himself off the ground and rose to his full height. He rolled his head on his shoulders, then looked toward the house he'd been watching.

Or rather, the female inside the house—Emma Moss.

He'd been here every night for the past week, watching, waiting, learning her habits and her routine, hoping to pick up on something that would confirm his suspicions.

So far he'd learned...absolutely nothing. Except she worked too much and seemed to be a vegetarian.

This was the first time he'd spent the entire night there, though. Usually he'd find a good vantage point in one of the trees surrounding her place right after sunset—about seven or eight at night—and he'd hang out until she went to bed around eleven. There was nothing much to see after that.

As far as he could tell, Emma was a loner. She had no family. No friends. She didn't even have a pet.

And wasn't that interesting in and of itself.

In spite of the fact he'd learned nothing to support what he knew about her, he didn't consider the past week a *complete* waste of time. Mainly because Emma Moss was fucking hot. Boring...but hot.

Even from halfway down her driveway hiding under a canopy of trees, he could see her well enough to know the female had been blessed with some good genes. Her body was lean and petite, and her face—framed by shoulder-length hair of some light, indecisive color...blond, maybe—could be on the cover of a magazine.

He'd love to be able to see that hair in the sunlight...run his fingers through it...lift it to his nose. He'd bet she smelled great with all the showers she took. One every night as soon as she came home, and probably again in the morning. She seemed to be the type.

Nik had just decided it was time to leave when he saw her bedroom light come on. Curious as to what her morning routine was, he leaned back against his favorite tree, crossed his muscular arms over his hard chest, and prepared to watch the show. His eyes followed the light trail as she made her way downstairs in the god-awful robe she always wore and walked into the kitchen and out of sight.

He waited where he was, thinking she wouldn't be there long. Probably just getting a drink.

Yup, there she goes, back upstairs, glass of water in hand.

He grinned widely, proud of himself that he'd guessed correctly, but between one second and the next, his smile turned into a scowl.

Man, I need to get a fucking life.

Emma walked across the bedroom and into her bathroom. A few minutes passed, then the lights turned off one by one as she made her way downstairs annnd...out the front door.

Nik shoved away from the tree. Shit! He needed to hightail it out of there, he wasn't ready to be seen. Besides, it was way too close to dawn. Still safe for him to be out, but just barely. He *really* needed to go.

Instead, he pulled his hood up to cover his light hair and silently moved to a more concealed vantage point behind the tree.

He watched as she strode across the porch to the top of the steps and stretched, grabbing her feet behind her—first one, then the other. Nik's eyebrows lifted when she bent over to touch her toes, giving him a full view of her ass. A pose that brought an interested lift to other parts of him, as well. She shook out her arms and legs, put her ear buds in, and headed his way at an easy jog.

As she came closer and closer, Nikulas became as still as the trees around him. Standing in the pre-dawn shadows of a large maple, he watched, mesmerized, as the most stunning creature he'd ever seen passed within mere feet of him, completely unaware of his presence.

Holy shit.

His lungs began to ache as she jogged by, reminding him to breathe, and he sucked in a big gulp of air. A second later, he wished he hadn't done that.

Her luscious scent hit him *hard*, and his body responded instantly, gums burning as his fangs elongated. Saliva filled his mouth and his muscles hardened in preparation to hunt. To feed.

Emma.

He'd spent the past week watching her from afar through the windows of her house, but nothing had prepared him for the sight, and smell, of her up close and personal.

His eyes followed her with an interest bordering on obsession. She moved with the easy grace born to a natural runner. Her...*oh yeah*...strawberry-blond ponytail bounced in the breeze, and her flawless, alabaster skin was just starting to flush a bit from the wind and exertion. He watched her cute little backside—in those tight running pants—bounce by him and out to the end of her driveway, where she turned right and headed down the rural road.

He scrubbed a hand over his mouth as he watched her.

FUCK me.

The burning of the sun's rays as it peeked over the horizon rapidly cooled his ardor, and Nik took off to head back to the tricked-out RV, about two miles from Emma's house, where he and Aiden—Guardian of Nik, Hunter, best buddy, tech wizard, and all around badass vampire—were holed up.

They'd found a clearing in a secluded area of the woods to park their pimped out mobile unit. It had started out as a Fleetwood Pace Arrow, which was worked over to include things like steel shutters over the windows, technology out the ass, weapon caches, and a souped-up engine (think *Meet The Fockers*).

Luckily for him, vampires were blessed with supernatural speed. He laughed out loud as he raced the fiery rays of the sun, feeling high off the adrenaline flooding his system and the close call with Emma. Nik barreled through the RV door like a SWAT officer, seconds away from turning into a bonfire and grinning like an idiot.

Aiden swung his chair around from the security monitors and watched, unperturbed, as his friend frantically slapped at the smoking areas of exposed skin on his arms and face.

"One of these days, mate, you're going to cut it too bloody close. And I'm the one who'll be chasing your ashes all over these bloody woods come nightfall, trying to collect enough to have a decent funeral. I will give you a brilliant elegy, and finish it just in time for Luukas to throw *me* into the sun for not doing my job of protecting you." Aiden squinted his eyes at his friend of over 300 years. "What's with the grin?"

Nik pushed his blonde hair out of his face. "Today is the day, my friend...or night rather. I'll call Emma at work and have her meet me after dark, somewhere public...that little bar down the road, maybe...and get her on our side."

"Do you know how you're going to manage that?" Aiden asked.

"You doubt my skills of persuasion, Aid? After all the years you've known me?" Nik scoffed. "Besides, how could she resist this handsome face?" He gave him his best roguish grin.

"You're sure she's the right girl? I would hate to kidnap the wrong one."

Nik stared at him. He had to be joking.

"Alright, I'd hate to kidnap the wrong one *this* time. And besides, those other times weren't really kidnappings, they were just weekend dalliances of mutual consent...for the most part."

Nik rolled his eyes and shook his head. This was a conversation for another day. Another day a long time from now. Like, never.

"It's her. I'm sure of it. There's no way she knows anything, though. She's totally clueless. As far as I can see, Emma Moss doesn't know who, or what, she is."

Aiden unfolded his six-foot one-inch frame from his chair and stretched his arms over his head. His shirt rode up, exposing a strip of flat, muscular stomach. "You really think she's unaware she's a witch? How can she not know?" He yanked his shirt down and pressed a button on the console that locked down the RV for the day. "How does she explain all of the unexplainable in her life? The premonitions? Things moving around on their own and such?"

Nik shook his head. "I've been watching her all week, man, and I'm telling you, she's completely clueless. She has no idea what she's capable of."

Aiden nodded, a thoughtful look on his face. "Well, that would explain why she hasn't gone after her sister, yet. I'll ring up the guys and tell them to prepare." Aiden turned back to grab his cell. "And then you and I need to get some rest, mate. I don't know about you, but I'm bloody knackered. And we've a busy next few days ahead of us."

2

The grass in the field has grown above Emma's knees and tickles her bare legs. It catches on the bottom of her short, summer skirt as she runs, pulling at the flimsy material. Her sister, Keira, is chasing her, and Emma laughs as she chances a look back over her shoulder. Keira is about to catch her, so she squeals and runs faster! Behind her sister, she can see the white lights of the Ferris wheel lighting up the night sky.

It's so pretty.

The tinkling of the carnival music fades as she and Keira run toward their car parked by the edge of the field. Laughing, they zigzag through the grass, trying to catch each other, stumbling every so often on the uneven ground.

Emma glances back again to find Keira has stopped running. The stuffed dog Emma won for her hangs limply at her side. Out of breath and giggling, Emma shoves her hair out of her face and stops, too.

"Come on, Keira!" Emma shouts, but her sister doesn't move, doesn't look at her. Gradually, Emma's smile fades.

Keira's eyes are white-ringed with terror.

Emma stares at her, confused. "Keira? What's the matter?"

The hair on the back of her neck lifts straight up. Someone, or something, is behind her. Something that has scared her normally brave sister into immobility.

Slowly, reluctantly, she turns around to face this thing that has so rudely intruded upon their night. The first fun time they'd had in the months since their parents died.

The sight before her takes a few seconds to sink in, as it's made from the stuff of nightmares.

Staggered along the tree line are monsters. Actual monsters. Grotesque creatures with skin oozing the rotting smell of death and bleeding, bulging eyes. Their bodies are tall and muscular, yet emaciated at the same time. Powerful arms hang almost to their knees. Long, yellowed claws curl at the ends of their fingers. They wear no clothing, and their genitalia hang obscenely between their legs.

The one closest to Emma opens its mouth wide, and saliva drips down sharp, pointed teeth. It pushes its nearly hairless, distorted head forward on its neck and hisses loudly at them.

Emma screams as Keira yells, "RUN, Emma! RUN!!"

Emma got to work at 7:55am on the dot, just like she did every morning. And like every morning, she walked through the reception area with a "Good morning, Linda!"

The receptionist put the romance novel she was reading in the desk drawer. "Good morning, Emma."

Emma waved her badge over the access pad, waiting for the security system to beep before she pushed through the door and strode to her cubicle. Locking her purse in her desk drawer, she sat down to boot up her computer. While she waited for the outdated thing to wake up, she took a sip of her soy latte and tried to shake off the effects of the dream she'd had.

She worked for an independent furniture company in their accounting department. Not the most exciting career, but it suited her. The work was routine, with very few surprises, which was exactly how she liked her life.

Or so she told herself.

At 8:00am exactly, her boss arrived. Smiling broadly, he stopped by Emma's desk. "Good Morning, Emma! You look especially nice today."

She glanced down at her clothes. She was wearing her usual work attire—black pencil skirt, silk hose, black, 2-inch heels, and a forest green blouse buttoned up to her neck. A black sweater thrown over her shoulders completed the ensemble. Her wavy hair was styled back off her face, and she wore minimal makeup.

"Um. Thank you, Mark." She felt a bit awkward as he beamed at her like he'd just won the lottery.

"I have some meetings this morning, so I'll probably be here late tonight catching up on the regular stuff. Let me know when you're leaving and I can walk you to your car."

"Sure. Thanks." Truth was, Mark walked her to her car almost every night since she'd started working here a year ago.

"I'll see you then." Mark rapped her desk once with his knuckles and continued to his office.

She sipped her latte and turned back to her computer.

"He likes you, Emma," Darlene, her co-worker in the cubicle across the aisle, whispered loudly.

Emma furrowed her brow and whispered back, "Mark is nice to everyone."

"Yeah, he is. But Mark doesn't stop and say good morning to everyone, or compliment what they're wearing, or offer to walk them to their car every night." With a knowing look, Darlene turned back to her computer.

Emma frowned at the back of Darlene's gray head. She decided to ignore the comments and turned back to her computer, which had finally gotten to the log in screen. After all, Mark was married with three kids. He was just a nice guy who was gentlemanly enough to walk her to her car after everyone else was gone.

Besides, she didn't date. Not since the "bear attack." Well, other than that one small fling she'd had with a Marine who'd been home on leave. Otherwise, she hadn't been out with anyone since Keira disappeared. And that was just fine with her. She liked her life the way it was. Orderly, unexciting, and peaceful. And yeah, sometimes a little boring.

Okay, a *lot* boring. But she didn't have to worry about anyone but herself. She did what she wanted, when she wanted, and she didn't have to explain herself.

Emma gave a heavy sigh. Not like she ever really did anything except work and exercise. And on the weekends she spent her time volunteering at the Women's Center, helping victims of abuse learn skills to be able to take care of themselves and their children. Anything to keep her mind off of her lack of a sex life, and the reason behind it.

Darlene handed her some purchase orders, pulling her from her thoughts. "Are you going to sit there staring into space all day, girl?"

Emma felt her face flush. "No. Of course not. Sorry." Shoving her personal problems out of her mind, where they belonged while she was at work, she logged onto her computer and started her day.

3

Nik woke instantaneously right as the sun was about to drop beneath the horizon. That was the thing with vampires. One minute you're dead to the world—literally—and the next you're completely alert. It was kind of cool, actually. You never felt groggy or hung over. Plus, there was the added bonus of expedited self-healing. A little blood, a full day's rest, and you woke up as good as new.

He stood up, slid on some sweat pants, and twisted his torso around to crack his back. Holding out his arms, he checked out his regenerated, unburned skin.

Cool.

Across the RV, Aiden sat cross-legged on his bed, dark head already bent over his laptop.

Aiden glanced up, eyeballed Nik, then turned his attention back to his laptop. "You know, mate, I really think you need to start exercising more. You're getting downright plump with all of this inactivity."

Nik barked out a laugh, throwing his pillow at him. He missed the head he was half-heartedly aiming for, hitting the bulletproof shutters over the window above the bed instead. "You *wish* you had a body like mine, man."

Actually, although Nik was slightly taller and bulkier, they were both built like MMA fighters. And they loved to fight like them too. Plus, you know, vampires...hello? Physical appearance never changes.

He returned Aiden's once over. "I guess we could both probably use a little exercise. That is, if you think you can keep up with me."

"Pffft. With that potbelly you're getting? I'll run rings around you. Just let me check in with Dante and make sure everything is on schedule, then we can squeeze in a quick match before you go meet up with Emma, yes?" Aiden didn't wait for an answer, strutting off in his boxers toward the area of the RV that served as his mobile recon center.

Nik grabbed a T-shirt and pulled it over his head, then strolled over to the fridge to grab some breakfast. What shall it be tonight? O Positive? B Negative? Didn't really matter. They all tasted like shit, but satisfied his nutritional requirements, for the most part. He did need to drink more than he would if he took straight from the vein, but he had a great delivery service set up from one of the local blood banks, so that wasn't a problem.

He got ragged a lot by the guys, especially his brother, for his diet choice. But they could all kiss his ass. If he wanted to drink bags of plastic-flavored blood, that was his business. And at least he didn't accidentally kill anyone.

Not anymore. Fucking never again.

Throwing his breakfast in the microwave, Nik propped himself against the counter to wait, drilling holes in Aiden's back as he talked to Dante, their head Hunter. "So what's up, Aid? Everything in place?"

Aiden raised his hand and waved at him to hang on, or to shut up, or both, and finished listening to what was being said on the other end of the line. "All right, commander. Sounds good, mate. We'll see you there."

He threw his cell on the table and turned his chair around to face Nik, who reminded him, "You know Dante hates it when you call him that."

Aiden grinned. "So he says. I think he secretly loves it. Anyway, all is good! In three days, they're going to be surrounding the bitch's lair. That will give us a little time to get Emma filled in and on board. We'll meet up with Dante, Shea, and Christian so they can catch us up on what they've found there, and we can get a plan of invasion together."

Nik chewed on the inside of his cheek as he considered the time frame. "We're going to need more time to work with her. She's going to have quite a challenge ahead of her to be ready in three days."

"There is that." Aiden leveled a cautious look at his friend. "You know Nik, I'm thinking, maybe we should keep her out of the actual fighting," he suggested. "Although having some witchy power on our side would be beneficial to our cause, we really only need her to keep her sister out of our way while we get Luukas."

Nik had to agree. "Yeah, you may be right. If she's as ignorant of our kind as I think, I don't know that she'd be any good to us anyway. She won't be ready." He blew out a frustrated breath.

"Fucking Luukas! I knew when he walked out that day something like this was going to happen. I tried to get him to stay, to take someone with him. I *told* him she was up to something. But he and his fucking ego think they're invincible. And now Leeha's got him, and we have to babysit an untrained witch."

Even if she is a total babe of a witch.

Pushing his hair off his face, he voiced his worst fears, "I can't even imagine what she's doing to him...or fuck, maybe I can." The microwave beeped. Opening the door, he grabbed his bag, but he'd lost his appetite.

"He's still alive, Nik," Aiden insisted softly. "She'd be daft to kill him. It would muck up all of her plans for world domination. And, she'd have no leverage."

"But if she can kill him she wouldn't need any leverage, Aid." Nik felt uncharacteristically somber as he looked to his friend. He didn't know what he'd do if Luukas was gone. Luuk was the Master Vampire, the most powerful of them all, and leader of their council. If anything happened to him, that responsibility would fall upon Nik as next in line. No damn way he was ready for that.

Although, if Leeha could manage to capture and contain *Luukas*, and it seemed she'd done exactly that, the rest of them were thoroughly fucked anyway.

They really should've burned her when they'd had the chance.

Aiden came over and stood in front of Nik. "Look at me, Nikulas. *Look* at me." Nik lifted his head. "If anything happened to your brother, we'd feel it. All of us. You know that. Luukas is still alive."

"It's been years, Aiden." Nik's voice was strained with the effort it took him to contain his emotions. "She's had him for almost seven fucking *years*."

Aiden squeezed his arm. "But he *is* still alive, Nik."

"Yeah. Yeah, I know." *But will he be sane after all this time?*

Aiden scratched his head. "What do you think her point was? Taking him? She hasn't contacted us. Hasn't started a war. Hasn't asked for any kind of ransom, or a deal, nothing."

Nik shrugged. "I don't know." He paused. "But she can't *have* him anymore."

"Then stop with all the gloom and doom, and let's go get him. I've been waiting ages to see Leeha again." He glanced around, looking for nonexistent eavesdroppers before confiding in a stage whisper, "I kind of fancy her, you know." Aiden grinned and waggled his eyebrows at Nik's shocked expression.

"You are one fucked up vampire, Aid."

"We established that when we met, Nik, I don't know why you still act so surprised." Aiden headed toward the back. "Finish your juice bag and let me throw some clothes on. I'll meet you outside in five."

Nik really didn't know if he could stomach anything after *that* particular confession, and so he sipped at his breakfast cautiously as he reminisced about the day he and Luukas had come across Aiden, bleeding in the middle of a battlefield. They'd hit it off right away, and had been inseparable ever since.

The bang of the bathroom door announced Aiden's return. "All set?"

"Yup. One sec…" Nik tossed his empty bag'o blood in the recycle container and picked up his cell phone. He hit speed dial for the number he'd programed in earlier and waited…one ring…two rings…three rings…Had he missed her?

"Accounting, this is Emma, how may I help you?" Her soft-spoken voice finally came across the line.

"Meet me at The Vineyard. 9pm sharp. Don't be late. I have information about Keira." Nik disconnected the call, set his phone down on the counter, and followed Aiden out into the cool night, both of them barefoot and wearing nothing but sweats and T-shirts. Silently, without a word or look between them, they split up and walked the perimeter, checking for anything threatening or unusual.

All was clear, so Nik walked to the center of the clearing and waited calmly for Aiden, who was now busy doing his Muhammad Ali dance. Such a showboat, that guy. But Nik wouldn't want anyone else with him when it came to a real fight. Aiden was a powerhouse. The fact that he was a complete lunatic only brought an extra element of surprise with them.

"All right, princess, let's go." Nik raised his fists in front of his face, sinking down into a solid fighting stance. "Time's a wastin'."

"Princess? *Princess??* That would be *Queen* to you, you Estonian bastard!" Aiden charged across the clearing, arms and legs pumping like pistons. Jumping high into the air at the last minute, he caught Nik in the head with a hook kick. With barely a stagger, Nik went with it and then ducked low and caught Aiden around the waist, tackling him to the ground with a *whoop!*

In less than a second, they were both on their feet again, circling each other. And then, it was Game. On.

Taunts and fists flying, they went after each other eagerly, only avoiding face shots. They saved those for their enemies. After all, why mess up their pretty mugs if it wasn't necessary?

Thirty minutes later, Nik called a halt to the fun. "Much as I enjoy kicking your ass," he grunted, "I need to shower and get ready to go see Emma." Holding Aiden's head between his thighs in a scissor hold, Nik gave him a noogie, burning his knuckles across Aiden's head and eliciting a string of curses from said head.

Releasing him, Nik jumped to his feet and ran into the RV, laughing aloud as Aiden rolled onto his stomach in the damp grass, yelling after him, "You'll not be getting away with that, Nikulas!"

4

Emma's phone rang right as she stood up to leave work. Leaning her head back and tiredly closing her eyes, she seriously considered not answering. But then, with a heavy sigh, she picked up the receiver.

"Accounting, this is Emma, how may I help you?"

"Meet me at The Vineyard. 9pm sharp. Don't be late." a very deep, very masculine voice said. A pause. "I have information about Keira."

Emma's breath froze in her lungs as she stared unblinking at her cubical wall. Information about Keira? About her sister? Could it be? After all this time?

"Who is this?"

But the caller had already hung up. She glanced at the clock on the wall. 7:09pm. She'd get there in plenty of time.

She reached for her purse. Wait...what the hell was she thinking? She didn't know who that was on the phone. She hadn't recognized the voice, and they hadn't identified themselves as an authority of any sort. It could just be someone playing a cruel joke. It had happened a few times before when Keira first disappeared.

But that was seven years ago. Why would someone do that again after all this time?

And what if it wasn't a joke? What if it was for real? Could she take that chance? Could she believe that maybe it was an actual lead about her sister? After all these years?

You bet your ass she could.

She slung her purse over her shoulder and yelled, "I'm leaving now, Mark. See you tomorrow." Without waiting for a response, she practically ran out of the office, nearly falling on her face when her cheap heels hit the slick floor in the reception area.

She was halfway across the parking lot before Mark managed to yell from the front door, "Wait, I'll walk you out!"

"I'm good!" She waved before she tossed her bag over to the passenger seat, hopped into the driver's seat, and started her eco-friendly gas-electric hybrid. Some quick hand over hand action backing out of her parking space sent a whiff of herself into the small space and Emma wrinkled her nose...*Ew*.

Hitting the gym at lunch for her kickboxing class was a necessary evil, but the time crunch didn't give her much time to clean up afterward, just a quick sponge bath. And she'd forgotten her deodorant.

She glanced at the clock. If she hurried, she'd have time to run home to shower before she went to the bar.

Jumping out of her car, she locked it with the key fob as she ran up the steps to her porch. The keys fumbled in her hands, and she almost dropped them three times before she finally managed to get the front door unlocked.

Bursting into her house, she ran upstairs, flicking on lights as she went. At her dresser, she yanked open the top drawer and grabbed some clean underwear, then yanked out the first pair of jeans she found and threw them both on the bed.

Hopping on one foot at a time to remove her heels, her work clothes were halfway off by the time she reached her closet. She threw her clothes in the hamper and her shoes into a corner.

Spotting her comfy lavender sweater, she tossed it onto the bed with the rest and streaked into the bathroom. Keeping her back to the mirror to avoid what she would see, she turned the water on.

It was an unconscious action after all these years—avoiding mirrors.

The cool water raised goosebumps as it hit her skin. Dumping shampoo on her head, she scrubbed her hair and body with the same suds, then stood under the water just long enough to rinse. The water never even had enough time to steam up the mirror.

Dressed and (sort of) blow dried, she threw on her sneakers, grabbed a protein bar to eat on the way, and ran out the door, barely remembering to lock it behind her.

It was 8:20pm when she walked into The Vineyard, pausing just inside the door to let her eyes adjust to the dim lighting. She'd never been to this place, even though it was only five minutes from her house.

The shoddy interior looked like every other small town watering hole. Same old red, leather booths. Same kerosene lamps along the wall. Dance floor—if you wanted to call it that—on the left, complete with a drunken couple slow dancing to a fast song. Bar straight ahead.

She proceeded that way. A drink to calm her nerves sounded like a good idea. Other than the inebriated dancers and a few stragglers, the place was fairly empty for a Friday night.

She sat down on an empty stool at the end of the bar and turned it slightly sideways so her back was to the wall and she could keep an eye on the entrance.

The bartender put down the glass he was cleaning at the other end of the bar and shuffled down to her.

"What'll it be darlin?" His voice was as ragged as his gray hair. But his pale blue eyes twinkled merrily. Grabbing a cloth, he sprayed the bar with disinfectant and wiped it down.

She liked him immediately.

"I'll take a Jack and Coke, please." She set her bag up on the clean bar and made herself comfortable.

"Strong drink for such a little girl," he teased, giving her a contagious smile.

He was missing a tooth, right in front. She couldn't help but smile back.

As he shuffled back down the way he had come, Emma looked around again. Upon further inspection, she saw that although the furnishings were old and the floor was beat up from all of the boots that had trod across it, the place was at least clean.

Maybe I should come hang out here sometime. Socialize and shit.

She snorted and rolled her eyes at herself. Like *that* would ever happen.

Emma never went anywhere except work and the gym. And honestly, she was surprised she still had this job after being there a full year. Usually she didn't last at any one place more than a few months before she'd have to quit and move on, and not always because she wanted to. She'd had some really cool jobs in the past, and had worked with some really nice people.

But, inevitably, *it* would happen. She'd get irritated with someone over something stupid, a stapler would fly off their desk and into a wall all by itself, and then the sideways looks and whispers would start. Her co-workers would now be afraid of her. They would stop coming by her desk for small talk. Stop inviting her to lunch.

It would be her childhood all over again.

Once, they'd even started a petition to have her fired due to "feelings of unease and inherent creepiness."

Inherent creepiness? Emma snorted to herself again. *Really?*

Her regular workout routine helped though. She found if she wore herself out physically on a daily basis, the "incidents" happened much less frequently. So she jogged and went to kickboxing class, sometimes doing both in the same day. Unfortunately, she hadn't figured this out until after Keira disappeared. What had started out as a way to help her cope with the trauma ended up having a life-changing side effect.

The bartender shuffled her way again. "Here you go, pretty lady." His elderly hand set her drink down in front of her without spilling a drop. "That'll be $3.50. Wanna start a tab?"

"No, thank you. I'll just go ahead and pay." Emma pulled her wallet out of her bag and dug out some cash. "I'm really not much of a drinker, you know. Just needed something to calm my nerves." She handed him a five. "Keep the change."

"Thank you, darlin.'" He turned to ring her up. "So! What brings you into our fine establishment tonight?" Propping his elbows up across the bar from her, the old man settled in for a chat. "I don't recall seeing you in here before. Though you do look kind of familiar...."

Emma turned her stool around to face him, not wanting to be rude. Taking a sip of her drink, she revealed, "Um, I'm meeting someone here actually."

"Mm hmm." Slapping his hand on the bar, he concluded, "A boyfriend! I knew someone as nice and pretty as you had to be taken." He attempted a sad face, but with his bushy eyebrows and sagging jowls, it was more comical than sad. "Though an old man could hope."

Emma felt her face heat up at the compliment. "Well, he's definitely *not* my boyfriend. So you may still have a chance." She winked at him.

"Is that right? In that case, let me buy you a drink."

Emma laughed as he turned around, pretending to look for the bartender. She was glad for the banter, it took her mind off of her nervousness. "Actually, I don't really know who it is I'm meeting here, other than the fact that it's a man. Someone called me saying they had information about my sister, who's been missing..." She dwindled off, not sure why she was sharing, other than it felt good to talk to someone.

He scrutinized her for a moment with his cloudy eyes, and then suddenly they sharpened with recognition. "You're Emma Moss! That's where I've seen you before. And it's your older sister, Keira, who's still missing, right?" He nodded to himself. "I remember now. I volunteered on one of the search teams."

"You did? Oh." She gave him a sad, grateful smile. "Well, thank you."

"They still haven't found any new information, huh?" At the negative shake of her head, the old man gave her a sympathetic shake of his own. "That's a damn shame, darlin'. It really is. I'm so sorry." He laid his gnarled hand on top of hers and gave it a slight squeeze. "My name's Ned, by the way."

"Nice to meet you, Ned," Emma responded politely.

He gave her a small nod, then his bushy brows furrowed down. "You don't know who this is that contacted you?"

Emma shook her head again and took another sip of her drink. "No idea. I received a phone call right as I was leaving work tonight. All he said was to meet him here at 9pm and that he had information about Keira."

She glanced up at Ned with an imploring look, and felt the need to explain. "I had to come and see what he has to say. She's all I have left..." She trailed off again as the door opened behind her, and she saw the kindly bartender squint suspiciously at the newcomer.

Glancing back over her shoulder to see who it was, she felt her breath leave her lungs in a *whoosh!*

Good God. Who was that?

The male who'd just entered was every bad girl's dream, and probably the good one's, too. She could practically feel her panties hit the floor just from looking at him.

Gauging him to be a little over six feet tall, he had dirty blonde hair that fell just past the top of his shoulders, with choppy pieces that gave it a careless appearance. Piercing blue eyes glowed—almost eerily—with a life of their own as he slowly perused the room. Clean-shaven, his slightly squared jaw was strong and confident. Sculpted cheekbones and a perfectly proportioned nose finished off one of the best-looking faces she'd ever seen on a guy.

Like, seriously. He put the fashion magazine models to shame.

Dressed in dark jeans, combat boots, and a long-sleeved black knit shirt—that did absolutely nothing to hide the lean, muscular body underneath—he was the most virile man Emma had ever seen.

Yet, in spite of his Hollywood pretty-boy looks, he had a predatory air of danger around him. It surrounded him like a physical substance, permeating the room as he stood casually just inside the door. Even the drunks on the dance floor sensed it, staggering as far away from him as they could get.

This guy was trouble. With a capital "T".

Emma was still staring in awe when his gaze swung her way, locking onto her and not letting go. She inhaled sharply as those eyes roved over her face, then her neck, and down to her breasts, lingering there for a few seconds.

A hot surge of desire tightened her lower stomach, surprising her, and she felt a rush of moisture as her innermost muscles clenched in response.

Lifting slowly back up to her face, his gaze burned through her for a long moment, like he was imagining her naked and knew she'd enjoy it.

Whoa.

He closed his eyes, and she watched him lift his nose and inhale deeply like he was scenting something, or someone, as an animal would scent their prey. The corners of his perfectly beautiful lips lifted knowingly.

That smirk was like a slap in the face. What the hell was the matter with her? Emma gave herself an internal shake. A good-looking guy walks in and she reacts like a hormone-laden teenager, when she should be worrying about the meeting about her sister.

She glared at the stranger. *Thank God he's not the informant. He's not supposed to be here until 9pm, and it was only—*

Emma jumped down from her stool and straightened her spine as the Greek god started walking—no, *prowling*—directly toward her. As he got closer, she took a deep, bracing breath and steeled her spine even more, determined not to let him affect her. He didn't stop until he was so close, she could feel the heat from his body.

"Hello, Emma."

5

Nik arrived at the local dive a little early for his appointment with Emma. Since it wasn't a personal residence, no invitation was needed, and he entered without any trouble. Pausing just over the threshold, he checked the place out, memorizing where the exits were out of habit. It wasn't hard. There were only two.

He wasn't surprised at the lack of a Friday night crowd. Places like this catered to regular customers who lived in the area. No one else would drive so far out of the way to get to such a small-town dive. It was one reason he had told Emma to meet him here. Without the crowd, they'd be able to talk.

She sat at the end of the bar. He let his eyes wander over her face and down to what he could see of her body. She was stunning in a simple sweater and jeans. Her hair fell in natural waves just to her shoulders, and his fingers itched to touch the bright strands, to see if they were as soft as they looked. Her cheeks were slightly flushed as she stared at him, wide-eyed. Her lips were slightly parted, her breathing shallow.

He imagined her looking at him like that as she lay naked and open beneath him, gasping as he pumped into her hot little body. His eyes narrowed at the wayward thought, and he felt his cock instantly respond.

As if she knew what he was thinking, her face reddened even more and he had to close his eyes a moment as he scented her body's response from across the room. He couldn't help it. He smirked at her, and saw her wide-eyed look change to a glare in response.

Was she angry at *him*, or at her body's reaction to him?

Nik allowed himself a moment more to enjoy pondering that question before reminding himself of the purpose of this meeting. The thought instantly sobered him. He headed toward Emma, and she jumped down from her stool to stand ramrod straight at his approach.

He didn't stop until there was less than a foot of air between their bodies, forcing her to look up at him as he loomed over her. She barely came to his chin, her slender form less than half his size.

His heart actually stuttered as his eyes roved over her face. Good Lord, she was lovely. So close to her, her scent nearly overwhelmed him, and it was all he could do not to scoop her up and take her with him, caveman style, back to his lair.

"Hello, Emma."

His voice was bedroom sexy. Way better in person. Or maybe she'd just been too shocked to notice when they'd talked on the phone for that brief time. Just listening to him say her name caused some very unladylike thoughts to jump, unbidden, into her head. Thoughts of popping buttons and tearing lace. Of bare skin sliding on bare skin.

She didn't even wear lace.

Emma stared at him until, giving herself a shake, she pulled her thoughts back into the here and now. Jesus, what was wrong with her? She'd never been this affected by a man, not even extremely good-looking ones.

Annoyed with herself, she stuck her chin out and demanded, "Who the hell are you, and what exactly do you know about my sister?"

He looked amused, if a bit surprised, with her directness. "Well, now, don't beat around the bush, sweetheart. Just go ahead and say whatever's on your mind."

She narrowed her eyes at him, but her insides quivered as she waited for a response to her question.

After a glance at the bartender who was still hovering near them, he suggested, "Why don't we find somewhere a bit more private to talk." It wasn't a question.

Emma studied his too-perfect face for a few seconds, then nodded once in agreement. Turning to grab her things, she gave old Ned a reassuring smile.

He took her hand as she placed it on her bag. "Darlin', you just give a yell if you need anything at all." He looked directly into her eyes while he spoke, making sure he got his point across. "And you just let me know when you're ready to leave. Alone." He gave the man beside her a pointed glare. "And I'll walk you to your car."

Men were always offering to walk her to her car. Did she really seem that helpless?

The beautiful male beside her tilted his head and looked at Ned with mild curiosity, like he would an animal at the zoo. "Do we owe you anything for the drink, old man?" he asked.

Ned shook his grey head slowly, staring him down. "The young *lady* has already paid."

Emma looked over at the newcomer just in time to catch him giving the elderly man a menacing smile.

"I'll be fine." She didn't know if that was true or not, but the bartender was no match for a guy like this, and she wouldn't have him risking life and limb because of her.

A strong hand wrapped gently, but firmly, around her arm. "Good! Come on, Emma."

Giving the bartender one last reassuring smile, she let the Greek god steer her toward an empty booth far from listening ears.

He led her to her seat, and then settled himself across from her where he kept one eye on the kindly bartender. "Would you like another drink?"

"No, thank you." She waited expectantly.

"A bite to eat? Are you hungry?"

Her nerves strung out as it was from the near confrontation at the bar, she leaned forward, got right up into his face, and slammed her hands on the table. "No! I don't want a drink! I don't want food! The only thing I want is to know is where the hell my sister is!"

Emma normally had a sense of self-preservation, but her patience with this was at an end. If he had some information for her, she wanted it. And she wanted it now.

"Calm down," he told her. "And I'll tell you everything I know."

Sitting back in a huff, Emma crossed her arms and waited for him to speak, idly wondering where her sanity had gone.

He leaned forward. "Emma, do you have any inkling of who or what you are?"

What is he talking about? "What do you mean?"

"I mean, *who* you are. Who your sister is. Who your parents were. And, more specifically, *what* they were?" He put his elbows on the table and linked his hands, drilling into her with those eyes, until she felt like he could see right down to her soul.

"I'm not sure I know what you mean..." Emma hedged, genuinely confused.

He continued to stare at her, his head tilted to the side, like he was listening to something she couldn't hear. After a moment, he seemed to come to some type of decision. "Emma, I'm just gonna put it out there. You come from a family of very powerful witches."

Well, that wasn't exactly what she'd expected to hear. "Witches," she repeated blandly.

"Yes," he affirmed with a nod.

Was this guy for real? If her family was full of witches, don't you think she would know?

She should've star sixty-nine'd him earlier, demanded more information before agreeing to meet him. Not that he had given her a choice. Clearly, he wasn't a cop or any kind of detective. Mentally unstable was probably more like it.

"I am so, so stupid," she finally admitted aloud. Disgusted with herself for falling for...whatever the hell this was, she grabbed her bag and stood to leave.

"Where are you going?" he demanded.

"I'm leaving. Obviously," she spat back at him.

"Emma, please. Sit down and hear me out." He held up a hand, halting her. "Please."

She paused next to the table. *I don't know why the hell I'm doing this.* "Fine. But I don't want to hear about whatever it is you think you know about my family. I want to know who you are. And I want to know what *you* know about the whereabouts of my sister."

"I promise I will tell you all of that, but in order for you to fully understand, I need to give you some background about my people, and about your family, that you are apparently unaware of." He waved his hand at her seat. "Please, Emma, sit down. As much as I hate to admit it, I need your help, and you need mine."

His tone sounded so sincere, it gave her pause. Slowly, she went back to her seat and sat down again, giving him a hard look. "Just so you know, giving me sad puppy dog eyes will get you nowhere with me."

His lips twitched. "Duly noted."

"Ok, wiseass, tell me about all this stuff I presumably don't know about. I'm listening." Crossing her arms again, she leaned back and waited for him to speak.

"Let me start over." He paused. "Emma, have you ever noticed any strange things that happen around you?" Another pause. "It's okay, you can trust me."

Surely, her expression alone clearly showed how much she disagreed with that comment, but just in case it didn't, she spelled it out for him. "What makes you think I would trust you with anything at all? I know absolutely *nothing* about you. I don't even know your name! Although you seem to know quite a bit about me. Or at least you think you do."

Emma had spent her entire life safeguarding her secrets from everyone except her immediate family; she was not about to give them up that easily. She didn't care how hot he was.

Or how lonely *she* was.

He ran a hand through his hair and started over again. He seemed to know he was totally blowing this. "I'm sorry, you're completely right. My name is Nik, or actually, Nikulas. Nikulas Kreek." He held out his hand.

She regarded that hand warily for a moment, and then hesitantly placed her palm against his much larger one. He closed his fingers firmly around hers.

The skin on skin contact instantly caused electric pulses to run right up her arm and straight down to her groin, where she felt a rush of wetness between her legs.

Her eyes snapped up to his, and her breathing became hindered as their gazes locked. Her heart pounded in her chest as the blood rushed through her veins.

She squeezed her thighs together to try to relieve the yearning between her legs that hadn't totally gone away since this man had entered the bar, and was oh, so much worse now.

Really, what is wrong with me?

Nik inhaled sharply, his nostrils flaring slightly, and she watched as those strange eyes of his seemed to shine even brighter. The muscles on each side of his jaw bulged out as he clenched his teeth, and his hand tightened around hers.

So. She wasn't the only one affected by the touch. Good to know.

6

Nik nearly groaned aloud as the scent of her arousal hit him. His body reacted immediately and against his will—his gums aching as his fangs descended, muscles hardening as his blood sped up to match the flow of hers. The thought of her wet and aching almost made him forget they were in a public place with watchful eyes.

He struggled to get himself under control as he clung to her small hand, fighting the hunger, the need to pierce her soft skin, afraid to move for fear of what he might do.

But then Emma abruptly pulled her hand from his, and the spell was broken. At the loss of it he curled his own hand in on itself to try to keep her warmth there.

Delicately clearing her throat, she repeated, "So, Nikulas, I ask again, who are you? Where did you come from? Because I know you're not from around here."

Nik discreetly rubbed the heel of his other hand over his throbbing erection and tried to concentrate on the conversation. "Originally? I was born in Estonia. But my brother and I, and some others in our...family, have been here quite a long time." He paused, contemplating how much to reveal about himself. "We actually live in Seattle, Washington."

"And what brings you all the way here to PA?" Emma asked.

Having readjusted himself in his jeans to a slightly more comfortable position, he focused again on her lovely face. "You."

"Me?" She scoffed. "Forgive me if I have a hard time believing you. I'm just a small-town girl living a very unexciting life. And we've never even met before tonight. How could you possibly have any interest in me?"

"Because that brother I mentioned? He's missing too. And I think he's with your sister, and I think you can help me when we find them." He held up a hand as she opened her mouth to interrupt him. "Just hold on. I'll answer your questions, but first, I need you to tell me exactly what happened the night your sister went missing. Everything. No matter how unimportant or unbelievable you think it is. You might be shocked at how little surprises me."

He watched, fascinated, as her every thought and emotion flitted across her expressive features. Doubt, confusion, hope, and finally...joy.

"I knew it!" She slammed her hands on the table again. "I knew she wasn't dead!" A full-on, dazzling smile broke out across her face, and Nik's lungs stopped working altogether.

Fucking hell. That smile—all white teeth and bright eyes sparkling with elation—lit up her entire face. He found himself unable to look away, even if he'd wanted to. It was like seeing the sun again after all of his hundreds of years of darkness.

This slip of a female was bringing out things in him he hadn't felt for…a very long time. And he didn't like it one damn bit.

Sitting back and placing a hand over his heart, like that would help it to start beating again, he blinked a few times to break the connection and attempted to disguise his reaction to her with a cough before asking, "And how did you know that?"

Emma stopped smiling and frowned at him instead. Squinting at him suspiciously, she answered his question with a couple of her own. "How do you know she's with your brother? And how do you know they're still alive?"

"Because if my brother was dead, I would feel it. Like, literally. Right here." He put his hand back over his heart. "And correct me if I'm wrong, but I think you have a similar connection with your sister."

Nik waited for her to deny it. She didn't.

"Look, I know you don't know me, and I know you have absolutely no reason to trust me. But that's exactly what I'm asking you to do."

He leaned forward again and trapped her hazel green eyes with his so she couldn't look away. "Emma, please. I need you to tell me what happened that night."

Looking away to watch the dancers, who had gone from slow dancing to *Just Like Heaven* to fast dancing to *Piano Man*, she gave him a lame story. "All I remember is being at the carnival with Keira. I remember walking through the field where everyone parked their cars, though it was pretty late so most people had already left. Ours was parked way out toward the tree line where the woods started. Next thing I remember, I was in the ER, and Keira was gone. They said it was a bear attack."

She recited the words with no emotion. Sitting back in his seat, he followed her gaze over to the dancers, who were now harassing the bartender for another drink. "You're lying." He tried, and failed, to keep the disappointment from his voice.

Her eyes whipped back to his face. "What did you say?"

"You're lying. I think you remember a whole lot more than you're letting on."

"How dare you?" she hissed at him. "Who the hell do you think you are, accusing me like that?"

Nik glanced over at the salt and pepper shakers, which had started to vibrate on the table.

"What reason would I have to lie?" she continued, completely oblivious to what she was doing. "You come waltzing in here, someone I've never even met, wanting me to give up all these supposed secrets you think I have, and when I don't say what you want to hear, you accuse me of lying?!" As Emma's voice got louder and louder, the shakers started bouncing into each other.

"I know you're lying, Emma," he admitted, distracted by the dancing tableware. "You totally suck at it."

She started sputtering, and he waved a hand at her. "Don't go puffing up at me and getting your feathers all ruffled. You do. You suck. You're a terrible liar. First of all, you couldn't look me in the eye when you told me that well-rehearsed crap you've probably been telling the authorities for years. Second, you're getting waaaay too defensive. Only liars get so defensive. And third—" With this he leaned across the booth until his face was inches from hers. "I can hear your heart. You'd fail a polygraph miserably, Em."

Emma frowned at him. Leaning back against the seat, she put some distance between them and inquired sarcastically, "You can *hear* my heart beat?" At his nod, she said, "So you *are* a dog." Then she shook her head in mock regret. "The hot ones always are."

Instead of being offended, Nik cocked his head to the side and gave her a charming smile. "You think I'm hot?"

"I am *so* out of here." Emma slammed down the remainder of her drink, grabbed her bag and stood up. "Don't contact me again." And with that, she turned and marched toward the door.

The salt and pepper flew at his head as she marched past. Nik caught them in mid-air, set them down, and slid out of the booth and followed her out. He pointed at old Ned and shook his head at him in warning that he'd better keep his happy ass right where it was.

Although he didn't look thrilled about it, the old bartender decided to be smart this time.

Outside in the parking lot, Nik ordered, "Emma! Dammit, STOP!"

"Go to hell!" Keys already in hand, she beeped her car open while still a few feet away. Wrenching the door open, she started to get in. But instead of the empty space she expected to find, she slammed into over six feet of hard-ass muscle that was suddenly between her and her escape.

Emma let out a little shriek, jumped back, and hit the inside of the car door with her hip.

"Ow!" Rubbing the sore spot, she glared up at Nik's unsmiling face. "How the hell did you do that? I didn't even hear you coming..." She snapped her mouth shut. "Know what? I don't want to know. Get out of the way, Nik."

"I'm afraid I can't do that, Emma." Putting his left hand against the door window, he caged her in. "Look, can we go back to your house?"

"What? NO! We most certainly canNOT go back to my house! I don't even *like* you! Now get out of my way before I scream. I want to go home! ALONE!"

"I'm not trying to get in your pants, Emma." His eyes roamed over her breasts before he'd even finished the sentence, and she huffed with indignation. "Not that it hasn't crossed my mind," he clarified. "But trust me, if I wanted to fuck you, you'd already be flat on your back and screaming my name."

Blood rushed to her face, and her skin flushed pink. She opened her mouth, then shut it again with an audible click.

Nik grinned, his ability to make her speechless impressing even him.

Clenching her jaw together so hard he could see the muscles jumping in her cheeks, she gave him one last, hateful look, then ducked under his arm, shoving her keys back into her bag as she stomped away again.

He closed her car door, then jogged across the pavement to catch up to her. "Emma, I'm sorry."

She kept walking, turned left on the main road and headed toward her house.

He tried again to get her to stop and listen to him. "Really, I am sorry. I don't know what gets into me sometimes."

She increased her pace.

"Hey, how about we stop all this silly bickering, and go back to your house so we can talk privately? I swear I'll behave myself."

Nik heaved a sigh as he watched her walk away. She was proving to be more of a challenge than he'd anticipated. Somehow, he'd let himself get the impression she was but a meek little thing.

Unfortunately, for her, that only piqued his interest more.

He set out after her again, the enticing sway of her hips a lure he couldn't resist, making him hard all over again. What the hell was wrong with him? He hadn't been this intrigued by a human female since Eliana.

Eliana.

God, he'd loved her all those years ago. But, it hadn't been enough to keep him from killing her, had it?

Nik stopped walking again, pain washing over him at the memory.

What would Emma think of him if she knew?

Why did he even care?

Suddenly, he heard her footsteps approaching, instead of receding. Nik's head snapped up. The sympathetic expression on her face surprised him.

Why was she looking at him like that? Did he look that pathetic? Was that *pity* on her face? Wtf? Embarrassed, he scrubbed at his face with his hands.

"So..." He cleared his throat before continuing. "Yeah, we should really get off this road and go talk. What do you say?" Trying to look as harmless as he could, he shoved his hands into his front pockets as he waited for her to decide what she wanted to do.

Conflicting emotions crossed her face while she decided whether or not to trust him. Little did she know she was coming with him tonight, whether she wanted to or not.

7

Emma didn't know what it was that made her stop and turn around, and now she wished she hadn't. If she hadn't, she wouldn't have seen the pain and sadness diminish his usual cockiness. She wouldn't have wondered what caused it. And she would never have felt the need to go to him, and offer what comfort she could.

A sound in the brush a few feet away whipped Emma's head around and made her heart hammer in her chest.

What the hell am I doing?

She was walking home down a little used, back road, in the dark, surrounded by dense forest. There were no streetlights, no light of any kind. The moon wasn't even out.

She looked left in the direction of her car, then right in the direction of her house. Finally, she looked at Nik. He was the lesser of evils, for now. Her desperate yearning for something, *anything*, he could tell her about her sister overshadowed her normally cautious nature.

"All right."

"Okay?" A surprised eyebrow lifted and a genuine smile made his face even more gorgeous. "We'll go talk?"

At her tentative nod, he glanced around.

"If you give me your keys, I can run up and get your car while you wait here, and come back and pick you up."

"No!" Emma took a deep breath to calm herself. "I'd just rather stay with you."

"All right." He turned around to lead the way.

Emma followed. "I don't like the dark is all," she clarified.

She didn't see the softening of his gaze, or hear his barely whispered, "I know."

Not for the first time that evening, Emma wondered if she'd completely lost her senses. Was she so desperate, or stupid, to believe some stranger would just show up out of nowhere, after seven years, and know something about her sister neither she nor the police had found?

Yes. Yes, she was. Her sister, Keira, was really gone. Not dead, but taken. Taken by the monsters in her nightmare, for they weren't just figments of her imagination. They were real. And they'd stolen her sister that night.

The hissing one had hurtled around Emma as she'd screamed. Throwing Keira over its shoulder, its claws had dug into the backs of her legs to hold her still. As her blood ran in rivulets down her thighs, its tongue protruded from the gaping hole of its mouth, greedily lapping up whatever it could reach. Hissing a final time at Emma, it had lurched off into the woods. The last thing she remembered was her sister screeching at her to "Run!" as the remaining monsters closed in on her.

Emma had spent three months in the hospital after her "bear attack". During that time, she'd buried what had happened to her deep inside, until she could recall nothing of what had occurred after the monsters appeared. But her own injuries weren't important. What was important was finding her sister. With a determination she didn't know she had, Emma spent the following year single-mindedly searching for her sister.

She'd harassed the police, local officials, anyone she could think of. Completely useless, all of them. Angry tears pricked her eyes just thinking about it. Lifting her hand, she quickly dashed them away, and concentrated on keeping up with Nik. She was so tired of crying, tired of wondering.

After that first year, the authorities had pretty much given up, and her sister's disappearance was buried in the back of a file room with all of the other unsolved cases. But Emma wouldn't give up. Keira was all the family she had left, and she was going to find her come hell or high water.

She just didn't know what else to do.

She'd contacted the city and gotten the name of the company who'd put on the carnival, and the employees who'd been there that night. Hunting them down one by one, she'd spoken to all of them, questioned them repeatedly. Nothing. No one remembered seeing anything or anyone unusual. No one had even noticed them leave the carnival. It's like Keira had disappeared into thin air.

She'd posted missing person alerts across the country every year. She'd spent hour upon hour online, trying to find evidence these creatures existed. Again, nothing. She'd exhausted all of her resources.

She didn't know why those things had taken Keira, and she didn't know where they'd taken her, but she believed her sister was still alive. She had to believe it. Or what else would she have left?

In spite of their two-year age difference, the sisters rarely fought. In fact, they'd always been the best of friends.

Maybe because they were each other's *only* friends.

Even when they were really young, and their mom would take them to the park, they never played with the other kids. It's not that they didn't want to, but the other kids always kept their distance.

The girls never understood why the other kids acted so weird around them. They would lie in bed at night in the room they shared, long after they should have been asleep, and whisper to each other about the "mean kids". And how they didn't need them anyway. They had each other.

As they got older and started school, nothing changed. They were shunned, avoided, and sometimes made fun of. They were never invited to sleepovers, or asked out on dates. They were always the last ones to be picked for teams in PE class, and only ended up on a team at all because the teachers made them.

"Special" is what Mom and Dad told them, when they asked what was different about them.

"Freaks" is what the other kids at school said about them.

They weren't picked on, or bullied, or threatened by the other kids. If they had been, Emma would've felt more normal, but they weren't any of those things. They were just ignored. The other students, and even some of the teachers, acted like they weren't even there. It was like they were invisible, and no one else saw them. They only saw each other, and it created a bond between the two girls that nothing could break. Except death. But Nik was right. If Keira were dead, Emma would know.

And she would do whatever she needed to—even trust a complete stranger—to find her.

8

Seattle, Washington

Shea scowled as Christian threw himself onto the oversized leather couch by the window overlooking the city. He propped his head on one end and his dirty boots on the other. The only female vampire on Luukas' council, she was also the only one who cared about things such as clean furniture.

"Hey! Easy on my furniture, manwhore."

His amber eyes flashed as he sat up. "Why? It's not like *you* ever bring any dates home to see it."

Shea shrugged. His barb stung a little more than it should have, though she'd be damned if she'd let him know it. "I just like my house clean."

He rolled his eyes. "Yeah, yeah. Is Dante coming, or what? I'm really getting tired of constantly waiting on his ass. I have things to do."

"Like blow all your money at the strip club?" She plopped down next to him before he could respond, just far enough away that they didn't accidentally touch. "Let's not fight, C. Fun as it always is, we have other things to worry about right now."

"Speaking of which…like, seriously, where the hell is Dante?" He reached over and smacked her jean-clad knee affectionately.

Biting back a hiss of pain caused by his casual touch, she only said, "He's on his way up. Give him a minute."

Shea leaned forward, propping her elbows on her knees. She was tired of having this same conversation with Christian over and over again.

Christian mimicked her position, turning his head to look at her. "What the hell is up with him, Shea? You're closer to him than all of us. What's his deal?"

She sighed inwardly. It looked like they were going to have it anyway.

"I really don't know," she told him honestly. "He's been like this since Luukas was taken. Hell, we've all been affected one way or another."

"Well, sure, but you don't see me living underground like a creature of lore. We don't have to do that anymore."

"He feels safe down there…if a bit wet." Shea smiled and changed the subject. "So, who's the floozy of the moment for

Christian the Lady Killer?" She threw a hand up. "Don't tell me! Let me guess her name. Candy? Bambi? No? Wait, I know, Porsche!"

"Lay off, Shea." Christian got up and wandered over to the kitchen counter separating the two rooms. "You know you're just jealous."

Shea regarded his broad, muscular back, hunched over the counter as he thumbed through the newspaper she'd left lying there. She wasn't kidding when she'd called him a manwhore. Did he ever tire of the endless parade of females sashaying in and out of his life?

The bastard was right, though.. She *was* jealous, though she would never admit it. She hadn't had a male companion since Luukas disappeared.

Something had happened to her that day. She'd first noticed it when Nik had gathered them all together to let them know their Master had never returned from his meeting with the she-bitch. After he'd filled them in, she'd gone up to him to give him a hug, show some support. But as soon as his arms had gone around her to return it, an excruciating pain had blasted down her spine, shooting out her limbs and hitting every nerve ending along the way. She'd pulled away with a hiss, and the pain had immediately gone away. Assuring Nik she was fine with an apologetic smile, she'd hurried out of the room, and hadn't purposely touched any male since.

Strange, but it seemed to *only* be males who affected her, no matter the species. Now, she fed exclusively on females. Sometimes she even fucked them, just to have some skin on skin contact, but she'd never admit it to her comrades. She didn't need the harassment. She wasn't gay, just lonely.

And she definitely didn't want to give the guys she hung out with any fuel for their sex lives. They were like her brothers, and she'd worked hard to build that relationship with all of them. She didn't want to ruin it by stirring up their girl on girl fantasies, with her as the star.

They all seemed to be dealing with Luukas' disappearance in their own ways.

The front door was suddenly thrown open, smashing into the wall behind it. Dressed in biker black, Dante's imposing figure filled the entire frame. Tribal tattoos ran down the side of his face and neck, vanishing under the neckline of the T-shirt stretched tight across his broad chest. His chilling appearance seemed to suck all the light and air in the room into the black void that was his existence.

Lifeless black eyes scanned the room, alighting briefly onto Christian, and finally coming to rest on Shea. A tiny spark of life appeared as he gazed upon her, but was just as quickly gone.

Christian calmly raised an eyebrow. "Is that really necessary, dude?"

Dante's lips lifted into a scary semblance of a smile as he ran a hand over his clean-shaven head.

Ducking his head, Dante stepped through the doorway and kicked the door shut behind him with a thud. He didn't come any farther inside, but leaned back against the wall in a deceptively casual stance, crossing his arms over his muscular chest.

He felt too exposed here in this high-rise apartment, with all of its windows and airiness. It made him edgy.

If he thought they'd do it, he'd make Shea and Christian meet him on his own turf in the underground below the city. The parts the tourists weren't allowed to see.

No one could sneak up on him down there. And no one could hear the screams with the city bustling above.

"Ok. We're all here." Shea stood up from the couch and joined Christian at the kitchen counter.

"Have you heard from Aiden?" she asked Dante.

"Yeah. Just got off the phone with him." His voice was gravelly and harsh from lack of use. Dante only spoke when he had to.

"Well? What did he say?" Christian's impatience was obvious. "Do they have the witch?"

Dante didn't acknowledge his impertinence, directing his answer to Shea. "Leeha's back in town. We're meeting them tomorrow night. The usual spot."

Shea nodded. "Ok. Good. So, we'll meet back here tomorrow at sundown then?"

Christian slapped his hands down on the counter. "Awesome. Good meeting. You two can work out the details. I'm out. See you tomorrow."

Shea watched him fly out of the apartment, and Dante frowned as her forehead creased with concern.

"Don't," Dante told her. "There's nothing you can do. He is what he is."

Shea gave her commander a sideways glance and sighed. "I know."

"I need you to get the vehicle ready for tomorrow. Check the weapons and ammo. We'll get a plan together when we meet Nik and Aiden." As an afterthought he added, "And feed, Shea. I need you at full strength tomorrow."

"I will." She paused. "I wish you'd let me share some of these duties with Christian, instead of letting him run off all the time."

He clenched his jaw at her petulant tone. She was questioning him?

She immediately dropped her gaze to her hands, folded on the counter. "I apologize. That was uncalled for. I shouldn't question you."

Dante eyed her bowed head. Though normally outspoken, he couldn't remember the last time she'd had a bad attitude. But lately...yeah...she really hasn't been herself. Maybe she needed someone to talk to.

But, he was not that person.

He supposed he could give her an explanation if it would get her ass in gear. "I give all these tasks to you, Shea, because I know I can depend on you. Not Christian. Not Aiden. You. Christian is a good Hunter, but these days he's more interested in where his dick is going to land next. Aiden is a good Hunter, but he doesn't have your mastery of weapons. It's good to have them at my back. But you, you are different. I trust *you* with my life."

She looked up. "Thank you, Dante. That means a lot to me."

He watched her a moment, then gave her a single nod. Pushing himself off the wall, he followed Christian out the door before she got all mushy on him or something. He had no time for that shit.

9

Other than a brief "who is driving" debate—which Emma won, because, *dammit*, it was her car—Nik and Emma spent the walk back to her car and the short ride to her house in thoughtful silence.

Nik gave in only because they were burning moonlight. He needed Emma packed and with him and Aiden by dawn, and he still had a lot of convincing to do if he wanted her to come of her own accord. And for some reason he couldn't explain, he found he didn't want to force her.

Emma parked along the side of the house and jumped out. Nik followed at a more leisurely pace, locking up her car for her.

They climbed the stairs to her front porch, and Emma paused at the door. "How about we just talk out here?" Without waiting for an answer she left her bag by the door and sat down in one of the old, wooden chairs. She looked nervous, probably wondering if it had been a good idea to bring him here.

"Sure, okay." Not wanting to alarm her more by arguing, Nik took the matching chair, slouching down and stretching his long legs out in front of him.

He leaned back and gazed up at the clear sky, still amazed at how much clearer the stars were to him now. He almost felt sorry for humans. They didn't have the capability to really appreciate a night like this.

"Are you just going to sit there staring at the sky?" she asked. "Or do you think maybe you could go ahead and tell me whatever the hell it is that's so damn important, it brought you all the way out here to harass me?"

Nik smirked to himself. Apparently, being nervous made her grumpy. He gave her the same look he would give a kitten who was misbehaving, but was so still so darn cute you couldn't be angry at them.

That seemed to piss her off even more. "Well?" she gritted out.

"Yes, I will tell you." He had rethought his approach, again, on the drive over. Maybe if he appealed to her sympathetic side... "I need your help, Emma."

He picked up his chair by the arms and angled it toward her. "I know you keep trying to avoid the subject, but I really need you to tell me what happened that night."

He could practically see the wall slam down.

"I've already told you. I really don't remember very much."

She was lying again. There was more to her story than she was telling him. But why would she lie? "Are you absolutely positive there's nothing else you remember? Nothing else you haven't told me?"

She sat silently a moment, and he swore he could hear her brain buzzing as she debated whether or not to trust him. Finally, she mumbled, "You wouldn't believe me if I told you."

"I might believe more than you think, sweetheart." The endearment rolled off his tongue without thought, and he could've bitten it. Just to shut himself up. He waited for her to snap at him again, but she must have been too preoccupied with what was going on in her lovely head to notice the slip.

She shook her head stubbornly, "I don't remember anything else."

Nik took a deep breath. He needed to earn her trust before she would open up to him. So, he took a huge chance. "Emma, I'm going to tell you something. And I need you to not freak out. Okay?"

Her forehead wrinkled up adorably. "Okay."

"I think maybe you've seen some things, things other people wouldn't believe, but I will. And the reason I will, Emma, is because I am something different myself."

She looked him over. "What do you mean?"

"I'll show you, but first I need you to believe me when I say I would *never* hurt you." He looked at her intently, willing her to believe him.

Emma was starting to look anxious. "You're scaring me here, Nik. Why don't you just spit it out?"

"Yeah, all right," he agreed, and hoped he wasn't making the biggest mistake of his life.

Using his previously learned reaction to this particular female, he rose from his chair and squatted down in front of her.

Leaning in until his senses were filled with nothing but Emma, he inhaled her sweet scent.

Instantly, he felt his gums burning as his fangs shot out. His mouth watered, and his muscles hardened as his blood roared through his veins, including his now painfully swollen erection.

Sitting back down in his own chair, he opened his mouth, drew his lips back, and showed her his fangs.

At first, Emma didn't understanding why he was just sitting there with his mouth hanging open. Then she looked closer.

Are those...? Noooo, it can't be. That's impossible.

Until they lengthened even more as she stared, even as she shook her head in denial.

He slowly lifted his hands up in front of him, palms out. "I'm a vampire, Emma."

Holy mother of God.

Emma sat frozen to the chair and stared at his mouth. At his *fangs*. She thought about the eerie glow his eyes had when he walked into the bar, of how he had appeared out of nowhere when she was about to get into her car.

Her heart sped up, and sweat started leaking out her pores as the adrenaline kicked in.

VAMPIRE. The word echoed around and around inside of her.

Terrifying images from the past suddenly crashed into her head, the sight of Nik's fangs releasing them from where they'd been firmly locked away.

Images of putrid grey skin with rotting patches hanging off, exposing raw muscle underneath. Bulging red eyes glaring at her heinously, and razor-sharp fangs...fangs dripping blood.

Her blood.

In her mind, she heard herself screaming in terror. Heard the monster hissing and grunting on top of her as pain ripped through her body, the others screeching as they watched and waited their turn.

Emma wanted to jump up and run, but she couldn't seem to get enough air. She blinked as her vision started wavering. "Oh, God." She couldn't even scream.

"Emma? Sweetheart?" His husky voice was filled with concern. "Are you all right?"

Emma felt lightheaded and gripped the arms of her chair with both hands until her knuckles turned white. She started seeing spots in front of her eyes, and her stomach felt nauseous. *Don't pass out. Don't pass out.*

She was going to pass out.

Just as her vision went dark, he grabbed her by the back of the neck, bending her over and shoving her head between her legs. "Breathe, Emma. Just breathe. It's all right. Nothing is going to hurt you."

As the blood rushed to her head, her breathing calmed and her vision gradually cleared. She took a moment to enjoy drawing air into her lungs, before knocking his arm away and cautiously sitting up to study him.

He gave her a full-fang smile.

Her entire body started to shake uncontrollably, and she scooted a little farther away from him. Tears came out of nowhere to unexpectedly fill her eyes until he was nothing but a blurry shape in front of her. She frantically wondered if there was any chance at all of her outrunning him.

Her eyes darted over to her car, judging the distance. She might make it if she ran faster than she ever had in her life. She could swipe up her bag on the way. She didn't even need to find her key. Her car started with a power button.

Would she be able to get a head start on him if she took him by surprise?

But what if he *was* faster than humans? She thought back to the event in the parking lot again, of how she'd slammed into his wall of a body. Was he really that fast?

She glanced over at him nervously.

"I'm not going to hurt you Emma. See? All gone." His smile returned, showing his pearly whites, and not a fang in sight. "I'm sorry to shock you like that. I didn't know how else to tell you without sounding like a crazy person, so I thought I'd just show you. I don't even drink from humans," he reassured her. "See? Harmless."

That got her attention.

"You d-don't d-drink blood? But, you said...you said...you're a... vampire..." she stammered.

Her focus drifted as she tried to reconcile the resurrected memories that were banging around in her skull to what she was seeing right in front of her. But they didn't add up. Nikulas was nothing like the monsters from her nightmares.

"Emma. Emma. Look at me."

Clenching her jaw to keep her teeth from chattering, she slowly raised her eyes to his.

"Sweetheart, it's okay. I swear," he told her gently.

After several minutes, and several more furtive glances at him, she managed to get out, "W-What exactly do you drink if not blood?"

"Oh, I do drink blood," he clarified. "Just out of a bag, not a body."

"A b-bag?" She was genuinely confused.

"Yeah. A blood bag. I have a friend who works at a blood bank. I get my nutritional requirements from people who donate it willingly." He gave her a big, fang-free, smile.

"Are there more like you? So...so...human-like?" She was almost afraid to hear the answer.

His forehead wrinkled up briefly as he confessed, "Yes. There are a lot of us, Emma. All over the place." Then he added, "You can ask me anything you'd like. I'll answer anything you'd like to know, and I won't lie to you."

"Do you all drink from blood bags?" It was a silly question. But, stupidly, she dared to hope. It was dashed with his honest answer.

"No. Actually, I think I may be the only one."

"Why do you do it?" she asked.

"I have my reasons." Judging by his tone, he was not going to elaborate.

"The others? Do they kill people?"

"Some of them," he said softly. "But I'm not one of those." He opened his mouth like he was about to say more, but then changed his mind.

After a moment of silence, he told her reverently, "I swear to you, you have nothing to fear from me."

Could she believe him? Now that the shock was wearing off and her nerves were calming down, she found she could think somewhat rationally again.

She was sitting on her porch, in the middle of the woods, with a...vampire. There. See? She could say it without passing out. "I guess if you were going to kill me, you would've done it by now."

A look of amusement passed over his face. "Is there anything else you'd like to know?"

She thought it over. "Can you go out in the sunlight?"

"No."

Morbid curiosity getting the better of her, she asked, "What would happen if you did?"

Grimacing slightly, Nik told her, "I would catch on fire and burn until I was nothing but a pile of ashes."

"Can you change form?"

"Like into a bat?" He laughed. "No."

"Is it true about the garlic and crosses? And holy water?"

"No, although I'd rather not eat garlic and I'm not big on religious decor. The only thing that can harm me besides the sun is a debilitating injury to the heart or being beheaded. That part of the lore is true."

Another question popped into her head, and she opened her mouth to ask, but caught herself just in time and snapped it shut.

"Is there something else you wanted to know?"

Her face and neck were burning, and she knew they were red, giving her thoughts away. She quickly looked away in an attempt to hide it. "No."

10

Nik bit down on the inside of his cheek to keep from laughing. Actually, he found her innocence endearing. Old-fashioned would not be a term he would use to describe himself, yet he thought most females these days were much too bold. And judging by the variety of colors she was turning, he could easily guess what she had been about to ask. "Yes, I can do that too."

"You can do what?" she asked, her eyes wide and innocent.

"I can have sex. That's what you were wondering, right? I wasn't lying when I talked about being in your pants before." As she got impossibly redder, he couldn't hold back his grin anymore.

"That's not what I was going to ask!" she exclaimed.

"You're lying again," he countered.

Clearing her throat, she swiftly changed the subject. "So, now that I know you're a...what you are. What do you know about where Keira is?"

Unwilling to upset her more after the shock he had just given her, he let her steer the conversation to safer ground. This time. "That's what I need your help with."

Frowning at him, she asked, "Don't you think if I knew where she was, I would've found her myself by now?"

Nik studied her. He sensed her frustration and tried to gauge how much more she could take. Although she seemed to be recovering quickly from his big reveal, she still looked a little off. It might be a good idea to give her a minute before he laid anything else on her.

Plus, although it didn't bother him, the temperature was dropping and she didn't have a coat.

"Why don't we go inside where it's warmer to continue our talk?"

She glanced at him, distrust all over her features.

"I give you my word you're safe with me. Have I done anything yet to make you think otherwise?" He gave her his most innocent face. It didn't seem to help.

"Come on. Let's go inside. I promise to behave. And..." Standing up, he stretched his arms over his head. "I'll tell you everything else you want to know."

It took her a moment, but his acting all chill must have worked.

She stood a bit shakily and walked to the front door. Not waiting for him to follow, she went into the house, letting the screen door bang shut behind her.

He watched through the screen as she turned on the lights, put her bag down and went into the kitchen to fill the teakettle with water.

He waited for her to notice he hadn't followed her in. Other than not being able to go out in the sunshine, this was the second most frustrating thing about being what he was.

Finally, she came back to the door to find him still standing on the porch.

"Why are you just standing there? You've been dying to come in here all night."

"Uh yeah, about that..." Sticking one hand in his pocket he reached up to rub the back of his neck with the other. "You need to invite me in," he grudgingly admitted.

Leaning back against the porch railing and putting his hands low on his narrow hips, he tried to make it look like this wasn't weird at all.

"I'm sorry?"

"You need to invite me in," he repeated. Casually surveying the area around him, he looked anywhere but at her.

"You mean you *can't* come in unless I invite you?" Reluctantly, he raised his eyes to hers with a sigh. He nodded, and watched a gloating smile spread slowly across Emma's face.

"Well, well. Doesn't this thicken the plot?" She frowned a bit as something occurred to her. "But you walked right into the bar tonight. How did you do that if you need an invitation?"

"The bar is a public place, not a private home. I only need to be invited into personal residences. Unless it's owned by another vampire, of course." He held her gaze.

"Huh." Emma leaned against the doorframe. "Maybe we should just continue this conversation from right where we are then."

She was laughing at him, now that she knew she was safe inside her home. "Come on, Emma. Invite me in."

He didn't like her being out of his reach. It made him nervous.

He chose not to dwell on the reason why.

"What if I don't?" she asked with a rebellious gleam in her eye.

Starting to really feel antsy now, he told her, "I can make you invite me in, but I'd rather not. I prefer not to mess with your head like that." He pushed away from the railing and walked up to the door. "And I don't think you would appreciate it either."

"I wouldn't," she said in all seriousness. "Promise me you'll never do that to me."

"I swear I will never alter your thoughts or memories." And he meant it.

But she wasn't done yet. "How exactly does this work? Do I have to invite you in every time?"

"No. Just once." His patience was wearing thin. It was getting harder to resist the growing urge to "suggest" to her that she just invite him in already, dammit, in spite of what he just told her.

"Can I take the invitation back once I give it?"

Nik pressed his lips together, and then grudgingly admitted, "Yes."

"Really? And how do I do that?"

Looking her square in the eye, he admitted, "You can rescind the invitation."

"And you have to leave?"

"Yes."

"Just like that?"

"Just like that," he confirmed.

She hesitated just for a moment. "All right, then. Come on in, Nikulas."

Finally!

Nik took a relieved breath as he yanked open the screen door and stalked over the threshold, forcing Emma to scramble back out of the way to avoid being plowed over.

Marching around her and heading into the house, he told himself this weird protectiveness he felt only stemmed from the fact that he needed her to help him save his brother.

"What are you doing?" she asked as he walked from room to room, checking the windows and looking in the closets.

Ignoring her, he continued to prowl around the lower floor of her home. When he reached the stairs, he didn't hesitate, but started climbing them two at a time, paying no mind to her frantic "Hey!"

He tromped around upstairs repeating the same security check, until he heard her yell, "You'd better not be getting my rugs all dirty with those boots you're wearing!"

He took a last glance around and then reappeared at the top of the stairs. "I just wanted to see your house. It's...nice."

He jogged down the stairs and walked right past her into the kitchen, where he pulled out a chair and nonchalantly sat down at the table, the picture of innocence.

Emma stared at him like he'd lost his mind, and maybe he had. Giving him one last unsure look, she went to the stove to make that cup of tea. Putting the water on to boil, she grabbed a cup and a tea bag, and then went over to sit across the table from him. "I would offer you something to drink, but I don't have any bagged blood here."

Nik held up a hand. "That's okay, I ate before I came."

"Oh." The teakettle started to whistle, and she got up.

Leaning forward and putting his elbows on the table, Nik looked down at his laced fingers. "So! Now that you know about me, do you think you can tell me now what really happened that night your sister disappeared?" He listened as she poured the hot water into her cup, and then dunked her teabag a few times.

When she didn't come back to the table, he raised his head to find her motionless at the counter. "Emma?"

He was about to get up to go see what she was about when she finally turned around. Her hands were shaking as she walked back to the table with her tea.

"I've already told you what I remember about that night." Her tea sloshed around in the cup when she tried to set it on the table.

"Here, let me help you." Nik jumped up and took it from her before she burned herself.

Emma gave him a funny look, but let him set the tea on the table while she found her chair. "Thank you."

"You're welcome." Nik set her tea down and then went to get the agave sweetener out of the pantry. He grabbed a spoon and brought both over to her.

"How did you know I like agave in my tea?" she asked him suspiciously as she added some to her cup.

Sitting down again at the other end of the table, Nik told her the truth. "I've been watching you."

She stopped stirring and her head snapped up. "Watching me? Here? When?"

Feeling not in the least bit uncomfortable at how this was going to sound, he told her, "I've been hanging around outside your house every night for the past week. Watching. Learning your habits..." he shrugged as he trailed off.

She stared at him a moment, then started stirring again. "Why?"

"I was trying to discern who you are, what you know...who you know...before I contacted you." He looked at her, kind of surprised to find nothing but mild curiosity on her face instead of the expected outrage.

"So you've been sitting outside my house every night?"

He nodded, unashamed.

"And what did you find out?"

She seemed genuinely intrigued. He'd expected her to feel intruded upon, offended, creeped out, but he wasn't sensing any of that.

"I found out that you work too much, and you come home too late every night. You run into the house, shower, eat, tea, TV and bed. Same time, same order. Every day." He paused, uncertain if he should continue. *Ah, what the hell.* "You're a vegetarian, or maybe just a healthy eater? You wear an old, blue, ratty robe...probably because it's familiar and it comforts you. Just like the routine you keep." Then he said quietly, "You don't like the darkness." He paused. "Last night I stayed here so long, I was still here when you got up to go jogging. You ran right past me."

"I did?" She sounded horrified. "But, I thought you can't go out in the day?"

"I can't. Not the direct sun. But it hadn't quite come up yet, and I'm *really* fast." He grinned at her. "I hightailed it out of here as soon as you got to the road."

She smiled slightly, a pensive look coming into her eyes just for a second before she seemed to catch herself. "Your stalking doesn't seem to have given you any useful information about me, though," she observed.

"On the contrary. I've learned all I needed to know." Thankful she wasn't freaking out on him again, he relaxed and sat back in his chair, stretching out one long leg.

Raising an eyebrow, he asked her, "One thing though...Marilyn Manson? Really?"

"I happen to like Marilyn," she said indignantly, taking a sip of her tea. "Besides," she murmured, "the music makes it go away."

"Makes what go away, Emma?" he prompted softly.

11

Emma looked down at her hands, wrapped around her warm teacup, and figured there was no dancing around the subject anymore.

But what if, in spite of his reassurances, he didn't believe her? What if he thought she was crazy? The things that attacked her and her sister that night don't exist in real life. She'd spent the last seven years convincing even herself they didn't, that she'd made them up in her mind to deal with the trauma she'd been dealt. And she'd nearly succeeded.

Then again, vampires like him weren't supposed to exist either. Yet there he was, sitting at her kitchen table, real as could be.

It was time to face reality. Much as she didn't want to talk about it, if Nik was legit and she wanted to help her sister, there seemed to be no more avoiding it. So, after a long silence, she finally admitted, "The nightmares. The music chases away the nightmares."

He sat very still. "What are the nightmares about, Em?"

Speaking very softly, like she was afraid they'd hear her, she stared out the window as she told him, "They're always the same. I'm with Keira and we're leaving the carnival. They hit all the little towns around here every summer, you know. It was a perfect summer night, and we'd had so much fun. We rode all the rides, played all the games, and ate every greasy thing we could find...and for once, no one had bothered us." A wistful smile played around her mouth as she remembered the last time she'd been with her sister. "It was getting really late, so we'd decided to leave. We were chasing each other through the field, running to our car. We were laughing..."

She stopped talking, lost in the memories she'd tried so hard to forget, intentionally recalling the details for the first time in years. Her mind recoiled against the memories, trying to go back into self-preservation mode, but she struggled through it.

"Keira suddenly stopped running, and I turned around to see why. She wasn't looking at me, but past me toward the tree line where our car was parked. She was white with terror. I thought maybe it was a bear or something; we have them around here sometimes. So I turned around to see for myself..."

Nik could feel her chaotic emotions, the main one being terror. It radiated from her across the space between them, and hit him right in the center of his chest.

The urge to go back in time and slowly, painfully, kill whatever it was that was making her feel so scared rushed through him without warning. He didn't want her to be afraid. Ever. He tried to look away, knowing his eyes would be glowing, full of the primal need for revenge rolling through him. But he couldn't tear them away from her face.

She paused, and tears ran down her cheeks as her hands started shaking again.

Nik's fangs slid down and his lips pulled back in a sinister snarl, instinctually preparing for battle. Muscles tensed and thickened, squeezing a low growl from deep within his chest.

Emma must have heard, for her tear-filled eyes found him. She raised her hand to wipe the moisture from her eyes, and before she could clear her vision, he jumped up from the table. She couldn't see him like this.

"Be right back." He rushed down the hall to the bathroom and locked the door behind him. In his current state, he'd forgotten to keep his speed at a human pace. He hoped he hadn't startled her.

Nik took several slow, deep breaths and tried to get a grip on himself. The close walls of the small half bath didn't make it any easier to calm down. Spotting a small window over the tub, he opened it wide.

What the fuck was wrong with him? He'd finally, *finally*, gotten her to talk, and he had to go all Neanderthal just because he felt she'd been afraid seven years ago.

Seven. Years. Ago. When Luukas had disappeared.

He had to find out the details of her sister's abduction, if that's what it was. Hopefully, his little *Flash* imitation hadn't startled her too much. She was dealing with enough tonight as it was. Upsetting her more was not going to accomplish anything.

Also, why had Emma been left alive to bear witness?

When the news of Luukas' capture had reached them, debilitating shock had rippled through the Council. There was no way anyone could overpower a Master Vampire, at least no one they'd ever known. And, unfortunately, they definitely knew Leeha. It was impossible for her to have overpowered him on her own.

Putting two and two together, Nik knew having a witch on her side was the only way Leeha could keep Luuk anywhere he didn't want to be. A witch, if powerful enough, is the only other being who can overpower a Master Vampire. But this type of ability was rare, and the whereabouts of all of the witches they knew had been accounted for.

It was only recently that one of the Hunters heard about Keira and brought it to Nik's attention. They hadn't even known she existed until just recently when they saw one of the missing person alerts. The Council wasn't certain how they'd missed knowing about a Moss witch, as they kept careful track of all the witches in their area. But their focus right now was getting Luukas back. They'd worry about the slip up later.

So, Nik and Aiden had set out to investigate. They'd discovered Keira was, indeed, a very powerful and practiced witch. And she had a sister who was looking for her, claiming she'd been abducted.

Had Keira really been taken against her will? Or had she been in on it the entire time?

Maybe they could've answered those questions if they could've found any trace of them at all. However, Leeha had pulled the greatest disappearing act she'd ever done.

Until now.

One thing was for sure; his Emma was an innocent victim in all of this.

His Emma. He really needed to stop thinking like that. She wasn't his. And she never would be.

Turning on the faucet, he splashed some cold water on his face and checked himself out in the mirror. Back to his normal self, he was eager to return to the kitchen. Hopefully she hadn't freaked out and withdrawn again. He didn't know if he'd have the patience or the time to get this story back out of her of her own free will.

He wasn't lying earlier when he said he could mess with her head, he totally could. Human minds were easily manipulated when need be. But he also wasn't lying when he told her he'd rather not do that. He didn't like playing with people's heads.

If the guys ever became aware of how he felt about it, they'd hand him his balls on a platter. It was bad enough they busted him about his feeding habit.

He made his way back to the table, at a more human-like speed this time. "Sorry about that. I, uh...needed a minute." He sat down and pushed his hair out of his face. "Please, continue. What was it you saw?"

When she just continued to stare out the window, he tried to prod her along. "*Was* it a bear?"

"A bear?" she repeated. "Um, no. It wasn't a bear. It was, um..." Her forehead wrinkled in concentration. "It was..." She rubbed her temples, like her head hurt just trying to think about it. "It was...I can't..."

Dammit, what the hell had happened to her that night? Moving very slowly, he pulled out the chair between them and slid over next to her. He figured this move would go either really good, or really bad, but he wanted to try to comfort her if she would let him.

She lowered her hands and wrapped them around her teacup. They were shaking again, so hard he was afraid the porcelain was going to bust apart on the table. He carefully covered her cold hands with his to still them.

She didn't pull away.

"Emma, you've got to stop this. You're going to rattle the skin right off your bones."

At his gentle teasing, a brief smile curved her lips. She sniffed and looked down at his hands engulfing hers. "I've just blocked out these memories for so long... It's hard to revisit them."

He left his hands where they were and smiled encouragingly until she continued, "It wasn't a bear. It was...they were... monsters. I don't know how else to say it. They attacked us."

"Monsters," he repeated. What in the world could she be talking about? Werewolves? The bitch that had his brother was most definitely a monster, but if you didn't know her, all you would see is a beautiful woman. Her minions were all normal looking "people", like him. He didn't think "monster" was a word someone would use to describe them physically.

"Can you tell me what they looked like?" He squeezed her hands, careful not to hurt her.

"Um..." She risked a quick peek at him for reassurance. "They were like something out of a horror movie—very tall and thin, yet muscular, with long arms..." Her voice started to quiver, but she pressed on. "Grayish, rotting skin. Red eyes. They had a mouthful of sharp fangs, and they wore no clothes."

Nik furrowed his brow as he tried to picture what she was describing. One of the locals he'd had watching Leeha's lair up north had mentioned seeing something that sounded similar. That's how they'd found out Leeha was back. He'd followed the thing and it took him right to her hideout.

He thought the civilian must have been mistaken, seen an animal or something. But he had no doubt Emma was telling the truth. If beings such as these existed, this was very disturbing.

"And these things took your sister?"

Emma nodded.

"Are you sure she was taken by force? She didn't go willingly?"

Pulling her hands out from under his, she sat back in her chair. "What are you saying?"

"I'm only asking because the female who has my brother would not have been able to overpower him without a witch helping her."

"And you think my sister is that witch."

"Yes, I believe so. According to my sources, she'd been gone only a few days before the night my brother went to meet the bitch who's holding him."

Emma crossed her arms over her chest. "Keira was taken by force."

Nik could feel the wall going up between them. He scrambled to undo the damage. "I know that's what you believe, but think about it. You didn't even know your sister is a witch. Isn't it possible there are other things you don't know about her?"

"Yes," she admitted after a moment. "I suppose that could be possible. But whether or not she was abducted against her will, I have no doubts about that," she insisted stubbornly.

"How can you be sure?" he asked.

Gritting her teeth, she said, "Because I was there. And because of this." She grabbed the neckline of her purple sweater and yanked it down below her collarbone, revealing a 3-inch area of shiny, puckered scar tissue.

12

Nik stared at her ruined skin, and swallowed hard. She'd been ripped open. No vampire would have left a mark like that. Not even a young, sloppy one.

His voice shaking with emotion, he asked her, "They did this to you? The monsters?"

"Yes," she whispered. Letting go of her sweater, she let it cover her again. "Keira may not have wanted me to know if there was something dangerous going on with her, but there's no way in hell she would have let anything hurt me. Especially if she had some kind of powers that could have stopped it."

Dropping his voice down to match hers, he whispered, "What else did they do to you?"

She didn't answer, but she didn't have to. The rigid way she was holding herself spoke volumes. A buzzing noise started up inside his head. He wanted to reach into her mind to see these things for himself. Fuck what he'd told her before. But he stopped himself. He needed to be here right now, not off on a killing rampage, which is exactly what would happen if he groped around in her memories. He was dangerously on the verge of losing it as it was.

Nik didn't think to question his reaction. He *would* kill them. He would hunt them down and fucking kill them. After he played with them a bit, like they had done to her. Every single one of those things that had dared to lay a finger on her.

If he thought his earlier reaction to her story was bad, seeing her beautiful skin marked with proof was much, much worse. And if Leeha was involved in this as he suspected? Nothing would save her this time. Burning would be too good for her.

"Nik? Are you alright?" Emma asked, bringing him partially back to the here and now. Her eyes were wide, captivated by what she saw.

He knew he was entirely vamped out on her. He couldn't control it. His fangs were fully extended and razor-sharp, and his lips pulled back as he let out a long, slow hiss. His facial features would be sharper, harsher, the skin pulled taut across the bones. And his blue eyes would glow almost silver.

He stared right at her, but it wasn't her face he was seeing. Tensed to attack, his hands were clenched into tight fists, his muscles taught and ready.

"Nikulas?"

Through the red haze of his rage, Emma's concerned voice came to him as if through a fog. With some difficulty, he refocused his full attention on to her.

Fuck. It was too late to run off to the bathroom again. He dropped his head down, trying to calm himself. This was bad. This was very bad.

Mentally kicking himself, he was about to move away from her when a gentle stroke on his forehead whipped his eyes back up to hers. She was touching him? There was no fear in her eyes, only a curious fascination.

Watching him closely for any kind of reaction, she ran her fingers along his cheekbone and up underneath his eye, and then slowly leaned toward him to get a closer look at his mouth.

Expelling a shuddering breath, his blood lust for violence turned into a completely different kind of lust as she came closer and closer to him.

Fucking hell.

Abruptly, he pulled away from her, stood up, and stepped away from the table, cupping his hands in front of himself to hide the bulge in his pants. "Sorry about..." He waved a hand in front of his face, pointing at his vampirish features. "I have a hard time controlling it sometimes if I get angry, or...whatever. The thought of someone hurting you—" He clenched his jaw, unable to finish. "Yeah. I'm gonna shut up now." Dropping his head again to hide from her gaze, he concentrated on his breathing. He needed to chill the fuck out.

Emma stood up from the table, cautiously walking over to stand in front of him. "This is all for me?" she asked. She reached out and laid a warm hand on his forearm, slightly squeezing the hard muscle under the cotton material. "Nik? It's okay, you don't have to hide from me."

What the hell was she doing? Why wasn't she running, screaming, from the room?

Unable to help himself, Nik groaned as her touch on his arm burned right through his shirt to the bare skin beneath. If she only knew what all he was hiding, like the throbbing bulge beneath his hands, she might not be so eager to lay her hands on him.

The tension in the air between them was a palpable thing. His entire body hummed from it, until he had to physically hold himself away from her. It made him feel more alive than he had in years, and he wondered if she could feel it too.

His control was rapidly slipping away at her touch, and he lifted his head. Her eyes were curious, but calm and warm. He knew his own had to be burning bright. Her close proximity to him wasn't doing a damn thing to help him calm down. His mouth watered at the thought of tasting her. Her lips, her neck, her breasts, her slick folds...her sweet blood.

He barely managed to rasp, "Emma, you need to back away."

She frowned slightly. "You said you would never hurt me."

"Emma, I'm so riled up right now...I just need you to..." *Kiss me. Touch me.* He breathed her deep into his lungs. "Go back to the table, and give me a moment." All he could think about was tearing off her clothes and shoving her down onto her hands and knees right there on the hard floor. Pounding into her from behind while he sank his fangs into the soft skin between her neck and her shoulder. Her hot blood searing his throat while he exploded inside of her.

Nik caught himself right before he groaned aloud again at the erotic images he couldn't seem to stop. "*Please,* Emma, just back away." He was so jazzed up; the predator in him poised to pounce at the slightest trigger.

"Okay," she whispered.

Nik continued to watch her with burning eyes and a clenched jaw, his hands still cupped in front of his hips. As she removed her hand from his arm, his eyes narrowed in on her. She stopped moving, her breasts rising and falling with quick breaths, then took a small step back.

Growling low in his throat, he tracked her.

She took another small step.

Nik's eyes never left her face. His body leaned toward her, try as he might to stay where he was.

Finally, she seemed to truly comprehend the situation she was in. Her eyes widened, and he heard her heart speed up as she panicked and jerked away.

Big. Mistake.

No sooner had she started twisting around, and he was on her. She never even saw him coming. Wrapping her in the vice-like grip of his arms, she was spun around and slammed back into the fridge behind him, his arms taking the brunt of the hit.

One hand wrapped in her hair, and the other low on her back, he held her immobile, groaning in her ear as he rolled his hips into her softness. His erection pulsed on her belly, hard and thick, and he felt it grow impossibly harder as she moaned in response to the feel of him.

"Emma." His voice was rough with strain as he tried to warn her. "I'm sorry." Holding her head still, his mouth crashed onto hers. Heedless of his fangs, they scraped her lips, drawing blood. She gasped at the assault, and he used the opportunity to deepen the kiss. Thrusting his tongue into her mouth over and over, he tasted her until she was kissing him back, her tongue dueling with his. Her soft answering moan and the tease of her blood on his lips urged him on, and he lost what little control he'd managed to retain thus far.

A small sound escaped her as he bit into her lower lip, his fangs so sharp they sliced into her flesh like a hot knife through butter.

Nik felt her stiffen with panic as he bit her, but there was no way he was letting her go now. As her blood hit his tongue and ran down his throat, it spread through him like wildfire, burning through his body and igniting every nerve ending.

MINE.

The word reverberated through him until there was nothing else but Emma. He kissed her, drinking from her swollen lips until she relaxed against him again. The taste of her was so completely unreal; he couldn't begin to describe it. He'd never had anything like her blood, not even Eliana had affected him like this.

Nik couldn't get enough. He fed greedily from her lips as he moved his hand down to her ass, pulling her softness into his hard cock. Her little body felt so good, so utterly perfect against him, he was about to come in his jeans just kissing her.

A low growl escaped him as she rose up on her toes and wrapped her arms around his neck, and he held her to him desperately. Licking at her lip to heal his wounds, he kissed his way over her soft jaw and down her throat, breathing in the heady scent that only belonged to her. Pulling her head to the side, he gently kissed her pulsing artery. He lingered there, the blood lust warring with his instinct not to hurt her.

The instinct won. For now.

Releasing her hair, he worked his way back up to her mouth as he ran his hands up over her back until he found the bottom of her sweater. Pushing it up, he slid his hands underneath it, unable to keep himself from touching her velvety, soft skin any longer.

13

Emma was on fire, her entire body pulsing with heat. She'd had a heart stopping moment when he'd first grabbed her, but as soon as he'd kissed her she'd responded to him instinctively.

He held her so tight, she was probably going to have bruises tomorrow, but she couldn't care less. She was completely surrounded by him—his hardness, his smell. Like soap and wilderness and pure male. She'd never felt anything like this. Not that she'd had much experience, but something told her she never would again.

His fangs scraped her lips, but she barely felt it. His tongue thrust into her mouth, distracting her until she kissed him back, moaning softly at the welcome invasion. At the sound, he ground his hips into her so hard she could feel him pulsing against her belly. Her nipples tightened against his chest until they hurt, her stomach clenched deep, and a rush of wetness soaked her panties.

Nik pulled his head back, and she moaned in protest, then stiffened when he held her still and struck, his fangs sliding through her lower lip. *No!* But the pain lasted only a fraction of a second, and was soon forgotten as he drank from her, every pull sending stabs of pleasure straight to her core.

Holy shit. He was drinking her blood, and it was *nothing* like what she had experienced with the grey monsters. Shocks of sensation streaked through her, and she wished she could somehow get closer. She wanted to crawl inside of him until they were one person. Sliding her hands up his hard chest, she did the next best thing. Wrapping her arms around his neck, she pulled him closer.

Releasing her lips, he pulled her head to the side and kissed his way to her throat, pausing over the artery there, and a small shiver of fear ran through her. But he didn't bite her, instead kissing his way back up to her lips as he ran his hands over her back and down to her waist. She felt him push underneath her sweater until he was touching her bare skin, and she sighed with pleasure against his mouth at the feel of his hands on her. She wanted him to rip off their clothes until they were skin to skin. Wanted to feel him run his eyes and lips all over her.

Panicking, she tried to push him away. "No! Stop!"

Nik growled dangerously and hung on as something tried to pull Emma away from him. He was running on pure animalistic need, and it wasn't until he felt her small fists banging on his chest and shoulders and heard her frantic voice, that he realized something was wrong.

"Nikulas!! Stop! Let go of me!"

What the hell?

He loosened his arms from around her just enough for her to get a good shot at his jaw. Her uppercut knocked his head back, surprising him enough that he let her go. She squeezed out from between him and the fridge and ran to the other side of the room.

Nikulas spun around to go after her, but stopped short when he saw her cowering in the corner of the counter with her arms wrapped around herself. The sight knocked some sense into him better than any punch could.

His ardor cooled instantly as he stared at her big eyes and swollen lips and messy hair. What the fuck was he doing? Licking his suddenly cold lips, he tasted the remnants of her blood.

MINE!

He gripped the sides of his head with his hands as he began to pace back and forth in front of the fridge. No. She couldn't be his. No, no, no, no, NO!

He thought it was just folklore. Like every other vampire, he'd heard the stories of how just one taste of their blood would reveal your fated mate to you. The one you would do anything for, the one you'd die to protect without a thought for your own safety, the one who would possess you completely. However, though vampires hooked up with humans on occasion, he'd never seen a true mating in all of his hundreds of years of being a vampire. Like everyone else, he blew it off as an old wives tale.

But the compulsion raging within him told a very different tale. The way her blood blazed through him confirmed it. His entire being protested even the few feet of space separating them, and it took every ounce of his control to keep himself where he was. He craved to feed her, to protect her, to spoil her, to make her laugh, to hear her cry out in ecstasy over and over. But mostly, he craved to feed from her.

He craved to love her.

Nik stopped pacing and met her anguished gaze with one of his own. No. No way. No fucking way this was happening. For her safety, and his sanity, he would not, *could not*, go there.

Even if it killed him.

Emma saw the pain and confusion in his eyes from across the room. Feeling like she owed him some sort of explanation, she felt shame heat her face as she managed to stutter out, "I'm sorry. I just...I have these...I don't like people to see me."

"I'm sorry, Emma," Nik began at the same time, "I shouldn't have done that...I...what?" He stopped speaking as what she was saying registered on his face. "What did you say?"

She just shook her head at the floor, and refused to say anymore. How could she possibly express the hurt, the shame she felt every time she looked at herself? How could she ever let someone else see that?

Peeking up at him from under her lashes, she saw him glance at the clock on the stove to her left. It was way after midnight. He shoved his hands into his hair to push it off his face. He looked torn, his eyes going back and forth between her and the clock.

He paced a few steps away and turned his back to her. Emma watched, until she realized what he was doing. Embarrassed to catch him adjusting himself, she quickly looked back down at the floor.

He turned back around and leaned back against the fridge, crossing his arms, all James Dean cool. "I'm sorry, Emma. I just...I lost control."

Understatement of the year.

"It won't happen again."

Too ashamed to raise her head, Emma felt a gaping cavern open up in her chest. It wasn't *her* he was so crazy about; it was just his vampire impulse to prey on the weak. God, she was so naive.

Tears filled her eyes as she let the rejection soak in. It was probably better this way. Because, really, why would someone like Nik want a girl like her? She was damaged, inside and out, and no one could fix her. And she'd just met him a few hours ago!

And, lest she forget, he was a *vampire*!

She swiped at her eyes. Steeling her spine, she lifted her chin and with a quick, "Don't worry about it," then she walked over to the table to grab her now cold tea and put her cup in the sink. "So, you got what you came for," *in more ways than one*, "what now?"

A heavy silence descended upon the room at her words. It lasted so long, she began to wonder if he'd left when she heard him say, "Now, I need you to pack a bag and come with me."

"Come with you where, exactly?" Turning around, she mimicked his unhurried pose, and wondered how she would ever get through spending any amount of time in close proximity with this male.

Nik narrowed his eyes at her, white teeth chewing his bottom lip.

She silently pleaded with him to just let it go. She was embarrassed enough. They didn't need to hash out what had just happened. It would be better to just forget about it.

Apparently, he agreed. "I need you to come with me to Washington. We recently found out Leeha is back in the area, and we believe she still has my brother. And your sister."

"Well, if you know where he is, then what do you need me for?" she asked. *Like anything could keep me away.*

"I need you there to talk some sense into your sister, just in case —" He held up his hand to silence her protest, "just in case she *is* there of her own violation."

There was no question in Emma's mind she was going to go with him. Their personal issues needed to be set aside. Getting her sister back was all that mattered to her. "What do I need to pack?"

Nik was already walking toward the stairs. "I'll help you."

Rolling her eyes, Emma followed him.

14

Shea locked the door behind Dante. It was ridiculous, she knew. Locking doors. She was an immortal, after all. Very few things could fatally harm her.

And a flimsy lock wouldn't keep out the things that could.

She leaned back and looked around her tidy apartment without really seeing it. Well, that meeting had been a complete waste of time. Why did she even bother going through the hassle of trying to get them in the same room?

It was just that they were all so distant with each other now. They used to hang out together, feed together, fight together, like any other dysfunctional family. What the hell had happened?

Shea sighed. Why did she even care? Maybe she was just tired. Weird, a vampire feeling tired. But she was. She probably just needed to feed, as Dante suggested. She'd hit the streets as soon as she checked and loaded their weapons and gassed up the Hummer.

She thought back to Dante's little speech. It had really thrown her for a loop. It was unlike him to be so revealing. Actually, she couldn't remember a time where she'd ever heard him say anything on a personal level about any of them. Much as she appreciated the gesture, it made her nervous. Why had he decided to go and get all mushy now? Did he know something he wasn't telling them?

The little hairs on the back of her neck tingled as a feeling of foreboding suddenly overcame her.

Dismissing it as nothing more than her overactive imagination, she shook off the feeling, and walked back to her room to start preparing for the mission.

"So, who is Leeha? And what does she have against...what's your brother's name again?"

Packed and ready to go, Emma took a last look around. She had left a message for her boss explaining she'd had a family emergency come up and wasn't sure how long she'd be gone. Hopefully she'd still have a job when she got back.

If not, well, she was used to that, wasn't she?

Other than locking up the house, there wasn't anything else she needed to do before leaving. She had no family or friends to call, no close neighbors. She didn't even have a fish.

"His name is Luukas. He's the Master Vampire over our colony. Leeha is a vampire who, with a few others, broke off from us to form their own Council. The problem being, she's completely fucked up in the head. She set her sights on Luuk to be her 'king' and rule next to her, even though vampires don't usually take other vampires as their companion. When he wouldn't give in to her, she got pissed, and didn't take the rejection well."

Setting her suitcase and backpack by the door, Nik told her, "Lock the door behind me. I'll go get Aiden and we'll come back and pick you up. It shouldn't be any more than a few minutes, so if you think of anything you've forgotten, don't waste any time getting it. We need to be on our way."

Standing in the kitchen doorway wondering if she should grab some food, Emma asked distractedly, "Aiden?"

"Have I not mentioned him yet?"

Emma shook her head.

"Aiden is my best friend and partner in crime. He came along to help me out on this trip. He's a pain in the ass Brit, but you'll like him. The girls always do." His mouth twisted, like he just had an unpleasant thought.

She raised an inquiring eyebrow, but he didn't elaborate, continuing his original train of thought. "We're camped out just a few miles from here. I'll run there. It won't take me long. Do not open this door to anyone but me."

She was going to be alone with not one, but two vampires? One of which, if what Nik had told her earlier was true, didn't drink from a bag but from a body. Emma didn't know if going with them was the best decision she'd ever made, but what choice did she have? This was the first honest to goodness lead she'd had on her sister since her abduction, there was no way she wasn't going to be in on it. And if her own life was on the line for doing it? She would happily take that risk.

He paused on his way out the door to tell her, "It's okay, Em. Aiden won't hurt you, I swear it."

His words did nothing to reassure her, but she nodded anyway.

"I'll be right back." Leaving her stuff just inside the door, he took off to go get the RV.

Emma locked the door behind him, and went back to the kitchen to grab some snacks to bring with her, just in case. Grabbing a recycled bag, she threw some travel ready stuff in, trying not to dwell on what she was getting herself into. Instead, she focused on seeing Keira again after all this time.

It'd been seven long years since the two girls ran hand in hand through the long grass. That day was the first time they'd had fun since their parents had died in a car accident earlier that year.

She set the bag of food down by the rest of her things, then sat down in the kitchen to wait and thought about what Nik had told her. It couldn't be true, could it? The witch thing? She wanted to disregard it, but the more she thought about it, the more sense it made.

Unlike Emma, her sister had always been involved in "extracurricular activities" growing up. She'd told Emma they were dance classes. But, how could she stand to take all of those "dance classes", when she had all of the same social issues Emma did?

Unless, it wasn't dance class she was going to at all. Now that she really thought about it, weren't there usually recitals when you were in dance? Performances? They'd never gone to anything like that. And she didn't remember any tutu's laying around either, for that matter.

Yet, twice a week, without fail, her mom would pack up her sister and off they would go for hours at a time. Keira would come home so exhausted she'd go right to bed. Where else would she have been going if not to dance classes?

And of course, there was always the fact the two sisters just weren't 'normal'. Although, as they got older, it did seem Emma's 'incidents' were more common than Keira's.

Was it true then? Did she really come from a family of witches? And they'd kept it from her all this time? Why would they not tell her?

Headlights coming down her driveway interrupted her musings, for now. Getting up, she turned off all of the lights except the one over the stove and waited for Nik to come to the door.

"Just pull up here along the side of the house," Nik told Aiden.

As soon as the vehicle stopped, he jumped out and leapt up the steps to the porch. Opening the screen door, he lifted his hand to knock, but the door swung open before he had the chance, and a backpack was shoved at him.

Scowling at Emma around the bag, he told her, "I told you not to open the door until you knew it was me."

"I did know it was you," she informed him. "Who else would be driving an RV down my driveway at one in the morning?" Picking up a recycled bag she'd added to her stuff and grabbing her coat from the hook by the door, she pulled the door shut behind her.

He slung the backpack over his shoulder and picked up her suitcase, then led the way to the RV. He heard her heart pounding as they walked up to the waiting vehicle. He stopped to reassure her. But she gave him a quick smile, took a deep breath, and squared her shoulders.

Okay, then.

Opening up the side door, Nik indicated for her to enter first, and then followed with her stuff. As he handed off her suitcase to Aiden, he made the introductions. "Emma, this is Aiden. Aiden...Emma."

"Hello." Emma smiled timidly, a blush creeping across her cheeks.

Nik looked over at his friend, trying to see him through her eyes. Just slightly shorter and smaller than Nik, he was lean and muscular in black, nylon running pants, tank top, and a grey hoodie with the hood up. Long lashed grey eyes bore into her from underneath dark brows. His nose was straight, his cheekbones high, his lips...all right for a guy, he guessed. With skin the color of a creamy latte and a slightly dimpled chin, he had the look of a desert prince, and he carried himself like one also.

Aiden looked from Emma to Nik and back to Emma again. Appraising gray eyes wandered over her small frame from her bright head to her sneakered feet and back again.

"Bloody hell." Muttering something to himself about "women" and "death of us all", he left them to take her suitcase to the back bedroom where she'd be sleeping.

"Um..." Emma looked at Nik, probably hoping he'd shed some light on his friend's greeting—or lack thereof. But he just shrugged his shoulders in agreement and followed his friend.

As he walked into the back sleeping area, he grinned a little as he heard her mumble sarcastically, "Nice to meet you too."

15

Emma looked around, checking out her new digs. At least they would be for the immediate future. "Oh, wow."

From the outside, the vehicle looked like any normal family vacation nightmare. From the inside? Gutted completely and remodeled for their use, it was a combination of spaceship control room, modern living quarters, and bank vault.

Stainless steel and black leather dominated the masculine decor. Instead of the usual chairs and TV set up behind the drivers seat, there was a corner desk with multiple computer monitors. A keyboard, mouse, cell phone, notebook, and satellite phone were all laying on the desk, and a swivel chair was bolted to the floor in front of it. A map was tacked to the wall above, red pins stuck into it here and there, including one smack in the middle of the location of her house.

All of the windows throughout the RV were covered with what looked like some kind of steel coverings, except for the front windshield and front door windows, which she was pretty sure were tinted darker than the legal limit. There was the usual driver and passenger seats, and a third seat behind the passenger's.

Behind her, there was a counter, a small fridge, some cabinets and a sink. Toward the back end, there were some sofa seats lining the sides with narrow tables parallel to them, a doorway which led to what she guessed was a bathroom, and the back room where the guys had disappeared with her stuff. To top it off, all of the doors seemed to be made of reinforced steel with multiple locks, even the driver and passenger doors.

She wondered where they slept during the day. There weren't any coffins lying around.

Setting her bag of snacks on the counter, she opened the fridge, and found it stacked full of bags of blood. More surprisingly, there was some bottled water in the door. And in the crisper? She found her favorite fruits. She stared at the apples (Fuji), and pears (Asian), and ignored the feeling in her chest at Nikulas' thoughtfulness. After a moment, she added her own pieces she'd brought with her. Opening the top cabinet, she found more of her favorite foods. Even her chai tea and the agave she liked in it.

She was still staring into the cabinet when Nik and Aiden wandered up from the back.

Nik cleared his throat. "I had Aiden run by the store while we were talking earlier. I gave him a list. Just some stuff I know you like." Rubbing the back of his neck uncomfortably, he wouldn't look at her when she tried to catch his eye.

Reaching over her head, he closed the cabinet door. "We need to get going Em. Unless you're hungry?" he asked.

"No, I'm good. Thanks." Stepping back from the counter, she silently berated herself for getting so emotional over some stupid fruit. It was just, she couldn't remember a time someone had been so thoughtful toward her. Not since her parents had died, actually.

As Aiden settled himself in the driver's seat, Nik told her, "We put your stuff in the back bedroom. Aid and I will crash out here on the couches come sunup."

Leaning forward, he got right down in her face. "When you wake up before us, do NOT leave this vehicle. Do you understand? Not for anything." When she'd confirmed she'd heard him, he added, "There are some books in the back room. Satellite TV. Shower items and towels are in the closet. Oh, no cell phone calls, and don't touch the computer."

"I don't have a phone, or anyone to call." Emma was well aware she was probably one of the few people in the world who didn't, but it would be a waste of money. The signal was so weak where she lived, she would never be able to call anyone on it, anyway.

As Nik went up front to join Aiden, she got the distinct feeling she was being dismissed. "Nik?"

Sitting down, he twisted his torso around to look back at her.

"Um. Thank you. For the food."

His blue eyes roved over her face. "You're welcome. Get some rest."

Emma gave him a small smile, then headed toward the back room, closing the door behind her.

Nik frowned as Emma closed the door behind her. Turning back toward the front, he caught Aiden's smug smile. "What?"

"I'm just quite relieved is all."

"About what?" Nik pulled up the GPS and set their coordinates.

"That Emma is such a crumpet. It'll make the trip much more interesting."

Nik's head whipped around. "You stay the fuck away from her, Aid."

Aiden glanced over, his brow lowered in exaggerated confusion as he started the RV. "For what reason? You have no need for any of that. You feed from a bag, and live like a monk."

He turned away, but caught Aiden's smirk out of the corner of his eye, and growled low in his throat.

"What? I won't hurt her. I just want to play a bit with our little witch."

"Aiden, you lay one fucking finger on her and I will lay you out. I am not fucking around. You are NOT to touch her. EVER."

"You take all the fun out of life for me, Nik. You know that?" Glaring out of the corner of his eye, he added, "I don't know why I even hang around with you. My stodgy ole mum was more fun than you are."

Staring straight ahead, Nik ground his teeth together, refusing to rise to the bait.

"Ah...I see how it is then."

Nik didn't ask what "it" was, but Aiden took it upon himself to state the obvious. "You fancy her for yourself." He laughed aloud. "You do! You fancy her!"

"Shut up, man." Nik pretended to ignore him as he cackled joyously from the driver's seat.

But Aiden would have none of it. "Come on, mate! Fess up! You fancy her!"

Nik absolutely refused to respond.

Giving up the game, Aiden assented, "Ah mate, why didn't you just say so? I would never come between you and a little shagging. Bros before hoes and all that." He smiled broadly at his friend. "I'm just happy you're finally showing some interest in a girl again. I was beginning to wonder about you, you know."

Nik speared him with a dangerous glare. "For the last time. I said...Shut. The. Fuck. Up."

Grinning widely, Aiden put up his hands. "All right, all right. Just having a little fun, mate. No need to get your knickers in a twist." Whistling a tune, he glanced at the GPS and turned right.

As they sped down the highway, Nik spent the next hour or so brooding out the window, while Aiden sang along to bad 80's hair bands he found on the radio.

If the pain in the ass only knew how right he was, Nik would never hear the end of it. He did "fancy" her. He fancied her right out of her life and into his. But since he wasn't going to do anything about it, was it really fair of him to be so possessive of her? No, it wasn't. What was he going to do? Follow her around for the rest of her life scaring off any male who dared to so much as look at her?

Actually, that didn't sound like such a bad idea.

Problem was, he didn't know if he'd be able to help it. Even now, he could sense her near proximity, and his instincts were screaming at him to go back there and make her his. Completely.

And *that*, he would not—could not—ever do.

Sighing, he checked the clock. They were making good time. Pending any issues, they should arrive at the airport about an hour before sunrise.

A sound coming from the back of the vehicle startled him from his thoughts.

"What was that?" Nik asked. Turning the radio down, he listened.

Aiden stopped singing. "What? I don't hear anything."

But Nik was already out of his seat and walking toward the back. "Just keep driving. I'll be right back." As he neared the bedroom where Emma was sleeping, his skin prickled and the hair rose on his arms.

Wtf?

When he reached her door, he stopped and stood perfectly still, listening. All was quiet for a moment, but then…

There it was again.

Flinging open the door, he charged into the bedroom and quickly searched the room. His eyesight was perfect even in the dim light.

Emma was writhing on the bed, whimpering. The smell of her fear came off of her in waves, and his fangs punched down hard as he prepared to protect what was his.

16

Caught up in the nightmare, Emma felt the monsters holding her down, smelled the putrid smell of them, and panicked. She could feel her flesh tearing where they were biting her, and tried to fight her way free.

The big one finally pushed the others aside and dropped down hard on top of her. Bloody saliva dripping from its mouth, it grabbed her wrists and slammed them into the ground on each side of her head, holding her down as it violently bit her, sinking its fangs into the flesh right below her collar bone. Sucking and slurping at her blood, it humped her obscenely, trying to work its way under her skirt without letting go of her wrists.

Emma tried to scream, but the weight of the thing on top of her prevented her from getting enough air. She felt its grossly swollen member pushing at her entrance through her underwear, bruising her, and tears rolled down her face.

The loss of blood was making her weak. They'd bitten her all over, shoved their members at her, humped her and each other as they fed, and threw her around like a rag doll. Refusing to give up, she gulped in a breath. Gathering the last of her strength, she tried to twist away from it.

She felt her wrist bones crack as it squeezed them in response to her struggles, and she let out a raspy scream as it renewed its effort with even more enthusiasm than before. Her strength was fading rapidly, and she screeched in agony as another snuck in from the side, twisting her leg roughly out to its mouth, popping her knee and ripping into her calf...

Finally free, Emma shot up in the bed, crying out and shoving the remainder of the blankets aside.

"Shh..shhh...it's okay, Em. It's me. It's Nikulas. It was just a dream, sweetheart. It's ok. You're safe."

Sucking in great gulps of air, Emma blinked rapidly and looked around as she tried to get her bearings. Grabbing the front of her shirt, she looked for the blood she could still feel spurting out of her, but there was nothing. Her bones throbbed with the phantom pain of past injuries, and tears ran down her face.

Raising her head, she sniffed and wiped at her eyes to find Nik on one knee on the bed, his pained eyes frantically searching her face.

She looked around the room to check they were alone, and then gave him a small, watery smile, whispering hoarsely, "Sorry about that. Bad dream. I have them a lot."

"Do you want to talk about it?" Nik looked terrible, almost like he'd been there with her.

Emma just shook her head and looked down at her knotted hands.

He reached out and covered them with his own, stilling her fidgeting.

"Please talk to me," he said. "Maybe it will help."

She gave a snort of disgust. "I doubt it." At his hurt expression, she added, "But thank you."

"Did they rape you?" he blurted out suddenly. He looked as shocked as she was at the question, even though he'd been the one to ask it.

But then he clenched his jaw with determination. "Emma? Did they rape you?" When she didn't answer, he demanded, "*Answer* me, goddamn it."

"No!" she burst out, and then more calmly, "No. Not for lack of trying, but...no."

He sagged visibly with relief, and took a deep breath. "I'm sorry. I just needed to know."

Turning her hands, he held them in his. "I'm sorry you were hurt, Em, I'm so sorry." A steely edge came into his voice. "I don't know what these 'monsters' are you told me about, but if we ever see them, rest assured they won't live to hurt you again."

Emma had no doubt.

Squeezing her fingers one last time, he stood up to leave, because he wanted to stay. "I'll let you try to go back to sleep.

We should make it to the airport by sunrise, and we'll hole up there for the day, then fly to Seattle at sunset."

Emma came up on her knees, grabbing at his hand again with both of hers. "Please, don't go! Please. Please, stay with me Nikulas. Just for a while?"

Nik paused by the side of the bed. There was nothing he wanted more than to stay with her. He would love to crawl right into that bed with her and touch her until she had nothing on her mind but him.

Glad she didn't have his night vision, he rubbed the heel of his free hand over the ever-present bulge in his pants, trying to ease the sudden discomfort there. "I don't know if that's such a good idea."

She sat back on her heels and let go of his hand. "Of course not. Forget it. I'll be fine."

Nik watched her nightshirt flirt around the tops of her thighs as she leaned over to take a sip from her water bottle.

Fuck. Me.

But the pain of his erection became bearable again when he noticed the marks on her smooth legs.

He met her eyes, then looked back down at her legs.

Emma followed his gaze and quickly pulled the blanket over herself, hiding the scars from his view. "Never mind, it's okay. You can go. I'm going to try to get back to sleep."

Nik needed to leave. He needed to say goodnight, turn around, and walk out. Instead, he stood there, the image of her ravaged skin seared into his brain.

Without a word, he sat on the side of the bed and bent over to unlace his combat boots, setting them neatly by the nightstand. He straightened the blankets around Emma, and she scooted down without a word as he tucked her in. Crawling in next to her on top of the blankets, he curled himself around her, threw an arm around her, and tugged her into the curve of his body.

He had no words as he lay there holding her, breathing her unique scent and listening to her heartbeat slow as she eventually relaxed and drifted off to sleep. Even when he heard her soft snores, he stayed with her, keeping her close. She shouldn't wake up alone again if the monsters came back.

The RV finally came to a stop. They must be at the hanger. He heard the steel shutters clang down and Aiden's footsteps as he headed back to one of the sofa beds. The thought crossed his mind that he should get up and grab a bag out of the fridge, then crash on the other couch, but he couldn't bring himself to leave the side of the tiny warrior he was protecting.

As Nik felt the rising sun pulling him down into slumber, he accepted the inevitable. He may not ever make her his in truth, but from now on, he would always be there to protect her.

Even if it was only from her own mind.

17

Two hours later, Nik suddenly sat straight up, leapt off the bed, and flung open the bedroom door. Hastening out into the sitting area, he passed by Aiden, who was just waking up himself. "Where is she?"

Aiden twisted around, causing a loud chorus of snap, crackle, pop to run up his spine. "Who?"

"Who? Emma! Who the fuck else would I be talking about?" Long strides ate up the length of the RV as he checked all the seats and then the door to see that it was still locked.

"How should I know? She's *your* witch. *You* should be watching her." Rubbing his hands over his face, Aiden shuffled into the bathroom to wash up.

"I'm *not* a witch." Emma's voice sounded behind him.

Nik's head whipped around to find her leaning in the bedroom doorway with a book in her hand. "Where the fuck were you?"

"I was right next to you, if you'd bothered to look around before charging out here to bellow at poor Aiden." She waved the book she'd been reading at him.

Now that she'd been found, he felt like a complete and utter idiot for going off all half-cocked like he had. And she was right. If he'd paused a second, he would have sensed her there. He'd had her blood. And even from that small amount, he would be able to find her anywhere within a mile radius. What the hell was the matter with him?

However, as far as he knew, she didn't know that yet. "No. You weren't. I think I would have noticed." Running his eyes over her black yoga pants and green top with approval, he added distractedly, "And I was not bellowing."

"Yes, you were!" Aiden called from the bathroom.

Scowling, Nik shot a dirty look in that direction. He gave her another once over before he abruptly turned away without another word and walked over to the fridge. He needed to feed before he trusted himself to be anywhere in the near vicinity of her without hauling her back into that bed and forcing himself on her. Ripping the fridge door open, he grabbed the first bag he found and threw it in the microwave, then stood there watching the countdown impatiently.

Emma sat down cross-legged on the empty couch across from Aiden's with her book. "Looks like somebody woke up on the wrong side of the coffin."

He ignored her as he reached into the microwave and got his breakfast, shaking it up to even out the heat. Snagging the tip of the bag with his teeth, he ripped it off and spit it into the trash, then upended the bag into his mouth, chugging it down like water.

Emma wrinkled her nose as she watched him.

It tasted disgusting, but he finished the bag, and even grabbed another. When he was finished, he found a water and turned to face her. "Did you eat?"

"I had an apple. You drink water?"

Ignoring her question, he frowned at her. "You need to eat more than that." Opening the cabinet, he rifled through the contents. "Can I make you something? There's oatmeal, soup—would you like some tea?" When he got no response, he stuck his head out to find her watching him with an unreadable expression on her face. "What?"

"Why do you care whether I eat or not?" she asked.

Why *did* he care? He was acting like a goddamn mother hen for Christ's sake, but he just couldn't seem to help himself. "Uh. It's just that we're going to be getting on the plane, and the flight's going to be pretty long."

"I can't eat on the plane? Don't they usually have a little kitchen?"

Closing the cabinet, he mumbled, "Yeah, probably."

Emma was silent a moment, and he was afraid to look at her for fear of what he'd see. She was probably laughing at him. But then she said, "Actually, if you wouldn't mind grabbing a pack of oatmeal...that sounds really good."

He grinned widely at her before he caught himself. The smile fell from his face as he turned back to the contents in the cabinet. "Sure. No problem. Long as I'm right here, anyway." Grabbing a bowl, he read the instructions on the box, and then dumped in the oatmeal and the required amount of water.

Throwing it in the microwave, he checked the back of the box again, and then set the time.

Emma was watching him, curiosity plain on her face. He could only imagine what she was thinking. One minute he was kissing her like his life depended on it, and the next he was brushing it off as an overreaction to the bloodlust. Then, he gets her here and sends her right off to bed, only to come running when she wakes from a nightmare. He tells her it's not a good idea to stay with her afterward, then ends up sleeping next to her all day. He wakes up in a horrible mood, grumbling at everyone, and ten minutes later couldn't be happier just to fix her some oatmeal.

He was starting to think they had it all wrong about females being the crazy ones.

Aiden sauntered out of the bathroom in cargo pants and his ever-present hoodie right as the timer went off announcing her food was ready. Throwing yesterday's clothes on his bed, he wandered up to watch Nik stirring her oatmeal. "I don't know how anyone can eat that mush." Wrinkling his nose, he eyeballed his friend. "You know, you're going to make someone a fine wife someday, mate."

Nik looked at him sideways, but refused to rise to the bait.

Aiden smirked to himself and walked over to his cell phone. "I'll give Bill a holler and see if things are ready."

"Who's Bill?" Emma asked as Nik brought her oatmeal to her. She smiled at him in thanks, but he refused to look at her, just set down her bowl and walked away. He heard her sigh, then pick up her spoon and take a bite.

"Bill is a friend of ours," Aiden told her as he plopped down in his office chair. "A human friend. He's going to be our pilot."

"And you trust him? I mean, I would imagine it must be frightening to have your lives in the hands of a human."

"Yes, yes, terrifying...Bill! Aiden. How are we doing out there? Mm hmm. Good! One hour. We're in the hanger. See you then." Turning his chair around to face them, he informed Nik, "We'll be ready in one hour. He's just fueling up. I think I'm going to go find a meal for myself. I'm feeling a bit peckish."

Grinning nefariously at Emma, who had stopped eating with the spoon midway to her mouth, he pulled on his boots and entered the code to unlock the RV. With a casual wave, he shut the door behind him with a bang.

Carefully setting her spoon back into the bowl, she asked, "When he says he's going to find dinner, he means...a human dinner?"

"He's a vampire, Em." Nik re-locked the door and came over to sit across from her. "Don't look at me like that. He won't hurt anyone. Aiden's prey of choice is usually a pretty little female who is more than happy to give him what he wants."

She looked slightly relieved, but not entirely convinced. "But don't you all worry someone will say something and your secret will be out?"

"Won't happen. He erases their memory before he leaves them." He didn't mention he only erased the feeding part, not the sex that inevitably came with it. Aiden liked to be remembered as the sex god he thought he was, at least until the female got too clingy.

Feeding and sex went hand in hand for vampires. It was hard to do one and not the other, as Nik's little performance last night proved.

Thinking of the intense lust that had overcome him in her kitchen, and the revelation afterward, had Nik rubbing his palms restlessly up and down his thighs.

"You can do that? Erase memories?" At his nod, she asked him weakly, "Are you going to erase mine when you're done with me?"

His eyes traveled over her. She had no makeup on, but her hazel-green eyes shone brightly from beneath dark lashes, and her strawberry hair was curling chaotically around her face. As he watched, a faint blush bloomed on her cheeks at his close perusal of her, and she lowered her gaze, hiding her eyes from him. She was absolutely lovely.

He didn't mean to say it, he really didn't. But it came out anyway. "No. I won't. I don't think I'll ever be done with you Emma."

At his softly spoken words, her gaze flew up and crashed with his across the small space of the vehicle. They stayed like that, the look between them saying more than words ever could, until Emma finally broke the connection by clearing her throat and looking away.

Getting up, she took her bowl to the sink and washed it, putting it back up into the cabinet. "Should I pack up some of this stuff to bring with us?"

Nik ran his hands through his hair, tugging at it with both hands. What the *fuck* had made him say that out loud? He really needed to chill the fuck out with this bonded shit. He was never going to do anything about these feelings he had. It wasn't fair of him to lead her on. Not even a little bit.

What the hell makes me think she'd even want to be with me anyway?

Taking a deep breath, he psyched himself up to harden his resolve against her. He shouldn't even like her. Her sister was keeping his brother hostage. Well, maybe not directly, but there was no way in hell Leeha would be able to hold him without her help.

Maybe Emma was just a really good actress. Maybe she knew about this all along. Maybe it was all a big plot to capture all of them. He was grasping at straws, he knew, but he needed to find *something* that would help him battle this obsession with her.

All of this ran through his head within just a few seconds as he stared at the table in front of him.

"Nik?"

"What," he snapped.

Visibly startled by the tone of his voice, Emma said, "I was just asking if I should pack up some of the food to bring along with us, or is there stuff on the plane?"

"Oh. Um. Yeah, I don't know. It would probably be a good idea." He went over to help her, removing her recycled bag from where he'd stashed it in a drawer. "We probably won't be able to fit it all. What would you like to bring?"

She found what she wanted and set it on the counter. "Would you mind grabbing the tea? I can't reach it."

Stepping up behind her he reached over her head to get it and the agave sweetener for her. He heard her breath catch in her throat as he pressed the length of his body against her back.

Nik immediately backed off and leaned back against the opposite counter.

She was still for a moment, and then continued loading up her bag. "What exactly did you mean before, when you said you'd never be done with me?"

He gave her nothing but a whole lot of silence in answer to her question. No way in hell he was answering that. Hanging his head, his hair hid his features as he stared at the floor, trying to think of a way to change the subject.

She repeated the question. "Nik. What did you mean?"

"Nothing. I didn't mean anything." He raised his head, and felt like a bastard as he saw doubt, confusion, and finally self-loathing pass over her face along with a myriad of other emotions.

She swallowed hard. "Are you not affected by me at all?" she asked softly.

The despondency in her voice was all it took to break down his resistance. Her anger he could deal with. Her standoffishness he could deal with. But knowing he was causing her pain, of any sort? He could *not* deal with that.

Grabbing her hand, he slammed it onto his aching erection. The constant, fucking painful erection he had whenever he was within six feet of her. He groaned aloud at the feel of her touching him even through his jeans. "Does this feel like I'm not affected by you Emma? *Does* it?"

18

Nik held her hand hard against his cock as he braced himself on the cabinet behind her with his other arm and curled his hips forward, rubbing himself up and down her palm. His head fell forward until his forehead rested on her hair and he drew a ragged breath. Her answering arousal filled his nose until there was nothing else between them. Her heart pounded in his ears as her blood rushed through her veins, just as hard as his.

The taste of her was sharp on his tongue, in spite of the fact he'd just fed. He needed to stop this, before he was unable to. Removing his hand from atop hers, he made to back away, but Emma grabbed him around the waist and pulled him back toward her while that other hand—oh yeah, *that other hand*—rubbed down his cock to his balls. His head fell back on a gasp as she gently squeezed them.

Holy shit. "Sweetheart, we need to stop."

"I don't want to stop," she said huskily. Moving both hands to the front of his jeans, she undid the button and grasped the zipper with shaking hands, but managed to get it down. As she slid her hands under the waistband and along his hips to push them down, Nik grabbed her wrists, effectively halting her progress. His skin felt tight and his lips were pulled back from fully extended fangs.

With a sound of frustration, she looked up, her eyes widening.

He gritted out, "We have to stop. Now. Or I'm going to bend you over that counter and fuck you. *Hard.*"

Instead of the effect he was hoping for, his words brought on a fresh surge of the scent of her sex. He felt her trembling, and knew she'd be soaking wet for him. He ached to touch her there, to feel her desire for him. To taste it. A deep growl rose up from low in his throat at the thought.

Leaning forward, she put her nose to his chest. Inhaling him deeply, she whispered, "Nikulas. Please."

He was losing his inner battle. She was like a soft, curvy 12 gauge, blowing away all of his arguments. Her whispered plea screamed at him to take her. Take her and make her his, and never let her go.

Releasing her wrists, he wrapped his arms around her head and shoulders and pulled her to him, struggling with the war raging within him between his desire and his fear. He heard her soft exhale as she slid her arms around his waist, her slender arms pulling him tighter against her.

A loud pounding at the door made them both jump away from each other. Nik grit his teeth as her face paled with guilt.

"Nik! Let me in!" Aiden shouted from outside.

Back in their own corners, they stared each other down.

Aiden pounded on the door again, "Come on! Open up! The plane is ready."

Giving Emma a look of betrayal she couldn't understand, he strode over and entered the code to let Aiden in.

Emma turned around and put her back to the door. Closing the cabinet, she scampered toward the bedroom just as Aiden climbed up the steps to come inside.

"Hallo, you two! What's going—"? He stopped as he lifted his nose and got a good whiff of the lingering scents in the air. "Ahhhh..." Smiling from ear to ear, he watched Emma hurrying to the back and then turned to Nik, staring pointedly at his unzipped pants.

"Interrupt something, did I?" His grin widened, and Nik stormed off to the bathroom without a word. The click of the lock echoed through the interior as he heard Aiden say, "Was it something I said?"

Turning on the water as hot as he could stand it, Nik yanked his shirt over his head and threw it on the floor. He let out a hiss as pants and boxer briefs slid over his still raging erection. It sprang free, hanging heavily at the juncture of his hips as he kicked them away and got into the shower stall. He moaned aloud as the spray of water hit him, his abs tightening and his cock kicking up in response. He needed some relief from this, or he was never going to make it to Seattle.

Palming his thick length, he slid his hand up and down the thick shaft. The water made it slick and he squeezed the head as he came to the top. He thought of Emma's small hand covering him, and his hips started pumping faster of their own accord, his grip tightening as he imagined it was her holding him. His breathing grew harsh and his heart pounded hard and fast.

Nik closed his eyes, and remembered the feel of her perfect little ass in his palm, her soft breasts pressed against his ribs as he kissed her the first time. He remembered sinking his fangs into her lip, her blood on his tongue...

Out of his mind with lust, he turned his head and sank his fangs into his own arm, feeding from himself. Bracing that arm against the wall, he continued to drink as he felt his balls tighten and his cock start to pulse in his hand. He came almost violently, exploding onto the wall in front of him as his whole body surged forward, instinctively looking for his witch.

Nik bit down hard on his arm to smother the roar that erupted from his chest. He rode out his orgasm for long minutes, until finally, with a few last strokes, he released himself. Removing his fangs from his arm, he licked the wound closed and dropped his head. His legs shook as he steadied himself against the side of the stall.

He stayed as he was for a long moment, eyes closed, arms hanging limply at his sides, hot water pounding on his hanging head, and trying to catch his breath.

Eventually, he straightened up and wiped the water out of his eyes. Looking down his ridged stomach to his still-hard cock, he came to the realization he was fighting a losing battle.

He'd hoped that taking care of it himself would at least release some tension. And it had. A bit.

Yet, it didn't change anything. He still wanted Emma. Every cell in his body craved her. He wanted all of her. Completely.

And it pissed him off because this was a distraction he did not need right now.

Speaking of which, he had a plane to catch. Quickly, he scrubbed his head and body clean and rinsed off, then shut off the water. He rubbed himself nearly raw with the towel, threw on some running pants and a T-shirt, then shook the water from his hair.

Grabbing his stuff, he went out into the RV to find Emma and Aiden already gone. Gritting his teeth at the idea of them alone together, he shoved his stuff into his travel bag, slipped on his sneakers, and slammed out of the RV, not even bothering to lock it behind him.

19

Emma walked to the runway alongside Aiden toward the small, private jet they would take to Seattle. The night air was chilly, but refreshing, and helped clear her head.

He had his duffle bag slung over one shoulder and was carrying her small suitcase in the other hand. Emma brought along her backpack and bag of food. Glancing sideways at her companion, she couldn't keep from asking sarcastically, "So, did you find someone to eat?"

Aiden raised his eyebrows, "Are you jealous, love?"

"No!" She shuddered slightly as he chuckled.

"Actually, I did find quite a delectable young flight attendant." Sneaking a peak at Emma—who had a sudden fascination with the nonexistent scenery—he elaborated, "A voluptuous brunette, with juicy arteries and *huge* tits..."

"Ug! Never mind!" If her hands had been free she would've slapped them over her ears. Since that wasn't an option, she just walked faster as he made gross smacking noises at her with his lips.

Where the hell is Nikulas?

Aiden easily caught up to her. "Seriously, love, do you really think I *eat* people? I'm not Hannibal Lector, though we do share the same hilarious wit, don't you think? I guess you really don't know me well enough, yet. But, no worries! We'll have plenty of time for that on the plane ride! By the time we reach Seattle, we'll be best mates, you and I." Scooting up in front of her, he walked backwards, his eyes sparkling at the prospect of harassing her all the way across the country.

Rolling her eyes, Emma looked back over her shoulder to see Nik following them at an easy run.

Oh, Thank God.

Swiveling her head back around, she ran smack into Aiden, who had come to a dead stop, and was staring at her with a hurt look on his face. "Oh! Sorry!" She exclaimed. "I didn't realize you'd stopped. *Directly in front of me.*"

With a sad frown and a puppy dog tilt to his head, he asked, "You really don't want to be my friend, Emma?"

Are you kidding me? "Um. I didn't say that, Aiden."

"But you rolled your eyes at me," he declared. "I saw you."

"Oh, nooo...no...I was just wondering what was taking Nik so long." She silently begged that the vampire in question hurry it the hell up. She should've waited for him instead of being so anxious to get out of that damn RV.

A breathtaking smile lit up Aiden's face. It really *was* too bad he was a total nut job.

"Oh! He's on his way. I see him coming now." He turned around and started walking again. "Come along then."

Dragging her feet, she followed, glancing back once more to reassure herself that Nik had nearly caught up.

Honestly, he made her a bit nervous, this one.

Nik closed the magazine he'd bought for the flight with an impatient sigh. The first half of the plane ride to Seattle had been uneventful, other than Aiden's insistent overtures of friendship to Emma, which consisted of him sitting in the luxury seat facing her, and intermittently regaling her with stories of his riskiest sexual exploits and trying to convince her that she was, indeed, a witch.

Around his tenth or eleventh try to goad her "witchy side" into appearing, her head fell back onto the headrest and she groaned with frustration. "Aiden! I'm telling you for the last time, I am NOT a witch! I can't see the future! I can't control the weather, or fire...or anything! And even if I could—*which I can't*—but even if I could, I shouldn't be trying to do any of that while forty thousand feet in the air!"

"So you're telling me nothing unusual ever happens when you're around?"

"That has nothing to do with anything—" she began.

"Just *try,*" he insisted, as she threw up her hands angrily.

They both turned to Nik.

"Would you please tell her she *is* a witch?"

"Would you please tell him I am NOT a witch?"

Talking over each other, they returned to arguing amongst themselves.

"I am not!"

"You *are*!"

Nik's patience, both with the arguing and the monopolizing of Emma's attention, had come to an end. *"Enough!"* Nik roared. "I am NOT the parent here, goddammit!"

"Of course you're not the parent," Aiden scoffed. "That would just be silly, as *Luukas* is the Master Vampire." Cocking his head to the side, he narrowed his eyes at Nikulas. "Something's eating at you. You just haven't been yourself since you brought Emma, here, aboard." Snapping his fingers, he exclaimed, "I know! Would it help if we talked about it?"

Nik widened his eyes, and with a furtive glance toward Emma, who appeared to be busy trying to look as disinterested as possible, told him, "No. It most certainly would *not* help to talk about it at this moment."

Sitting back in his seat, Aiden crossed his legs and steepled his fingers beneath his chin. "I disagree. I think it would help immensely to get a certain *something* off your chest, so to speak."

He was going to kill his best friend. He really was. Slowly. And so very painfully. "I'm warning you, Aid...Shut. Up."

"Oh, come on! Let's hash it out, as they say. We have nothing else to do at the moment, and we still have a few hours until we land in Seattle. I promise you'll feel better." With a naughty smirk, Aiden winked at Emma.

Nik's mind spun, frantically trying to think of a way to shut him the fuck up. He needed something to distract him.

"Emma. You are a witch." He hated throwing her under the bus, but if it would distract his so-called friend…

"What?!" she cried.

"I told you so!" Aiden crowed happily to Emma.

Well, what do you know? It worked. He was really going to have to remember that trick. "Your family comes from a coven of witches that dates back as long as we do, probably longer. I tried to tell you about this last night, and I understand your reluctance to hear it, really, I do, but—"

She put her head in her hands. "I. Am. NOT…"

Slashing his hand sharply through the air, Nik cut her off. "You ARE. *Every* woman in your family, and some of the men, as far back as we can remember, have been witches. Your *mother* was a witch."

"My mother??"

"Your *sister* is a witch. Unless there's been some weird mutation in your gene pool when it comes to you, specifically, you have to be one too. The only thing that changes is the level of power from one person to another."

Emma sank down into her seat, like the wind had been knocked out of her. "If this is true, how did I live my entire life and not know? *Why* wouldn't I know?"

"I have no idea." He was just as baffled as she looked.

Aiden chimed in, "Maybe if we tell her some of the history?"

Nik nodded and Aiden continued. "See, basically it boils down to this: There are two kind of vampires, good ones and bad ones. We," he indicated Nik and himself, "are the good ones, and we call ourselves, simply 'Vampires'. The other group is known in our world these days as the 'Legion'. Now the Legion, they are some *wonky* vampires. Leeha, their leader, is the worst one. She's fabulously mad, and quite beautiful. Her arse alone makes a man want to...to..." He stuttered to a halt, and settled on appreciative grunting noises as he squeezed the air with his hands.

"I don't think Emma cares about her ass," Nik cut in, picking up where Aiden had left off. "But as he was saying, she is totally fucking psycho, and her followers are right up there with her."

"Occasionally," Aiden interrupted, "when a vampire is turned, they come out of it just, not quite right."

"Long story short," Nik continued, "Leeha is one of those Vampires. She was made a vampire illegally. Kidnapped as a human child by one of our males. He secretly raised her as his daughter, and on her 25th birthday, he turned her without permission from Luukas."

Emma interrupted to ask, "Why would he need permission?"

"Because if we let every Vlad, Count, and Elvira make vampires willy-nilly, the population would quickly get out of control and we would run out of humans to eat." Aiden said as matter-of-factly as if he'd been asking her to pass the salt.

Nik scowled at him. "Anyway, when Luukas found out, the male who did this was tried by our Council and sentenced to death by fire. Leeha was spared. At the time, we believed she wasn't to blame for his actions. We've since learned she was not as innocent as she appeared."

Pausing to gather his thoughts, he stretched his long, muscular legs out in front of him and crossed his ankles. Emma's eyes flickered over his body, and he bit back a smile as she tore them away and asked, "What made you reconsider?"

"We found out later from the servants in his household he had raised Leeha to believe she would one-day rule by Luukas' side. We've no clue where he got that idea. He'd taken her from her human family when she was quite young; he's the only parent she remembers. When she turned about 14, he began preparing her to be queen. He abused her as no daughter should be abused, and justified it by telling her she needed to have sexual prowess to be able to win over the Master Vampire." Nik flashed his fangs, his lip curling up in disgust.

"So vampires do have relationships with other vampires?"

"No. Never. Which is why we were so shocked when we found out what he'd been telling her. Sometimes they'll, uh, hook up, but they never stay together in a long-term thing. Once in a while though, a Vampire and a human will mate."

Little lines of confusion appeared between her brows. "But aren't humans just food for vampires?"

Nik's blue eyes burned fiercely into hers. "Not always, no."

"See, Em...I feel like I can call you 'Em' now...Is that okay?" Aiden blurted out. At her distracted nod, he ignored Nik's scowl and repeated, "See, Em, vampires don't mate with other vampires because they can't sustain each other. We can feed off of other vamps, it doesn't hurt us, but it's kind of like eating a rice cake. You can't live off of it. We need viable, live, human blood to survive. And since feeding and sex are so closely intertwined, it makes sense to have a human if you want a significant other. Personally, I find monogamy quite boring, I would never tie myself down to just one flavor, but to each his own."

"But Nik drinks donated blood, from a bag."

Before Nik could defend his actions, Aiden added "And you can clearly see how he suffers for it."

Nik shifted uncomfortably as she scrutinized him from head to toe.

"He looks fine to me."

"Thank you." With a smile for Emma, Nik flipped off Aiden.

"What does the human get out of it? Other than being a food bank?" Emma asked.

"What do they get out of it?" Aiden exclaimed. "They get protection, a longer life! They get to stay young, and beautiful! And, love, *most importantly*, they get to experience mind-blowing vampire sex."

"What Aiden is trying to say," Nik blurted, "is if a human is taken as a vampire's mate, he or she will actually exchange blood with the vampire. Not as much as we drink, of course, but a little of our blood will go a long way."

Emma made a face. "That's so gross."

"Don't knock it till you've tried it, poppet." Aiden waggled his eyebrows at her.

She looked at him like he was nuts and turned her attention back to Nik. "So, what exactly would your blood do?"

"Um. Well, if we exchanged blood, I would be able to find you anywhere. I would be able to protect you should anything ever happen. Also, my blood would keep you young and healthy, and you'd grow stronger than a normal human. You'd never get sick. You'd heal faster. You would be as immortal as I am as long as you were with me."

"As long as no one cut off your head or ripped out a vital organ." Aiden chimed in.

"What would happen if I stopped drinking it?"

"You would begin to age at that time, picking up right where you left off."

While Emma mulled that over, Nik tried to get the conversation back on topic, "Anyway, all this stuff isn't important for you to know right now."

"Mmmm, I don't know." Aiden tilted his head and tapped a finger against his chin in mock consideration. "I think it is *very* important for Emma to know all of this 'stuff', and the sooner the better the way things are going."

He ducked to the side to avoid the water bottle Nik chucked at him. It hit the floor and rolled toward the front of the plane. He gave Nik a hurt look. "You know, I'm beginning to feel a bit unappreciated here. I think I may just go hang out with pilot Bill for a bit."

Shaking his head in disbelief at Aiden's back, Nik waited until the cockpit door clicked shut before continuing. "So, long story short. Leeha decided to take it upon herself to make her father's wishes come true. Luuk went to meet her one night, and we haven't seen him since.

Emma looked down at her folded hands, then back up at Nik. "But, how do you know for sure Leeha has him? Could something else have happened?"

"Maybe. Except she called and told us she has him."

20

"Did I leave out that part?" Nik asked as Emma's mouth fell open. He chewed the inside of his cheek. He could've sworn he'd told her.

"She told you this? When? Did she say anything about my sister?"

"No. She just told us she has Luukas."

"She didn't mention anything at all about Keira?" A note of desperation flavored her voice.

He shook his head.

"Then tell me again why you think Keira is even with her," she said indignantly.

Sitting forward to rest his elbows on his knees, he admitted, "Actually, as I told you before, we don't know for sure..."

Emma sat up straight in her seat and folded her arms over her chest

"Don't go all ballistic on me. A few months after she claimed to have Luuk, one of the guys heard about your sister going missing. We knew of your family heritage already, and we put two and two together."

"That still doesn't explain to me why you think she's there," she insisted.

"Like I told you, we think she's there because the only way Leeha would be able to hold Luuk anywhere he didn't want to be, is by having some way of keeping him weakened enough he couldn't escape. There are only two ways of doing that. She can starve him, obviously, but that takes time. Older vampires only need to feed a few times a month, so how would she hold him there long enough to get him so malnourished his power would be weakened to the point where he couldn't escape?"

"I know, I know." Her voice dripped with sarcasm. "A witch."

"Exactly. A witch. Having a powerful witch on her side would give Leeha the upper hand. There are spells that can weaken even a Master Vampire like my brother. And your sister, is the only witch we know of who can't be accounted for during the past seven years."

"I just can't believe my sister would have kept a secret like that from me," Emma muttered, "Or that she would ever do something like this. She'd never purposely hurt anyone. She just wouldn't."

The hurt he could hear in her voice tugged at his insides. "I'm sure she had a very good reason for doing it."

"Yeah, I guess." After a breath, she asked, "How did you know about my family? Is there some kind of supernatural online community I don't know about or something?"

He barked out a laugh. "Yeah! Allsupes.com - Meet other supernatural beings in your area! Vamps! Find your favorite blood type in our human donor database! Wolves! Looking for that perfect bitch? Just answer our questionnaire..."

Emma squinted at him in annoyance as he threw his head back and laughed. "I'm so glad you can amuse yourself at my expense. Wait, did you say 'wolves'?"

He nodded as he wiped at his eyes and tried to get it together. "Yeah, wolves. Like werewolves, you know?"

"*There are werewolves?*" Emma's face was so shocked, Nik started laughing all over again.

"Nikulas! Would you *please* stop!" Emma had to shout to be heard over all the noise.

"Sorry. I'm sorry." He took a deep breath and wiped his eyes again, fighting to control himself. "Okay. Sorry. Um...no, there isn't a website. At least not that I'm aware of. And yes, there are werewolves. You may meet some of them in Seattle. They like the colder climates. They run kind of hot. I'm surprised you've never run into any living out in the country where you do."

"I don't get out very much," she said.

Sitting back in her seat, she looked bewildered as she tried to absorb the fact that everything she'd thought she'd known about the world was false.

"Vampires, and witches, and wolves. Are faeries real too? Magical elves? Dragons?" She waved away his answer with a muttered, "I really don't want to know." After a moment, she turned her head to look at him. "So, my family? How did you know about us?"

"I've never met your mom or sister, but vampires and witches have worked together throughout the years for the 'greater good', so to speak. And the Moss family has always played a prominent role in that association with us, up until recently." He smiled at her. "You witches agree to help us, and we agree not to feed on you. Unless it's by mutual consent, of course."

Ignoring that last comment, she asked, "Helped you how?"

"Witches from the family in our area have helped us control the Legion. And before that, there were different reasons. Vampires are notoriously territorial, so fights spring up all the time between each other or between us and another species. As witches are the only ones who can really hurt us, it was in our best interest to form an alliance with them right from the start."

"So what you're admitting to me, is that I'm the only one on this plane who could hurt you?"

He nodded. "Depending on your power, yes."

"Is that smart of you to tell me?"

"Are you going to hurt me, Em?" he asked her in a low voice.

"Of course not," she answered softly.

"Good." He searched her face before dropping his eyes to the pulse in her throat. As he stared, the beats came faster. Harder.

He cleared his throat, breaking the spell. "And as much as I hate to admit it, Aiden is right about one thing. We should work with you on helping you to control your 'witchy side' as he likes to call it."

"I still think that I would know if I was a witch," she insisted.

"At the risk of sounding like your worst Freudian nightmare, why don't you tell me about your childhood? Whatever you remember. What about, like, premonitions? Or, did anything ever happen if you were feeling really emotional? Like really angry or something?"

She looked down at her hands, twisted in her lap. "Yeah, I've had some weird things happen when I'm upset. Keira, too. We never really talked about it. It was just something that happened. I don't think we even realized it wasn't normal until we started school."

"Your parents never mentioned anything to explain why this stuff happened?"

"No. Not a word. They just acted like it was no big deal for things to fly across the room when I was mad I couldn't have dessert, or whatever." She gave him a pained smile. "As we got older, the incidents tapered off, unless I get really upset. Working out seems to help."

"Yet, amazingly, nothing has flown through the air to smash over my head during any of our previous conversations. Other than some jumpy salt and pepper shakers at the bar, of course. Why do you think that is?"

She shrugged. "I don't know. You've certainly deserved it a few times. And it's not like I haven't thought about it."

Hiding his smile at that last comment, he asked, "Did you never wonder why these things were happening?"

She shook her head. "I've always just felt like I didn't belong. I never had any friends, except my sister. She had the same problems in school as I did, but it never seemed to bother her as much. I've always just thought she was stronger than I am. I guess I never really questioned it."

"I'm not uncomfortable around you." Reaching across the narrow aisle, he took her small hand in his.

She jumped at his touch. Ever since their encounter earlier, he'd made it a point not to be anywhere within three feet of her, not wanting to tempt himself more. But after hearing the loneliness in her voice, he felt the need to prove to her he meant what he'd said.

After a pause, she threaded her fingers through his. "What you were saying earlier? About when humans and vampires mate and what happens when they exchange blood? Does that work if it's only one way?"

He knew this question was coming, he'd seen it click in her head earlier. Looking down at their joined hands, he gently played with her fingers, hoping she wouldn't remember the ass he'd made of himself when he'd woken up. "I can sense you when you're nearby, because I've had your blood, if that's what you're asking."

He narrowed his eyes at her as she bit back a smile. Guess it was too much to ask that she didn't catch on to that. She didn't tease him about it, though.

"What exactly do you mean by 'sense'? Just that I'm there?"

"Where you are, and your general sense of well-being. I can feel it if you're angry or upset. Or sad, like you are now. But I've always been able to do that. It's just stronger now. Does that bother you?" He watched her reaction closely. "Em?" He started pulling his hand away.

But she closed her fingers tighter around his to keep him there, and told him firmly, "No. It doesn't bother me."

Letting out the breath he didn't realize he'd been holding, he carefully squeezed her hand in response before he released her. "Good." Then he attempted to steer the conversation back on to safer ground. "When we land, if you're not too tired—"

"What is this Nik?" she blurted. "With us? I mean, are you just playing with me for your own amusement? Is that it? The naive human? Or witch? Or whatever I am?" Her voice trembled. "Because if that's what you're doing, please just...stop."

"Emma—"

"Are you just acting like you're interested in me to keep me here so I'll help you? Because you don't have to do that, either. I would help you anyway if there was any chance at all of me finding my sister."

"It's not that simple," he argued.

"Sure it is, Nikulas. If it's just your...predator instincts, or the thrill of the chase, or whatever, causing you to run all hot and cold with me, knock it off. I have enough on my plate right now without having to deal with any more confusing emotions caused by you."

Nik launched himself out of his seat to pace up and down the aisle, tugging at his hair with both hands in frustration. *Dammit Em, just let it go.* "That's not it. I haven't...I wouldn't do that."

"Then what, exactly, is it?" she asked sarcastically.

He paced faster, not even bothering to put forth the 'human' façade, and clenched his teeth together so hard his jaw hurt. "Shouldn't you be afraid of me, Emma? I'm a vampire, for

Christ's sake! You've been attacked before! Why the *fuck* are you not afraid of me?"

"Just answer the damn question, Nik!" she snapped.

He came to an abrupt halt directly in front of her, and just shook his head. The misery in her eyes ripped him apart. But, how could he explain something to her he barely understood himself?

Apparently, she'd gotten her answer. "Okay, then. So, we'll work together to try to find our family. Other than that, please leave me alone." Taking off her seatbelt, she lifted her chin and rose out of her seat. She wouldn't look at him as she headed to the restroom at the front of the plane.

His anguished voice tore from his chest against his will, stopping her dead in her tracks. "I can't."

She froze outside the bathroom door. "What did you say?"

His eyes burned as he admitted, "I can't leave you alone. I *want* to, I do. I'm trying, but I fear I *can't*."

"Why not?" she asked softly.

"Because you're MINE," he grated through his teeth.

Her forehead scrunched up in confusion. "What?"

Planting his hands low on his lean hips, his head fell forward in defeat. Fuck it. He may as well tell her. She'd find out eventually anyway, one way or the other. "You're *mine*. I can't leave you alone, but I can't have you either. And it's tearing me up inside."

Agony flowed from him like a living, breathing thing, filling the cabin. It was so palpable, he heard Emma lose her breath when it first hit her.

Cautiously, she walked toward him until she was close enough to touch. "Nikulas, what are you talking about?"

He inhaled a ragged breath and lifted his head. His tortured eyes locked onto her face. "You're *mine,* Emma. My mate. Given to me by fate, fucking bitch that she is. I knew the moment I tasted your blood." He gave a derisive laugh. "I always passed it off as just a fable, you know? A story passed down through the years from the elders. But it's not. It's real. It's taken me over 600 years, but I've finally found you. And I can't *fucking* have you."

Emma was obviously struggling to understand. "Why can't you have me?"

He didn't answer at first, just ran his eyes desperately, hungrily, over her face, stopping at the pulse beating in her throat.

"Because I'll kill you."

21

Christian walked through downtown Seattle. Man, he loved this city. He loved the gloomy weather. Loved the hustle and bustle of downtown and Pike Market. Loved the different neighborhoods, each so distinctive in their own way. Loved the ferries, the islands, the mountains. He even loved the homeless population. No one really noticed when they came up missing.

Disposable humans. Always a good feature of the place Dante called home. And being that he was an important part of their group, it kept them all out of trouble, and allowed them to stay here.

Christian didn't understand the way the old ones behaved sometimes. The way they didn't care. Maybe it was because they'd been *inhuman* for so long, they'd forgotten what it was like to be human. Maybe, in a few hundred years, he'd become just like them. Not caring if his meal lived or died. Not caring if somebody's mom or dad or brother or sister didn't come home. Not caring if families got ripped apart and destroyed.

But today was not that day. Today, he would carry on as usual. Fucking, feeding, and sending them home. Safe and sound.

Hitting 6th Ave, he headed toward Belltown, threading his way through the crowd of people outside Nordstrom's. There was a cute little dancer he'd been eyeing up at a strip club there. He glanced down at his watch. He should arrive just in time to talk her into taking the night off, and spending it with him. Or at least an hour or two of it.

Then he'd be off to find another female. And another. And another. Until the rising sun chased him back to the sanctuary of his apartment, right next door to Shea's.

He never brought a female home with him, preferring to keep things as anonymous as possible, erasing their memories when necessary. And it was always necessary. If he brought them home, he'd see the faces of the women he used everywhere he looked. He could barely live with himself as it was. He needed a place that held no memories of what a complete and total asshole he was.

Shaking it off, he cut through an alley behind the theatre. He could be disgusted with himself later. Right now he wanted—no, needed—to get to the strip club, and the bleached blonde who would be arriving there on the bus in about five minutes.

Christian came to the end of the alley. Pulling his cell phone out of his front pocket, he looked down to check the time, but a noise behind him had him glancing over his shoulder. Suddenly, his cell phone fell from his hand and smashed apart on the pavement.

He never made it to the strip club.

Ushering Emma off of the plane, Aiden steadfastly refused to answer any of her questions, insisting she needed to discuss this stuff with Nik. There was just one problem with that. Nik wasn't speaking to her.

Immediately after his revelation on the plane, the pilot had come over the speakers to let them know they were about to land in Seattle, and the shot of reality seemed to wash over Nik like a deluge of ice water. He'd ordered her to sit down and put on her seatbelt, assisting her when she'd just stood there, staring at him dumbfounded. Then he'd taken his own seat and refused to talk to her or even look her way while they touched down.

As soon as the plane had stopped, he'd made a run for it. He had his bag and was at the hatch and off the plane before she'd even gotten a chance to unbuckle herself.

With no explanation for, or reaction to, his friend's cowardly behavior, Aiden had come and helped her with her stuff again, escorting her off the plane and into the private car waiting to take them to their home.

She'd never been to Seattle, or any big city for that matter, so Emma let Aiden distract her as he played tour guide from where they sat in the backseat. It was a beautiful city, even in the early morning hours and with the drizzling rain, and she was constantly craning her neck around to look out all of the windows.

Nik sat up front with the driver, not offering any input, not even when Aiden obviously made up outlandish tales about some of the history. As a matter of fact, he didn't seem to be listening to them at all.

As they'd landed way before rush hour, it didn't take them long at all to arrive downtown. Emma stared, wide-eyed and open-mouthed, at all of the towering high-rises. She was sure she looked liked an ignorant country girl, which, she supposed, she was. But she didn't care. The glass buildings sparkled in the rain, some so high she couldn't see the tops from the car. It wasn't dreary like you would expect, not like back home. It was shiny and glittery.

She wondered if she'd get to see the top of the Space Needle while she was here. After she found her sister, of course. Then she glanced at Nik and sighed heavily. Probably not.

In no time at all, they were driving into an underground parking garage below one of the more modern looking high-rises. Pulling into a designated parking space, their driver shut off the car and got out to open the door for Emma.

"This is where you live?" she asked Aiden, as he was still the only one speaking to her.

"Mm hmm. You look surprised."

"I was just expecting something more like The Adams Family, or something."

He laughed. "I am so sorry to disappoint you, love, but you'll soon see that this building is the perfect vampire lair. We had it constructed to our exact specifications. The area vamps live in the top half of the building. Well, except for Dante. Humans occupy the lower floors. It helps us to keep our anonymity, and the humans are not aware of the special "amenities" the building contains. No coffins, however, or bats, or gargoyles. Those are so 18th century. But," Grabbing their stuff from the trunk, he followed Nik to the elevator. "We *do* have secret underground tunnels! Come along, Em!"

Thanking the driver, she hurried after them, catching up to the guys right as the doors opened. Following them in, she stood awkwardly between the two vampires as Aiden hit the button that would take them to the 19th floor. As the doors closed, the tension in the cramped space became increasingly uncomfortable, and Emma counted the floors as they rose, wishing the stupid elevator would hurry up.

Nik stood behind her and slightly to her left, so stiff and still he looked like he would shatter into a million pieces if a feather landed on him. The only one who didn't seem affected was Aiden, who was slouched in the corner, whistling merrily.

The elevator whooshed them up smoothly to their floor, and within seconds she was walking out into a small, yet opulent foyer. Limestone floors complemented the clean lines of the walls, which rose up to high ceilings, dotted with recessed lighting. The white walls were covered in modern paintings, or were they prints?

She walked closer. Nope, those weren't prints. She was no expert, but by the looks of the rest of the decor, she imagined those paintings cost a pretty penny.

They continued down the short hall until it opened up to the main living area. Emma's mouth dropped open again. Straight ahead, the entire wall was constructed completely of glass, giving her an unobstructed view of the Puget Sound. She desperately hoped they didn't cover the windows when the sun came up, although she didn't see how they couldn't if they wanted to avoid the sun's rays. It was too bad. She'd bet she could see Mt. Olympus on a clear day.

To her left, there was a galley style kitchen, open to the main room on one side with bar seating for six. The appliances were all stainless steel. The modern-looking cabinets were walnut. Across from the kitchen, in the corner, was what looked to be an office area, enclosed by more glass, so as not to interrupt the view. A sitting area took up the right side of the apartment, made up of a couch, some end tables, and a couple of comfy looking chairs all facing a marble fireplace. Thick area rugs were scattered about, giving the space a cozy feel. Nearer to her were a couple of doors to her right, one leading to a guest bath and the other was probably the coat closet. Hallways led off to either side of the space, and she guessed that must be where the bedrooms were.

She strolled over to the windows and looked out at the still dark sky while the guys put their stuff down and locked up for the day. She wondered if Keira was out there somewhere, looking at the same sky.

A wave of melancholy washed over her. She missed her sister so much. She didn't care what she was, or rather, what *they* were. She didn't care if she'd lied to her. She just wanted her back.

After a short, muffled discussion with Nik she tried hard to ignore, Aiden called out, "Em! Follow me, poppet. I'll show you to a room where you can sleep."

Turning away from the view, she said goodnight to Nik, but got nothing but a terse nod from him in response. She barely resisted the childish urge to stick her tongue out at him. Someone had to be the adult in this relationship, after all.

Ambling along behind Aiden down the hall past the kitchen, she asked, "You guys live here together? Just the two of you?"

Aiden must have deemed this was a safe question to answer. "Of course not, love. We have our harem of females that we keep here to feed our lusts." With a lascivious grin, he quirked an eyebrow. "Both kinds."

Rolling her eyes and muttering—"I don't know why I even try speaking to you like a normal person."—she turned her attention to the bedroom he'd brought her to.

A king-sized bed dominated the space, which, she was thrilled to see, faced the continuous wall of glass. The "headboard" of the bed was actually a half wall, which acted as a divider between the bed and a small sitting area directly behind it. A plush couch with bright pillows faced the wall mounted TV, with a coffee table in between. Bookshelves lined the walls on either side of the screen, and another fireplace was underneath it. The entire room was all walnut and blues, fresh and clean. She loved it.

"I'm jesting Emma," Aiden told her. "Well, mostly. I have offered the suggestion to Nik many times, but he insists we don't have the room."

She wandered around under his watchful eye, touching this and that and peeking into the bath and the walk-in closet.

"Those would be Nikulas's clothes you see in there," he answered her questioning look. "This is his room. He insisted you sleep in here and not be banned to the couch like a common house guest."

"But where is he going to sleep? The sun will be coming up soon." She tried, and failed, to keep the worry from her voice.

"Don't fret. Every window in this building was specially made. There's a layer of gas between the thick panes. When the sun comes up, it activates the gas, which will then, in turn, block the rays enough to where they won't hurt us, but allows us to enjoy the light. We also have these handy things." Hitting a button by the light switch, narrow panels slid open along the walls, revealing dark curtains that traveled across the entire wall, blocking out any light. "Just in case of an emergency."

"I can't take his room. Really, I'll be fine out on the couch."

"Not up to me, love. I just follow orders." Re-opening the curtains, Aiden paused in the doorway. "Nikulas will come around, Em. He's just a little upside down right now." With that cryptic remark, he tipped his imaginary hat to her and said goodnight, closing the door quietly behind him.

Well, what should I do now? As comfy as that bed looked, she didn't know that she'd get any sleep in it, knowing who slept there every night. The tip of her tongue wet her bottom lip as she wondered if he slept in pajamas...or not. Or maybe he wore those loose, cotton pajama pants? And nothing else? That would be hot.

Stop it, Emma. Grabbing her small suitcase, she tossed it up on the bed and dug out a clean T-shirt to sleep in. Maybe a cold shower would cool down her libido.

22

Nik stood in the kitchen alone, attempting to suck down a blood bag without gagging, watching the lights dance across the water. Aiden had gone to his room to pack and rest before they headed out this coming night.

He listened to Emma rustling around in his room and wondered what she was doing. He liked the thought of her in there. A lot. He wanted to go talk to her, but what the hell was he going to say? *Sorry about all that 'I'd kill you' shit. I was just messing around. Ha Ha.*

TMI was becoming a major issue whenever he was anywhere in the near vicinity of that female. What the fuck had he been thinking, telling her about all that fated mate shit? She probably thought he was some psycho stalker now. That is, if she hadn't already.

Although he felt like they'd always known each other, the truth of the matter was it had only been a day. One day. Barely a full

24 hours. It was crazy even to him. He could only imagine what Emma thought about it. She didn't even have the weird vamp shit to help.

Nik rubbed the back of his neck. He just needed to get through the next few days. Afterward, he'd be busy with his brother, and she could go home with her sister, and they'd never have to see each other again. Things could go back to normal. Maybe take Aiden up on that harem idea he was always bugging him about, or something.

Pft. *Yeah, right.* The guys teased him *now* for living his life like a monk, he had a feeling it was only going to get worse once Emma was gone, if that was even possible.

Tossing the now empty blood bag, Nik grabbed a glass and poured himself a large shot of whiskey, not that it would do much good. Alcohol didn't affect him anymore, which was great, or he'd be a goddamned alcoholic by now. He still liked to slug it down though, more for comfort than effect, and he quickly downed that glass and poured another. Tossing that one back as he had the first, he rinsed out his glass and gathered up the courage to go talk to his female. It was time to quit being a pussy and go in there and tell her how it was going to be, which was strictly business from here on out. She'd help them when they found Luukas, and then she'd be on her way back across the country, lost sister in tow. Fated mate shit be damned.

Mind made up, he headed to his room, not bothering to knock. But, Emma wasn't there. Walking around the bed he checked the couch, which was empty. His heart gave a heavy thump in his chest. Where did she go? He'd been standing right there in the kitchen the entire time. She couldn't have snuck past him.

Nik made himself stop, take a deep breath, and focus. She was in the room. He could feel her. Her stuff was still here, and the suitcase was open on the bed. His head whipped around as he noticed the bathroom door was cracked open, and the soft light above the sink was on.

He was standing in the open doorway before he was even aware he'd moved, a deep breath of relief filling his chest. Emma was there, in nothing but a towel, her hair pulled up to reveal her graceful neck. Holding the towel closed with one hand, she reached in with her other to turn on the water, holding it under the stream as she waited for the temperature to adjust. As he watched, she dropped the towel she'd been wrapped in and stuck her hand in for a final check.

Ahhh. Fucking. Hell.

As the graceful line of her spine and her hot little ass were revealed to him, his cock punched up so hard, he sent up a silent thank you for stretchy running clothes. Her body was lean and strong, yet still retained plenty of feminine curves. She was absolutely perfect.

Scrubbing a hand across his mouth, he nearly sliced it open on his aching fangs.

If there were anything left of a gentleman in him, he would leave and give her her privacy. Turn around right now, and walk right the fuck back into the kitchen. Yeah, he should do that. He could come back later for that talk. When she was fully clothed.

He was about to step back into the bedroom. Really, he was. But then she shifted slightly as she removed her hand from the water and pulled back the curtain to step under the water.

What the fuck?

The light was soft in here, as it was easier on his sensitive eyes, so he hadn't noticed right away.

More scars, similar to the ones he'd already seen, ran across her hip and down her one leg. Ragged tears that had healed unevenly where they couldn't be stitched closed. She looked like she'd been torn into by rabid dogs. How had she possibly survived wounds like that? And there was another one on the muscle between her neck and shoulder, and another on her side above the opposite hip, one of her calves, her arms, her legs...

"Stop!" he ordered. "Don't. Move."

Emma let out a small shriek, nearly jumping out of her skin as Nik's voice boomed and echoed in the small room. Bending down to retrieve the towel she'd just dropped, she wrapped it back around herself before turning around to face him. "What the hell are you doing in here? Get out!"

Catching her first good look at him, she immediately took a step back, almost falling into the shower. He was totally vamped out again, and not just in an "I want to fuck you and/or drink you" kind of way. He was utterly enraged, and perfectly lethal.

"Nik? What's wrong?" Looking around, she didn't see any immediate danger lurking about. What was he so riled up about? It never crossed her mind she could be in danger from him.

He didn't immediately answer. His glowing eyes raked over her, like he could see right through the towel she was clutching. "Take off the towel, Emma," he ground out.

"What? No! I will not!" Pulling it tighter around her, she ordered sternly, "Nikulas. You need to leave."

He narrowed his eyes, and she could see the muscles jump as he clenched his jaw. "Take. It. Off." He started advancing toward her. "NOW."

Emma began to panic. No, no, no! How much had he seen? Tears filled her eyes as she begged him, "Nik, please. *Please*. Leave it alone." Stepping back into the shower, with a death grip on her towel under the onslaught of water, she got as far from him as she could. She didn't want him to see the rest of her body. She was ugly and scarred and...and...ruined. He'd already seen enough. More than enough.

A harsh sob was wrung from her chest as she suddenly comprehended why he was reacting the way he was. Horrified he'd seen so much, she gripped that towel so hard her fingers hurt.

The wretched sound that burst from her drew him up short, and he stayed just out of arm's reach of her. "Emma...I want to see them. I *need* to see them."

She shook her head frantically. "No. No, Nik."

Reaching out a hand toward her, but not touching her, he said, "I'm not going to hurt you. I'm sorry. I didn't mean to scare you. I'm *sorry*."

Dropping his hand back down to his side, he just stared at her for long moments. When he did finally speak, his voice was hoarse with the emotions shining from his bright eyes. "What did they do to you?"

She trembled visibly in the warm water, desperately clutching her drenched towel to herself. "Please..." she whispered.

L.E. WILSON

Why wouldn't he just leave?

23

Fury surged through Nikulas. He couldn't control it. Fury at himself for scaring her, and fury at the things that had torn her up like a piece of meat. If there was any doubt in his mind the things she'd described existed, it wasn't there anymore.

Stepping into the shower fully clothed, he ignored her protests and pulled her trembling body into his arms. She wasn't broken. He would hold her pieces together. His strong, brave, sweet girl. His little warrior. She had nothing to be ashamed of.

He held her head to his chest and wrapped his other arm tightly around her back, holding her to him like she was the most precious thing he'd ever beheld.

She is, he realized.

Tearfully, she whispered, "I just don't want you to see..."

"How stunningly gorgeous you are? You're right. Probably not a good idea. I don't know that I'd be able to control myself. It would totally ruin my long running status as the monk of the group here."

It took her a moment, but then...her muffled laugh was the sweetest thing he'd ever heard. "Somehow, I don't believe that," she mumbled into his wet shirt.

"It's absolutely true. The guys tease me relentlessly about it." He was trying to distract her, and it worked.

"How is that possible? I mean, you're...you...and you look like...you do."

"That's a story for another time." As he felt her start to relax, he loosened his grip and leaned back to look down into her face. "Okay?"

Peeking up at him from beneath her lashes, she gave a small shrug as she awkwardly tried to hike up her towel while still in his arms.

"I'm sorry for barging in like I did. I should have let you know I was in the bedroom." He wanted to rip the towel off of her. Wanted to demand she tell him, in detail, what those things did to her. So, she wouldn't have to bear the pain alone anymore. But he did neither of those things.

In an act of sheer willpower, he kissed her on top of the head and took a step back. "I'll leave you to your shower. There's more towels in the closet right there."

Emma stayed him with a hand on his arm. "Thank you."

He gave her a little smirk. "For barging in on you unannounced, invading your privacy, and yelling at you?"

"No." She laughed again, holding her sopping towel with one hand and running her fingers through her steam dampened hair with the other. "Not for that part. For not pushing the matter. And for lying." She let go of his arm.

But he stayed where he was, frowning down at her. "Lying?"

"Yeah. You know. About the 'gorgeous' thing and all that." Color rushed into her face as she lowered her head in embarrassment. "I'm far from it, but I appreciate the gesture."

Nik's anger returned full force. Gripping her chin, he tilted her face up to his until she was forced to look at him. Her eyes were wide as he gently squeezed her jaw, just enough to make sure he had her full attention. "I NEVER lie, Emma. You would do well to remember that."

Loosening his grip, he ran the backs of his fingers across her cheek and down her neck. "Everything about you is perfect to me, don't *ever* doubt that. Your face, your hair, your scent, your voice, your soul...even your scars. Especially your scars. Every single second I'm near you is absolute torture for me. You couldn't even begin to comprehend the amount of willpower I have to have not to throw you down onto this cold bathroom floor right now and fuck you senseless. Every single second of every single day. I don't care where we are, or who's around. It's always like that when I'm near you."

The words rushed out of him. And when it was over, he could do nothing but stand there. Aching for her. Silently willing her to touch him. Did she believe him? He couldn't tell.

Suddenly, she rose up on her toes and softly kissed his jaw. God, she smelled so good. He wanted her to kiss him again, wanted to taste her, wanted to run his tongue slowly from her lips to her groin and everywhere in between.

Nik let his eyelids slide closed as he felt her lips touch his skin again. A low growl rumbled within his chest. He couldn't contain it. His self-control was quickly slipping away. The sweet scent of her building desire rose around him, and he knew if he touched her there, she'd be soaking wet and ready.

He heard her racing heart and the soft roar of her blood rushing through her veins. His mouth watered at the memory of that blood. He'd never wanted a female like he wanted Emma. He wanted her naked and writhing beneath him, her hair mussed and her skin slick with sweat. He wanted to feel her lose control and scream his name. Wanted to make her come over and over again.

Opening his eyes, he looked down at her flushed face. He knew it wasn't the heat of the shower bringing the color to her cheeks. Her hazel eyes were bold and bright with desire as she stared up at him. Her lips slightly parted. Her breath coming in soft pants. It would be so easy to devour that luscious mouth of hers. All he had to do was lower his head just a little. He could be very careful.

Moving quicker than she could track, Nik lowered his mouth to hers. He didn't touch her, only ravaged her sweet mouth, being very careful of his fangs this time.

It wasn't enough. He wanted more.

Clenching his fists, he fought his instincts. They raged through him, urging him to take her. He felt one of her hands come up to rest on his stomach, and his muscles tightened in response. She hesitated, then moved up his chest and shoulder to push into his hair and hold his head to hers while she kissed him back with enthusiasm.

Though his hands were fisted at his sides, his mouth on hers held her against him as effectively as his arms would. He kissed her like a starving man. Kissed her relentlessly. Growling low in his throat at the taste of her.

He wanted to pull her to him and wrap his arms around her. He wanted to tear off his clothes, push her up against that shower wall, and bury his length in her. He wanted to sink his fangs into her plump vein as she came, and then pound into her while her blood ran down his throat, until he erupted inside of her. He wanted to crawl inside of her sweet flesh until they were one.

And then he wanted to do it all over again. And again. And would probably rip her apart and suck her dry without even realizing it.

Just like Eliana.

Holy hell, he wanted this woman, but he couldn't trust himself to be careful enough with her if he fucked her. There was no damn way he'd be able to control himself when it was complete agony just to kiss her. But maybe...

Emma let out a little sound of protest as Nik broke off the kiss and stepped back again. He took a moment to calm his breathing as he silently tried to talk himself out of what he was thinking.

In the meantime, he allowed himself the luxury of letting his eyes roam over her. Her eyes were bright. Her lips swollen from his kisses. Her nipples were hard little pebbles underneath her wet towel.

She lifted a hand and swayed toward him, but he grabbed it in his before she could touch him, and quickly spun her around to the back of the shower. "Put your hands on the wall."

"Nikulas? What are you doing?" Emma tried to twist herself back around to face him, but he wouldn't let her.

"Do as I say. Put your hands on the wall, above your head."

After a slight hesitation, she did. The towel fell open in the front, but the wet material stuck to her back.

"Don't move your hands, no matter what. Don't touch me. You hold up that fucking wall like it will come crashing down on us if you don't. I don't think I could control myself if you touched me anymore, Em, and I don't want to hurt you."

He heard her suck in a breath as he moved up against her back, blocking the shower spray, and pressed his aching cock into her backside. He felt as hard as the stone tiles under her palms.

Leaning into her from behind and putting his arms around her waist, he put his mouth to her ear. "I want to touch you, Emma. I want your breasts to fill my hands. I want to feel how wet you are. I want to make you come and I want you to scream my name when you do it. I won't hurt you. I won't bite you. I swear. Do you trust me?"

She didn't even hesitate this time. "Yes."

With a hungry growl at her answer, he didn't give her any time to change her mind. Gathering her hair out of the way in one hand, he pressed his lips to the back of her neck, careful to keep his fangs in check, as he slid his other hand across the satiny skin of her stomach. Running his palm up her ribcage, he squeezed her full breast, kneading her gently and then plucking hard at her nipple, making her gasp and arch her back.

"Perfect," he moaned. "You feel so perfect."

Moving his hand to her other breast, he felt more scars there, and had to quickly tamper down the rage that rose up. Needing to distract himself, he closed his eyes and lost himself in the feel of her.

He continued to tease her nipples as he let go of her hair and slowly moved his other hand across her flat stomach, over her hip, and down to settle low on her belly. Holding her tightly in place, he rolled his hips into her shapely ass.

Emma pushed her hips back, rubbing along his thick length. Her breath came in short pants, and she moaned.

Nik tightened his hands on her. "Do NOT move," he hissed. "You do that again and I'll have you down on the floor with my cock inside of you before realize what's happening."

Emma whimpered at his words, and Nik became still. "Shit. I'm sorry." He took a deep breath. "I can stop." *I think.*

"No! Nikulas, please," Emma begged. "Don't stop touching me."

He didn't move for a long time. Her words, raw with need for him, hit him so hard he had to take a moment to get himself under control.

When he thought he could control himself, he tugged her nipples with one hand as he slid his other hand lower on her stomach. He hesitated slightly, steeling himself, before cupping her silky curls.

But it wasn't enough. Her scent curled around him and her body trembled in his arms as he slid his fingers into her slippery folds. She was soaking wet and ready for him, as he knew she would be. Emma's moan was drowned out by his own as he stroked her.

"Jesus...You're so fucking wet. Is that just for me, Em." It wasn't really a question. He knew the answer.

"Yes," she breathed.

She moaned louder as he continued to gently rub her slick nub. Pushing one of his knees between hers, Nik forced her legs farther apart, opening her even more to his touch. He kissed her neck as he slid one finger inside her, then two, stretching her. She was tight and wet, and his muscles began to ache at the level of self-control he had to maintain. He pumped his fingers in and out of her, imitating the movement with his hips.

His fangs lightly scraped her skin, and he felt a tremor run down her spine, and her slick sheath gripped his fingers even tighter as they pumped in and out of her. Under his other palm, her nipples tightened as he expertly worked her higher and higher.

Emma began to tremble in his arms, her muscles straining as she threw her head back against his chest. Her fingers curled into claws on the hard tile. "Nik? I don't..."

"Shhh...It's okay, sweetheart. I've got you. You feel so fucking good. Let go. I've got you."

Nik held her even tighter to him as he pulled his fingers out of her and slid them up to her swollen clit. As he gently rubbed her faster and faster, she arched her back, pushing herself into his hand. Her hips moved, matching his movements.

Nik pinched her nipple hard. "Come for me, Emma. Come NOW," he ordered.

And with a hoarse cry, she exploded, her body convulsing almost violently in his arms.

Nik continued touching her as she rode out her orgasm, then gently brought her down. He held her, harsh breaths exploding from his chest as he fought the urge the take her against the shower wall and finish what he started.

Holy fucking shit, she was beautiful. Watching her come was the most erotic thing he'd ever seen. And he'd seen quite a bit. Unlike other females he'd known, his Emma was completely raw in her reactions to his touch. She didn't try to put on a show, wasn't practiced. She was innocence and beauty, and she was his.

HIS Emma. The truth of that floored him. She was his. And he was well and truly fucked now. He never should've touched her like this. Never should've smelled the delicious scent of her desire. Never felt her innocent, but completely raw reaction to him. Never watched her face as she threw her head back into his chest when she came. It made him want to keep her. Forever.

But he couldn't have her. It wasn't possible. He'd never be able to control himself enough to make love to her without sinking his fangs into her luscious vein. He was barely hanging onto his control by a thread now. And he was terrified that once he got another taste of her, he wouldn't be able to stop.

The thought tamped down his lingering desire. Taking a deep breath, he inhaled her scent one last time. Then, Nik released her and forced himself to step back into the shower spray.

Dammit. This never should have happened.

24

Emma felt Nik move away, physically and emotionally. Her hands slid down the wet tiles with a squeak as she dropped her arms and grabbed the edges of her wet towel, pulling it tight around herself.

Her face burned. Whether it was from embarrassment or the lingering effects of her orgasm, she wasn't sure.

She wondered if he would do that again.

Oh my God, what the hell was she thinking? What must he think of her? She'd practically guilt-tripped him into doing those things to her. Nik still hadn't said anything, and she dreaded turning around to face him.

Her eyes filled with tears. She'd just let him violate her like a common whore, instead of respecting his wishes to keep some distance between them. And she'd loved it. She could only imagine how he was feeling. He probably couldn't get away from her fast enough.

"Emma..." Nik began in a strained voice.

But she turned around and cut him off with a jerk of her head. She wiped her tears with the heel of one hand and gathered the tiny shreds of her remaining dignity around her. "I'm sorry, Nik. I don't know what I was thinking." Emma laughed wryly. "Actually, I obviously wasn't thinking. You don't have to say anything." She ignored his shocked expression. "It's okay. Let's just forget about it."

She looked away and waited for him to leave her to her shower, where she could fall apart in private.

"Un-fucking-believable," he spit out.

Her head snapped up, and she was met with eyes brimming with rage.

She clenched her jaw. He had no right to be this angry. After all, he's the one who'd barged in on her. "Just go, please."

Stepping all up into her personal space, he took her chin and forced her to look at him. "Em-ma!"

Emma fought to keep more tears at bay, her chin and her inner wall of defense lifted high. "What."

"We need to talk about this, Em."

"There's nothing to talk about, Nik."

"Yes, there is."

"NO. There isn't." Yanking her chin out of his hand with a quick jerk, she forced a measure of calm into her voice. "Now, please—leave."

Nik stared at her, a lost expression on his face. He tried again. "Emma. Please, talk to me."

"There's *nothing* to say, Nik."

"I disagree, Emma." Nik took her face gently in both hands. "You have nothing to feel ashamed of, do you hear me?"

She felt her cheeks burn and tried to look away from him. He thought he knew what she was feeling. He didn't.

But Nik would have none of it. "What happened here...that was a perfectly natural thing. What happened to you seven years ago, that wasn't your fault, and it doesn't make you any less. You can't let it ruin your life."

Emma refused to look at him. "I know that. I've done the therapy, and I *have* had sex since then you know."

Nik recoiled at her words, dropping his hands from her face and moving away from her. "So, if this isn't about your feeling ashamed of the act, it must be *who* the act was performed with."

A sharp pain ripped through Emma's gut at the hurt in his voice, but she said nothing.

He gave a harsh, derisive laugh. "Yeah, you know what? You're right. There's absolutely nothing to talk about." Yanking the shower curtain closed behind him, Nik sloshed over to the bathroom door.

Emma stared at the closed curtain with a heart full of regret. She'd seen the flicker of pain in his eyes. But it was there and gone so fast she'd almost missed it.

"Will you stay?" she called from behind the curtain. "I mean, not here, but in your room?"

She started to think he'd already left, when she heard him reply, "Yeah, I'll stay."

"Good."

Emma listened as Nik closed the door firmly behind him. After checking he was really gone, she pulled off her sopping towel and hung it on a rail inside the shower.

As the warm water hit her still tender breasts, she stifled a moan. How long had he been standing there before he'd said anything? She prayed she had covered herself fast enough and he hadn't gotten more than a glimpse of her ravaged skin.

Other than her doctor, no one had seen her undressed since that night. Not even herself. She avoided mirrors whenever possible. With the one lover she'd had, she'd always insisted on the lights being off. He hadn't complained. She didn't think he'd been that into her anyway, and she'd felt the same. It had just been two consenting adults staving off the loneliness for a little while.

Funny. She tended to forget about her scars completely whenever Nik touched her.

Grabbing the shampoo, she quickly lathered up while she still had some hot water. As she massaged her scalp, she closed her eyes and tried to enjoy the feeling. But as soon as her lids slid down, Nik's handsome face appeared. Smiling at her. Teasing her.

Fixated on her in her kitchen, right before he pounced.

A surge of lust went through her again, so strong she nearly moaned out loud before she caught herself. Emma wiped the shampoo from her face. She really needed to stop this. She couldn't fall for him. He was a vampire, for God's sake. If she had an ounce of sense she'd be terrified, and would be counting the hours until she could be far, far away from him.

However, she wasn't afraid. Not at all. Not even when he got all freaky scary looking. She didn't understand it.

Or maybe she did. Taking a deep breath, she admitted the truth to herself. A truth she'd known deep down since the moment he'd walked into that bar. She'd never been more attracted to a man than she was to him. Inside and out. She didn't care that he wasn't completely human. She didn't care about what had happened to her in the past.

Emma made a decision right then and there. If he wanted her, she wouldn't fight it.

But, that was the question, wasn't it? Did *he* want *her*? He ran so hot and cold, it was impossible to tell if it was just bloodlust, or was he as consumed with her as she was with him?

As she finished scrubbing herself clean, she thought about what he had started to tell her on the plane. What the hell had that been about? What had he meant by all that 'fated mate' talk?

She knew he wanted her sexually, he sure as hell had proven that, but was that all it was? Is that all a relationship with him would be? Or did it mean more than that?

And why did he think he would kill her?

These questions and more spun around in her head as she got out and dried herself off. Pulling on her oversized T-shirt, she realized she hadn't brought her robe in with her. Of course, she hadn't expected company either.

Cracking open the door, she saw Nik sitting on the end of the bed with his back to her, staring out at the Sound. He had changed into a pair of dry sweats and a black tank top. His feet were bare. He tilted his head slightly toward her as she tiptoed over to her suitcase and found her old robe. Pulling it on, she went over and sat down next to him.

They sat together, lost in their own thoughts, until Nik finally broke the silence. "I'm sorry..." His voice was husky, and he cleared his throat before continuing. "I'm sorry, again, for walking in on you. I can be a little overbearing at times."

"I've noticed."

Needing to do something to break the tension between them, she put a hand on his muscular bicep and gave him a little shove. "What happened to the pain in the ass vampire who loved to amuse himself at my expense?"

With a sheepish glance her way, he murmured, "You seem to bring out the worst in me. I don't know what it is. I'm usually a pretty laid back, happy-go-lucky kind of guy."

Emma didn't know how to respond as he rose from the bed to pace back and forth at vamp speed, nothing but a blur until he appeared at either end when he turned around. Here and there she would catch a glimpse of tensed jaw muscles and drawn brows, and even a flash of fang.

Emma remained where she was, watching, waiting patiently for him to work out...whatever he was trying to work out.

A few seconds later, he stopped, appearing abruptly in front of her. Fists clenched at his sides, he wouldn't look at her.

"What is it?" she asked.

He met her eyes. "You were right before, what you said on the plane. From now on, any interaction between us needs to be strictly business. That's it. We'll find our siblings, and then you and your sister can go back to Pennsylvania and we can forget all of this—" He indicated the two of them. "—ever happened."

Even though she had been the one to originally suggest it, she was nonetheless more than a little bit hurt to hear him agree. With all of his erratic behavior, she rarely knew what to expect from him, but it wasn't this. "It's a little bit late for that, isn't it?"

Nik resumed his pacing.

"So, what are we doing here, Nik? Other than playing 'feel up the witch' of course..." she mumbled under her breath.

Swinging around in front of her so fast he startled her, Nik ground out, "Don't do that."

"Don't do what?"

"Don't demean what happened between us," he fumed.

"Us?" she scoffed. "There is no 'us', Nik. You refuse to let there be an 'us'."

"I'm not arguing about this anymore, Emma." He went back to pacing.

Emma chewed her bottom lip, her thoughts spinning as she watched him appear and disappear, like some kind of out of control strobe light. She should just let it be. Respect his wishes. He was just trying to protect her, after all.

But, the thing was, she didn't believe there was anything to protect her from. She'd never once felt like she was in danger when she was with him. Ever. No matter what they were doing. Maybe she was being naive, but she trusted her instincts. And her instincts told her not to give up on him. There had to be something she could say, something she could do, to convince this stubborn idiot it didn't have to be that way.

She had no idea what that was, however.

"So, just like that? When this is done, we just...forget about each other?"

"That's how it has to be, Emma." Resolve hardened his posture.

She lowered her eyes so he wouldn't see the pain reflected there. "I liked you better when you were teasing me all the time."

"Emma..." he admonished.

She didn't want to ask this. She really didn't. But she had to know. "It's because of what you saw just now, isn't it?" When his brows lowered, she clarified, "My scars?"

"No. No!" he emphasized. "Emma...this is...this really has nothing to do with you. It's just the way it has to be."

"I think it has everything to do with me."

He rubbed the back of his neck. "It's just better this way. Please, trust me on this."

"Does this have something to do with you thinking you would kill me?"

Nik dragged his hands through his hair. *Why not just fucking tell her?* Maybe it would scare her enough that she'd be smart and stay the hell away from him.

"Yeah, all right." He'd give her the abbreviated version. "I loved a girl once, or thought I did, a long time ago. Her name was Eliana." Leaning against the window wall, as far from her delicious scent as he could get, he crossed his arms over his broad chest. "She was human, like you." He took a breath to steady himself. "We were together for about a year when I came home late one night to find her already asleep in our bed. The Council had just been in a battle with another Master Vampire. He and his followers had challenged Luukas' authority. It happens occasionally. We won, but it was a hard, bloody fight. I was still amped up from it when I entered our room. The bloodlust blinded me, and I fell on her like a beast, tearing her nightclothes, not even giving her time to wake up." Self-loathing filled him, and he began to pace again. "I fed on her while I...well, that's what we do. Except I lost control. I took too much. I drained her dry while I fucked her." Pausing directly in front of her, he willed her to look at him as he forced the words out. "I killed her Emma. I fed on her until her heart stopped beating, rutting on her the entire time. I didn't even notice until her body began to get cold underneath me."

Her horrified expression burrowed into his brain like maggots, never to be forgotten. Yes. This was for the best. He could live with this gaping hole that was ripping apart his chest as she finally looked at him like the monster he was.

He'd learned to live with Eliana's death. But if he killed Emma, even accidentally, he would *never* be able to live with that. What he felt for her, well, there was no comparison to it. He would rather walk into the sun.

He walked slowly toward the door. Even now wanting to stay with her. But he couldn't look at her. Couldn't stand to see the look on her face again.

"Be ready to go at sundown. Tonight, we're going after our siblings."

25

"What the fuck did you do?"

"Ow! What the hell?" Nik cursed violently as Aiden woke him, gently, with a backhand to the head. Raising his arms automatically to protect himself from more attacks, Nik shook his head and forced himself to wake up. He felt strange. Kind of loopy and unusually lethargic.

Grabbing him by the front of the shirt, a thoroughly angry Brit hauled him up to a sitting position. "What the fuck did you do to Emma?"

Nik shoved him out of the way, rolled off the couch, and ambled to the guest bath to wash up. "Fuck off, Aiden."

Not to be put off that easily, Aiden was right on his heels. "What the fuck did you do, Nik? She looks positively wretched in there!"

Whipping around, Nik snarled, "What the fuck were *you* doing in her room?"

"What do you care? You seem to be doing your damnedest to push her away from you."

Aiden held his ground as Nik got right up in his face. He flashed his fangs and hissed in warning. "Stay out of it, Aid. It's none of your fucking business." He turned and stomped to the bathroom, slamming the door in his friends' face.

Aiden banged on the door. "It is my business, you twat! I happen to like Emma!"

Nik turned the shower on in response.

Aiden yelled about the sound of running water. "You think I don't know what's going on with you two? I've heard the stories too, you know! Never believed them until now...but you shouldn't fight it, Nik! If the stories are true, you need her now, or you will perish, slowly and painfully! That means dead, Nikulas! Like, *dead* dead. No coming back to life this time."

Naked and dripping with water, Nik wrenched open the door. "Better me, than her," he gritted through his teeth. "Now, shut the fuck up, and let me get my shower." He slammed the door in his face again.

"We'll just see about that, you bloody arse," Aiden called.

Emma dreaded leaving her refuge where she'd been holed up since Nik's visit last night, or was it this morning? She frowned. Her newfound sleep schedule was causing her to get her days and nights all confused. She'd had a long, restless night...or day, rather...and the mirror in the bathroom confirmed she looked exactly how she felt.

Like hell.

She supposed she'd asked for this. If she hadn't kept on pushing and pushing him, he wouldn't have felt forced to tell her about his past and she could still be naively fantasizing about the hunk of gorgeous vampire in the other room. But no, she had to back him into a corner until he'd had no choice but to come out swinging.

She should be relieved. She hadn't been acting like herself since tall, buff, and fangy came strutting into her life. It was like that filter in your brain...the one that censors what you say and how you act before you actually do it... had up and disappeared completely. But mostly, she just felt stupid, like one of those girls always chasing after a guy who obviously didn't want her.

By the time Aiden had come in to wake her, she'd been sitting in the same spot on the couch for hours staring at the blank T.V. screen. Sleep had eluded her. No surprise there. But at least there were no new nightmares to deal with.

See? Silver lining.

"Em? We'll need to be leaving in about an hour." Aiden eyed the dark circles and puffy eyes no amount of cold water could fix, a look of concern on his face. "Can I get you anything, love?"

"No, thanks. I'm fine." She tried for a smile and rose unsteadily to her feet, stiff from sitting in the same spot for so long.

Aiden eyed her up and down, and then reluctantly closed the door behind him as he left, leaving Emma to her thoughts.

After all these years, it seemed surreal she may be seeing her sister again in only a number of hours. She should be worrying about how dangerous it was going to be to get her out. About what she was going to say to Keira once they did. If they were all going to make it out of there alive. Because she had no doubt in her mind, if her sister was helping that horrible woman, she was doing it against her will.

But all she'd thought about the entire day were Nik's eyes burning into her soul as he'd told her he'd brutally killed the last girl he'd loved in an act of mindless bloodlust.

His story had been stuck on replay in her head all day. She knew he'd meant it as a warning to her, and she had no doubt what he'd told her was the truth as he believed it. But something about his story was nagging at her. Something just didn't add up. She'd seen Nik all "vamped out" a few times now, and not once had she ever feared he would hurt her. He'd always, without fail, been mindful of his superior strength, gentle even.

And the first time he'd kissed her? When he'd nicked her lip and then straight out bit it? He could have easily lost control that night, gone for her throat and sucked her dry, but he hadn't.

And last night, in the shower. Emma felt a rush of heat at the memory. The things he'd done to her. He'd been in complete control the entire time. And after, he'd walked away, which only confirmed her theory even more.

She'd felt completely overwhelmed by him, yes. But in danger? Never. Not once.

Granted, although she'd been in a life-threatening situation before, she'd never been a soldier. She didn't know how it felt to be in a struggle for your life and come out on top, high from the fight with adrenalin pumping through your body.

But Aiden would.

Emma turned off the water she'd been using to wash her face and brush her teeth and heard raised voices in the other room.

Drying her face and tossing the towel on the sink, she hopped into a pair of jeans and changed her shirt. Barefoot, she flung open her door just in time to catch a glimpse of a very pissed off, very wet, and very *naked*, vampire slamming the guest bath door in Aiden's face.

Whoa.

Speechless for the second time in as many days at how beautiful he was, she didn't immediately remember why she was standing there, until she noticed Aiden stalk off in the direction of his room.

"Aiden! Wait!"

His fierce expression immediately softened. "Em? What's wrong, love?"

"Would you come here for a minute? Please?" She gave him what, she hoped, was a winning smile.

"To your room? But, Emma, what will everyone think?" One hand placed theatrically over his heart, he looked over his shoulder.

"But, you've already been in my...in Nik's room. And no one else is here."

"Hmm. True enough. Well then, I guess there's no harm in it." With a shrug, he headed her way. Squeezing past her to get through the doorway, he muttered under his breath, "But please don't tell Nikulas. He's upset about us as it is."

Was that what all the yelling had been about? "There is no *us*, Aiden." Closing the door so their conversation wouldn't be overheard, she leaned back against it as he sat down on the side of the bed.

Leaning back on his elbows, he gave her a lusty wink. "You just keep telling yourself that, poppet."

Emma barely caught herself before she rolled her eyes at him. She would rather avoid another scene like the one on the runway. Changing the subject would be her safest route. "Aiden, you've been in battles since becoming a vampire, right? Fights?"

Sitting up, he gave her a knowing grin. "You want to see my battle wounds. Alas, vampires heal quickly, and never have scars. However, I have a great one where I was completely gutted when I was still human—"

"No, I don't! Wait...you were gutted? Really?"

He lifted up his shirt, giving her an eyeful of mouth-watering, rock hard abs and yes, a horrific scar running diagonally from the bottom of his ribcage to where it disappeared under the waistband of his pants.

Coming closer to get a better look, she was suitably impressed. "Holy cow. How did you live through that?"

"That would all be due to Luukas and Nik, who found me on the battlefield with my insides hanging out, and who gave me this second chance at life. Otherwise, there's no doubt in my mind I would have died that day." Pulling his shirt back down, he started untying his running pants. "I have others, though they're not as good as that one, but still impressive. Want to see?"

Emma jumped away and slapped a hand over her eyes. "No! Would you please just answer my question? And keep your pants on!"

"First time I've heard *that* particular statement come out of a female's mouth," he remarked.

"Aiden!!"

"All right, all right, don't get your knickers in a twist. Obviously, yes, I have been in some really gnarly fights."

She took a quick peek through her fingers to make sure his pants were, indeed, still on, before lowering her hand. "As a vampire, I would imagine all the blood and fighting really gets to you. Makes you really...um...excited?"

He cocked his head to the side, narrowing his eyes with suspicion. "What are you getting at, Emma?"

"Um. I was just curious, for no particular reason, how much all of that affects you? Would you say you completely lose control from the blood lust? Would *everyone* around you be in danger? Even after the fight is over?"

"Why ever would you be concerned about that?"

Thinking quickly, she tried to come up with a feasible reason. "I was just, um, thinking about what we're going to be doing tonight. There will probably be a lot of fighting, and the other vampires who are meeting us there don't know me. I was just wondering if I should be worried? For my own safety, I mean, from you guys."

She cut off her nervous babbling, hiding her eyes behind lowered lids as he studied her with sharp eyes that saw way too much, but she had a feeling it wouldn't help. She was a terrible liar, and vampires were entirely too attentive to detail.

Aiden stared at her for so long she started to fidget under his rapt attention. She could almost feel him silently probing around in her head for the truth…and maybe he was. Emma made a mental note to find out more about vampire abilities.

"Come on, love, don't play coy with me," he finally said. "That's not what you're fretting about." Checking the clock, he continued, "We don't have a lot of time before we need to leave. Let's cut to the chase, shall we? What are you really wanting to know? Spit it out. I won't judge, I promise."

"All right, fine." Dropping the act, she hesitated briefly as she wondered if she would be betraying Nik's confidence by speaking about this. However, if the two of them have been friends as long as they say, Aiden probably already knew all about it.

She shoved her hands in her pockets to keep herself from fidgeting, and tried to sound blasé. "Last night, Nik came in here and told me a story about something he did. An accident—" That was as far as she got.

Jumping up off of the bed, Aiden smacked his forehead with his palm. "*That's* what he did to you! He told you about Eliana! Sneaky bastard." Clasping his hands behind his back, he paced a few steps away, then abruptly turned and came to stand directly in front of her. "Emma, I've decided there are some things we need to discuss. Nik will want to kill me when he finds out I've spoken with you about it, but I would hope you would prevent him from doing that."

Emma shook her head in bewilderment. "I don't see how you think I could keep Nik from doing anything! I have no control over him."

"Ah, but you do. Much more than you know." Gesturing toward the couch, he suggested they sit down.

"We need to make this short and sweet, so I'm just going to lay it on you, all right?" When she eagerly nodded her agreement, he continued, "I don't know if Nik has mentioned this to you, but the signs are all there that you are his mate, chosen by the gods to be his one and only for as long as you both shall live."

"Actually, he did mention something about that," she hedged.

"Did he mention that once he's had your blood, he will slowly fade away until there is nothing left of him if he doesn't continue to have it?"

Emma fought down a rush of alarm. "No. He, uh, didn't mention that. We were interrupted in the midst of that discussion by the plane landing in Seattle."

Muttering under his breath, "Stupid, stubborn Estonian," Aiden kindly filled her in. "Neither of us have actually ever seen or heard of this happening, but according to the stories passed down through the ages, vampires will know when they've met their mate after they've had a taste of their blood. That this will happen is inevitable, as upon first seeing them, the vampire is drawn to said mate to the point of obsession, even before they've fed from them. I have to ask, has Nik fed from you yet?"

Heat flooded her face and neck. "Just one time, and just a little. He, uh, he kissed me and his fangs are so sharp—"

Aiden cut her off. "I don't need the gory details. Mostly because I'm envious." He gazed longingly at her lips for a moment before he suddenly slapped his hands together, startling her. "Okay! So, this is where we're at. Now that Nik has fed from you, he needs to continue feeding from you, or he will die, Emma. Simple as that. Die the true death. It will take a while, but it will happen. I'm not certain why this is so, but it's the one detail that is bashed into our brains from day one of becoming a vampire."

She tried to imagine Nik "feeding" from her, his fangs latched onto her neck. But far from being repulsed at the thought, she felt a rush of desire so strong she was glad she was sitting down.

Embarrassed, because she knew Aiden would know what she was feeling, she cleared her throat and asked, "How long is 'a while'?"

He lifted one eyebrow, but said nothing about her reaction. "I'm not sure, exactly. This kind of thing is pretty rare. We're just going by what the elders have told us. However," He sighed. "I've already noticed a few things amiss with him. He'd never admit it, of course, but they're there. He's already starting to weaken, starting to reject that nasty bagged blood. Thank the gods."

Nik was weakening? Emma's heart clenched in her chest. "So, next question. Let's be realistic here. What if he doesn't want me?" She'd already made a fool of herself over this guy; she was not about to continue doing so. But there was also no way in hell she was going to let him die. Not if there was anything she could do about it.

Aiden grinned at her. "Oh, he wants you. Have no worries there, love. Why do you think he's been such a bloody arse since you've come around?" He didn't wait for her to answer. "Although, I guess you wouldn't know, since that's the only way you've ever seen him." Then he added, "I'm also going to assume you're not opposed to the idea of being with him? Even though he's a vampire? You two are practically shagging every time I leave you alone."

She surprised both of them by confessing honestly, "I've never been more attracted to anyone in my life, in spite of everything that's happened to me. But what do we do now? He believes he'll kill me if he's with me."

Speaking of which, this brought her back to her original inquiry. "*Would* he kill me, Aiden? Like he did Eliana?"

"I don't think there's much of a chance of that," Aiden hedged. "Vampires are extremely territorial and protective over anything, or anyone, they consider theirs. I believe that protective trait will keep him from letting anyone harm you, including himself, although he may need some convincing. Eliana was unfortunate. However, though he cared a great deal for her, she wasn't his mate."

Lowering his voice, he confided, "Personally, between you and me, I think there was something a bit off with that female. That whole thing seemed a bit dodgy to me. I think there's more to that story than any of us know, including Nik."

The bedroom door suddenly flew open. It crashed into the opposite wall and was left hanging askew on its hinges.

Emma jumped up guiltily from the couch, coming face to face with over two hundred and forty pounds of thoroughly enraged vampire standing in the doorway, wearing nothing but a towel wrapped around his narrow waist.

26

Too alarmed to appreciate the view of Nikulas' naked torso, Emma anxiously racked her brain to come up with an excuse for her and Aiden to be in there with the door closed. "We're not...this isn't what it looks like!"

Aiden, on the other hand, did not appear to be intimidated. "Nikulas! Just the leech we wanted to see! We need to have a quick life and death chat with you, mate. It will just take a second. Why don't you come sit with us?" He patted the cushion Emma had abandoned.

Fists clenched at his sides and fangs bared, Nik growled, "Get away from her, Aiden."

Aiden smirked at Emma. "See what I mean? A complete arse. If it were anyone else but me, there's no doubt I'd be learning I can't fly by now."

Nik stalked further into the room, his eyes never wavering from Emma. "Leave us," he snarled in Aiden's direction.

One side of Aiden's mouth twisted as he contemplated the ceiling. "I think you owe me an apology first." Crossing his legs, he swung one foot up and down. "And I won't be leaving until I get it."

As Nik's fury reached the eye-glowing level, Aiden's foot stilled. He yawned, then slowly stood up and stretched his back. With a wink and a, "I'll see you in a few, poppet", he casually sauntered through the busted doorway.

Emma watched him in disbelief. She couldn't believe it. The loon was leaving her here alone with a growling, enraged vampire.

She scowled at Aiden's retreating back. Or maybe she could. Ignoring her pounding pulse, she tried not to sound as nervous as she felt. "We were just talking, Nikulas."

"Talking," he sneered. Taking several deep breaths, he lowered his voice. "You are to stay away from him, do you understand?"

Now he was just being ridiculous. They'd only been talking. "He's your best friend!"

"He's also a notorious womanizer," he gritted through his teeth. "And I don't want you anywhere near him when I'm not around."

"You're being ridiculous, he—" Before she could finish what she was saying, he was around the couch and all up in her personal space.

"I said, STAY AWAY FROM HIM!" he bellowed inches from her face.

Nervousness forgotten, she shoved at his bare chest with both hands. "Back off, blood sucker! I'm dealing with enough here without having to deal with your irrational jealousy! In the last 48 hours, I've been told I'm a witch, told there are such things as vampires, kissed senseless, given my first orgasm, dragged from my home, and brought on a recon mission to rescue my sister from some deranged, immortal, sadistic bitch. I'm tired, I'm hungry, and I've had just about ENOUGH out of you!" She shoved him again. It was like hitting a stone wall, so she stomped around him. "I'm going to get something to eat, and then we're leaving to go get my sister, because I want to GO HOME!" Abruptly coming to a halt, she turned to him again and shoved her finger in his face. "YOU are not to speak to me again until you can stop yelling."

Leaving him standing there slack-jawed, she flounced out of the room to go make something to eat, only to find Aiden sitting at the bar, beaming at her.

As long as she was at it... "And you! There's something seriously wrong with you, do you know that?" She waved her hands at him. "Other than the whole being a vampire thing."

As she stomped angrily around the kitchen to make a peanut butter sandwich, Aiden looked down at his shirt front. "What ever do you mean? There's nothing wrong with me."

A few minutes later, Nik—dried off and fully dressed—wandered out of his bedroom to come and sit next to Aiden at the bar. With a sheepish look at Emma, he told them, "Sorry about all the yelling, and for being such an asshole lately. I'm not sure where all that's coming from."

Emma shot daggers his way, while Aiden sought to make amends. "No worries, mate. And I apologize for clocking you in the head earlier." Giving each other a masculine, one-armed hug and pat on the back, all appeared to be forgiven. "Get yourself a bag, you'll feel better."

Nik got up from his stool and cautiously sidled around Emma, giving her a wide berth. She glared at him out of the corner of her eye and slapped her bread together.

Aiden frowned at her and pointed with his chin toward Nik, silently beseeching her to follow suit.

In response, she narrowed her eyes at him and savagely ripped off a bite of her sandwich with her teeth.

His eyes widened, but then he smiled at her warmly. Lord only knew what was going on in that crazy head of his.

She waited until Nik warmed up his blood and made his way back to the other side of the bar before she spoke. "So, what's the plan for tonight guys?"

"The plan," Nikulas grimaced as he took a sip from his bag. "Is to meet up with Dante and the rest of our crew, and then go kill things."

Dante punched the elevator button that would take him down to the passageway leading to his living quarters. This elevator was the only accessible way to get there, other than a small tunnel he'd dug out himself.

No one else knew about that tunnel, not even Shea, and no one ever would. The private rooms it led to were not areas anyone else needed to see.

The Seattle Underground, the original city, wasn't a place most vampires would think was suitable to live in during these modern times. They preferred the freedom of being able to live above ground amongst the humans. Gods among men. But Dante felt right at home there in the damp darkness. It suited him.

And he had no desire to interact with his food, other than to hunt them.

Well, that wasn't entirely true. Sometimes, he would *play* with his food. It satisfied something deep and dark within him, to hear them pleading for their life. He got off on it. Male or female, it didn't matter. They'd beg him like the pathetic animals they were, the smell of fear and urine and blood dominating the room, until he tired of their screams and finally put them out of their misery.

Dragging what was left of the broken bodies through the underground, he'd emerge into the fresh air to toss them into the Sound for the sea creatures to eat. Otherwise, the stench became overwhelming, and others would begin to notice.

The elevator doors opened and Dante got in. As they closed behind him, he changed his mind at the last minute and hit the button that would take him to the underground parking garage instead of all the way down to his rooms.

He was uneasy about the mission they were about to embark on, more so than usual. Failure was not an option, or they would lose Luukas forever. He wasn't sure how he knew this, but he did. The waiting to leave had him ready to jump out of his own skin.

He needed to feed. And he needed the release the pain would bring. Other's pain, and his own.

The doors opened, and Dante stepped out into the garage. He turned his head as a black SUV came careening around the corner, swerving way too close to where he stood.

He smiled. Looked like his meal was coming to him.

Tires squealed as the driver noticed him standing there, and Dante saw him wrench the wheel to the side to try to avoid him. He didn't so much as flinch as the side of the vehicle missed him by a mere few inches before it screeched to a halt just a few feet away. The back doors opened, and two males got out.

"Hey man, are you okay?" One of them asked Dante, coming up on his left.

The other snuck around to his right.

Dante lifted his upper lip in a sneer. The piece of shit thought he could sneak up on him? He turned his head to see what he was up to, felt the sting of a needle in the side of his neck…and then there was nothing but darkness.

27

The matte black Hummer pushed deeper and deeper into the mountains, blending in perfectly with the darkness that surrounded it. It was slow going, the road they were on well hidden from the main freeway, and rarely used. Most people didn't even know it existed, or where it led.

As they swerved around fallen branches and water-filled potholes the size of small ponds, Emma braced herself in the back seat and thanked God she wasn't prone to motion sickness. Although she was probably going to be black and blue before this ride was over.

In spite of the rutted road and Nik's reckless driving, Emma was nonetheless relieved to be back on the ground. Time being of the essence, they'd taken a private helicopter to Vancouver, lifting straight off of the roof of the apartment building.

Aiden let out a frustrated noise as he tried, again, to contact the rest of their team. After receiving the go ahead to head to their meeting point, Dante and the rest of the team had gone radio silent. "I'm not getting anything," he repeated for the fourth time. "Where the bloody hell are they?"

"Have you tried the other channels?" Nik asked. "Or tried calling Christian directly?"

"Yes. Yes. I've tried everything." Pulling out his cell phone, Aiden hit a button. The speakerphone came on, and they all listened to the rings on the other end of the line. After the fifth one, voicemail picked up, and one of the most sinister voices Emma had ever heard gritted out, simply, "Dante", as if daring the person on the other end to leave a message. It actually made the hair stand up on the back of her neck, and she was very glad it was Nik and not this "Dante" vampire who'd come for her.

If the phone had been in her hands, she would've hung up immediately. And thrown it out the window for good measure.

But Aiden, true to form, was not intimidated. "Commander! Where the bloody hell are you?" Hanging up, he picked up the radio again and asked for anyone listening to respond. Still nothing.

Nik drove on as he chewed on the inside of his cheek, his expression thoughtful. "We'll go on to the meeting point. Maybe something happened to their radio."

"All of them?" Aiden scoffed in disbelief. "I've tried to reach all three of them via cell phone *and* radio."

For the first time since Emma had met him, he sounded worried. "Where the hell are they, Nik? What if they were discovered?" He chucked his radio into the console. "What if we're driving directly into a bloody trap?"

A look of concern passed between the two vampires.

"Wait a minute." Emma had just grasped what Aiden had said. "We're storming the sadistic bitch's lair with only three others to help?" She'd been nothing but a mass of nerves since leaving the apartment, but she'd been consoling herself with the thought they would be meeting an army of vicious vampires who were going to storm in there and rescue Luukas and Keira —all cavalry style—while she stayed safely in the background until if/when the time came that she could go get her sister.

No one would get hurt except the bad guys, and she and Keira would hug and cry and go back to their normal boring lives. They'd forget all about the past seven years, and all this witch nonsense. And most especially, one particular vampire. Blood bond be damned.

Was that really so much to ask?

With a quiet sigh, she knew it was wishful thinking. She'd never condemn Nik to die. No, she would do all she could to figure out some kind of arrangement between them. One they could both live with. "Live" being the prominent word there.

"Five of us are normally more than enough to get the job done. Besides," Nik suddenly turned off onto an even smaller road, more like a trail actually, right through a thick stand of trees. "A large party is more easily spotted. Easier to surprise the enemy this way."

They drove another 20 minutes or so before Nik finally slowed and pulled off to the side. Turning off the engine, he looked back at Emma, a finger over his lips indicating for her to keep quiet.

Sitting very still, she listened with them. She didn't know what she would hear or see before they did, but she tried anyway.

Suddenly, without a look or word between them, Nik and Aiden opened their doors and got out of the vehicle. Quietly telling Emma to "Stay here, and lock the doors" they melted into the night, leaving her alone in the dark. Crawling up to the front seat, she locked the doors as directed and tried to see where they'd gone, but there was nothing but blackness. They'd disappeared in the blink of an eye.

After ten of the longest minutes of her life, her breath caught on a scream as they suddenly appeared again in front of the Hummer, scaring the hell out of her. She didn't know if she'd ever get used to the speed of vampires.

Nik came over to her side and indicated for her to unlock the doors while Aiden went to the back to get their packs out. Opening the driver's side, he grabbed her by the waist and effortlessly plucked her out and set her on the ground. "Looks clear. Go with Aiden while I camouflage the vehicle."

She started to ask him why it was okay for her to be alone with Aiden *now*, but not at the apartment, but changed her mind when she noticed the lines of strain around is blue eyes, still bright even in the dim light coming from the vehicle. Instead, she just nodded and decided to save her teasing for another time.

Emma tromped through the undergrowth after Aiden, branches and wet leaves whipping against her legs. She was glad she'd put on her heavy jeans, and not her more comfortable yoga pants.

She wanted to ask him if they'd heard or seen anything to indicate the others were in the area or on their way, but didn't know if it was safe to make any unnecessary noise, so she held her tongue.

Aiden moved silently through the brush in front of her, like the predator he was. Following close behind him, she sounded like something more along the lines of a large elephant, or maybe even an entire herd of them.

"Through here, love." Holding back a bundle of lush, green branches, Aiden ushered her through an opening in the side of a large rock face. It was so well hidden, she would've never noticed it there, which she guessed was the point. Once inside, she walked forward a few paces but couldn't see enough of where she was going to continue, so she stopped and waited for Aiden. He re-covered the entrance, and the darkness became absolute.

She jumped as she felt him slide by her. "Hang on to my backpack and stay behind me. Watch your step. I dread the talking to I'll receive if I return you to Nikulas with so much as a skinned knee."

"You make me sound like his property." Reaching out blindly in front of her, she found his pack and held on.

"You *are* his property now, love, no matter what he wants to believe. Don't delude yourself into thinking otherwise." They started walking slowly through the tunnel. "Until he dies, or you do."

"Will he really die if he doesn't feed from me?"

"Yes. Eventually."

"And he knows this?"

"Yes."

"Then why hasn't he spoken to me about it?"

"Because he's a bloody Estonian bastard, that's why."

She wasn't sure what his heritage had to do with Nik's reluctance to feed from a live person, but all conversation was put on hold as she concentrated on following Aiden without falling on her face.

After about 2 minutes of walking blindly through the tunnel, he stopped. "Let go of my pack Em, and stay here."

"Where are you going?" she squeaked. Her voice echoed, and she could hear the constant "drip, drip, drip" of water somewhere off to her right. When he didn't answer right away, she began to get anxious. Chewing on her bottom lip, she tried to see something, anything, around her that would give her an indication of where she was. But there was nothing but blackness, and her imagination went into overdrive. What if there were rats down here? Oh, God. She hated rats. Or spiders? Or worse, snakes??

She could feel herself starting to go into a full-blown panic. "Aiden!"

"I'm just going to get us some light. I would imagine you can't see very well in here."

He didn't sound very far away, and she took a halting step toward him before remembering he'd told her to stay where she was.

"Don't fret Em, I'm just right here. Your heart sounds like a bloody freight train, love. Calm down. We vampires only have so much control, mind you."

"Sorry." She didn't really think Aiden would actually hurt her, but took a long, calming breath just the same. There was a rustling sound, and then a flashlight beam.

"You had a flashlight this entire time?" she hissed as she held up a hand in front of her face. "Is there any particular reason you didn't use it until now?"

He shrugged. "I didn't need it until now." Shining the light around, he found what he was looking for—an old fashioned torch. "Wouldn't want to waste the batteries," he explained.

Taking the torch down from its holder, he dipped it into some kind of noxious smelling liquid in a barrel along the wall, then took a lighter from his pocket and lit it. Placing it back in its holder, he turned off his flashlight.

"There we go!" He disappeared into the shadows, reappearing again when he lit another torch.

Emma looked around in awe as she slowly walked further inside. They had traveled down a narrow tunnel through the rock to a natural underground cavern. Smooth limestone walls, swirled with lighter and darker browns, led up to a soaring ceiling at least thirty feet above her head. Under her feet, dirt had been packed down to make an even floor. She could still hear the water dripping off to her right, but didn't see its source.

Her gaze came back to Aiden, who was putting his flashlight away, and she glowered at him.

Nik silently entered the room just then. His gaze went back and forth between her and Aiden. He raised an eyebrow. "Did I miss something?"

Rolling her eyes, Emma walked into the middle of the room where a circle of stones surrounded a fire pit. "Just Aiden... being Aiden." She plopped down on one of the large, flat-topped rocks surrounding it for seating, threw down her backpack, and pulled out a bottled water and a protein bar.

Taking a closer look around, she saw the remnants of past visitors. "So I take it you guys have been here before?" she ventured.

Aiden puffed out his chest. "I found this place years ago. Quite the thing, isn't it? We use it as our meet up area whenever we feel the need to come up here and check on our sweet Leeha."

Emma was confused. "So you've known all along she's in this area?"

They both nodded.

"Then why not come up here until now? If you knew all this time where your brother—*and my sister*—were, why were they not rescued seven years ago??"

"We did come here," Aiden hastened to reassure her. "But the place was deserted. Not a sign of anyone to be found for years. But, we have scouts come up occasionally to keep an eye out for her, and we just recently found out she was back." He held up his index finger. "The question is: why come back now? She has to know we'd be watching for her." He gave Emma a wink. "Perhaps she missed me." With a secretive smile, Aiden headed to the back of the room where some wood was already cut and stacked up against the wall.

Nik sat down on the rock next to her, and gestured to the water bottle she held stuck halfway to her mouth while she blinked, speechless, at Aiden. "Go easy on that stuff, sweetheart." He took a peek into her bag. "Just in case."

She turned back to Nik and lowered her arm. "How long do you expect us to be here?" She'd been under the impression it wouldn't be more than a day or two at most.

"Not long, hopefully, but it's always good to be prepared. I can't have you starving to death on me." He smirked at her, looking a bit like the carefree Nik she'd first met, but she wasn't in the mood.

"No, we can't have that, can we? Because if I die, so do you."

His smile faded as quickly as it had appeared, and he glared over at his best friend, who was suddenly very busy counting the pieces of wood stacked up in the far corner of the cavern.

"What the fuck, Aiden? I told you to keep your fucking mouth shut about all that shit."

Aiden's face was the picture of innocence as he pushed off his hood and scratched his head. "You did? Are you quite certain? I don't exactly recall..."

Nik shot up off of the rock he was sitting on. "You're a son of a bitch, you know that?"

Aiden pulled his hood back up over his short, dark hair and calmly met Nik look for look. "What the bloody hell did you expect me to do, mate? Let you kill yourself over your misguided belief you can never be happy because of what you think happened with Eliana?" He suddenly appeared in front of his friend, moving too fast for Emma to track. "You're my best friend. More importantly, I'm your Guardian. As such, I am required to do everything in my power to keep you healthy and alive. It's bad enough I already let you get away with drinking that fucking bagged blood. I cannot—I WILL NOT— let you commit suicide because of an unfortunate accident that happened in the past."

"It's not your choice, Aiden."

"Sod off, Nikulas. It IS my choice. And I choose to not stand idly by and let you do this." Grabbing Emma by the arm, he hauled her up to stand next to him, ignoring Nik's immediate warning growl at the sight of his hands on her. "This is a good woman right here. This is a strong woman. She would be a brilliant mate. *I like her.* And she cares about you, you bloody arse."

Emma glowered at him and his manhandling, and yanked her arm from his grasp. "Look," she told Nikulas. "If you don't want to be with me," Her face began to heat, but she forced the words out. "For whatever the reason. That's okay."

Nik dropped his head back, looking heavenward. He didn't seem to find any help there, so he thrust both hands into his hair in exasperation. "Emma—"

"We can figure something else out, Nik." She grabbed his hands as she looked up at him imploringly. "You don't have to die! I can just donate into a bag or something."

Turning his hands, he carefully gripped her small fingers in his. "You don't get it. I would rather die, than hurt you."

"You're not listening! I could *donate*, like blood donors. That would work, right?"

Neither of them noticed Aiden quietly slip away and leave the cave.

"You drink out of those gross bags, anyway. It could work!" Why was he still arguing with her?

"No, sweetheart, it wouldn't. Your blood weakens once it's left your body. It would be nearly the same as drinking the stuff I do now, only lacking what I need to survive. You wouldn't be able to give enough. It would barely prolong the inevitable, and in the end would have the same result as not drinking it. Please, just let it be," he begged.

But Emma wasn't finished yet. "Well, so, what if you did the same thing then? Would that help? We can swap blood without ever having to be anywhere near each other. I can...I don't know, put it in a smoothie or something." She grimaced at the thought, but if it would keep him alive, she would do it.

"No, Emma."

"Yes! I'd be able to give more. It would work."

Sadly, insistently, he shook his head. "No."

"Would you *please* stop being so damn stubborn, and—"

"Emma, I said *no*."

"Why the hell not, Nikulas!" Yanking her hands from his, she stomped a few feet away from him, swiping at the angry tears on her cheeks.

28

The cave rumbled, and Nik glanced around with a frown. But this was no earthquake.

Large rocks and hunks of wood vibrated throughout the cavern. Some were even hovering a few inches above the floor. His little witch was losing her temper, and was probably about to bash him in the head with it all. The air was heavy with magic. It filled the room until he felt it crawl across his skin like it was alive.

Now would probably be a good time to try to calm her down. "Em...sweetheart..."

"No! No, Nik!" She swiped at her face before she turned around, but he could still see the moisture from her tears. "How can you ask me to just walk away from this? Do you think *I* would be able to live with myself, knowing I was the cause of your death? You're being an obstinate ass!"

She threw her arms up in the air. "There! I said it. You're being an ass, Nikulas! I actually agree with Aiden on this one point."

A rock the size of a soccer ball hit the opposite wall with a crash, and her head whipped around to stare at the smashed pieces in shock.

Nik ignored it, all of his attention on Emma. "Emma, listen to me. Please."

She turned back to him, and opened her mouth to yell at him some more. The physical display of her rage hovered higher off the ground now. The objects buzzed with so much power, it sounded like a large swarm of bees.

Nik fought his way through her magic, reaching out to her with his ravaged emotions. He understood her frustration. But if she thought this was easy for him, she was wrong.

So fucking wrong.

She must have felt him, for the cavern became quiet as her temper—and her weapons—settled down. "Fine," she snapped at him. "Talk."

Now that he had her undivided attention, Nik found himself at a loss for words. Shoving his hands into his pockets, he looked around for some help from Aiden. Where the hell was that loud-mouthed Brit when he needed him?

"Well?" Emma's voice brought him back to her.

Nik took a deep inhale and braced himself. It scared the hell out of him to open up to her, but she had the right to know. "It won't work because...because I'm fucking crazy about you Emma. I was crazy about you from the first moment I saw you, puttering around your house in that hideous, blue robe."

Her forehead scrunched up and she rubbed at her temples. "Then what's the problem? I don't understand."

"I can't do that to you, Em. I can't ask you to rearrange your life for me. I won't. I won't use you like that."

Both hands yanked at his hair as he paced back and forth, trying to think of something that would convince her to see things his way. But he instinctively knew she wouldn't believe anything but raw honesty from him. So, that's exactly what he would give her.

Nik became perfectly still, strong in his resolve. "To me, you are the most utterly perfect female I've ever seen, or talked to, or touched. The things you've been through, your bravery, your attitude in spite of it all…they leave me in awe of you. I'm not worthy of a female such as you."

He paced away and back again. "I've seen things…done things…in my life that weren't exactly honorable. I'm not a good male."

The more he spoke, the more he felt the lingering anger in her dissipate. She dropped her eyes, hiding from him as she wrapped her arms around herself. "I think you're exaggerating. I'm not anything special." Her jaw set and she looked up at him. "And I have to disagree with that last statement."

Her modesty only endeared her to him more. "I'm not worthy, sweetheart. I'm not." He speared her with his gaze. "But, when I tasted you—" His voice broke at the memory. "I tasted you, and it was all over for me. It doesn't have to be for you."

He held himself stiffly before her with his heart and soul outside of his body, raw and exposed. "I would never be able to have any kind of 'arrangement' with you, even if it were possible. I would never be able to watch you go through your life from the sidelines. Watch you have other lovers." His lips pulled back in a snarl at the thought, and his fangs slid down in aggression. "Watch you laugh, and cry, and not be there with you. Not be able to hold you, to comfort you. You're MINE, Emma. But I can't have you. I don't trust myself not to hurt you. Or worse."

"Nik—" she faltered.

His heart pounded like it was about to jump out of his chest, but he kept going. "In a way, I'm afraid of you, Em." Shaking his head, he denied the obvious reason why before it could be spoken. "Not because I'm dependent on your blood now. Not because I'm afraid to die. I've lived more than my share of lifetimes."

She scoffed playfully at him, and he smiled at her attempt to lighten the mood. "I'm like, half your size, and human. What is there to be afraid of?"

"Exactly. You're too fragile. I couldn't be there all the time to protect you. What if something happened? What if it happened because of *me*? What if I..." He stopped, unable to finish the thought. "I wouldn't be able to take it, Emma. I feel more for you, in these few days I've known you, than I've ever felt for any other female. Or anyone, for that matter. I'm afraid, Em." Then he shook his head again. "No, not afraid. I'm *terrified* of the pain of losing you. I would rather bring an end to myself and leave you to live a long, healthy, natural life than make you into my own personal feeding bag. I've lived a long time, had more than my share of lives. It is enough."

"You don't have to lose me, Nik." Emma's eyes glinted with frustration.

"It would happen someday. You're too fragile. Too...human." His voice broke with the emotions rolling through him. "And then what would I do, Em? What would I do without you?

Without your smile to light up my nights? Without being able to hold you? To talk to you?" He tried for a smile, but couldn't keep it there. "Death wouldn't come for me soon enough."

Emma closed the distance between them and wrapped her arms around his lean waist. She hugged him hard and buried her face in his chest. He barely heard her confession.

"Nikulas, I feel the same way about you, as impossible as it should be."

His eyes fell to the top of her bright head. Allowing himself this moment to enjoy, Nik wrapped his arms around her and lovingly returning her embrace. "That's impossible. You barely know me." His smile was as fragile as his emotions as he teased her.

She smiled back at him. "I'm a sucker for pretty boys with cocky attitudes."

A look of hope briefly lit up inside of him, but it fluttered out again almost immediately. "You'd have to give up your life to be with me."

"I'm good with that," she promised.

"What about your sister?"

"She's a big girl. She can take care of herself. And I'd be able to visit once we get her home."

He set her away from him. "I can't take the chance, Em. You'll be okay. This whole mating thing, it doesn't affect you the way it does me. You can go on to live a long, happy, and normal life."

"Why is this only *your* choice? Don't I get a say in any of this?" She stepped back into his arms, and he didn't have the heart or the willpower to push her away again. "I choose *you*, Nikulas. You're just going to have to deal with it."

"Emma." A noise came from the tunnel and he cocked his head, listening. Pulling Emma behind him, he placed himself between her and the entrance, his body suddenly tense. But after a moment, he relaxed. "It's Aiden." With one last, longing look at her, he went over to get the wood Aiden had abandoned from the corner and set about making a small fire.

Dammit, Aiden. The guy had perfect fucking timing.

Aiden came around the corner into the cavern, whistling an energetic tune. "Hey, you two! Get things worked out, did we?"

No one answered him as Nik broke logs over his knee and Emma crossed her arms in front of her with a huff. "No? Still? Pity, that." Looking back and forth between the two of them, he must have astutely deemed Emma to be the safer choice, and wandered over her way.

Nik watching his every move.

"No luck, huh?"

Sliding down the wall behind her, she sat cross-legged on the dirt packed floor. "Nope."

Joining her, Aiden asked hopefully, "Not even just a little?"

"*Your* friend, Aiden, is a bloody Estonian bastard."

"Yes. Yes, he is," he commiserated with her.

Nik glared at the two of them sitting there with their heads together. When the hell had they gotten so chummy? "I can hear you! I'm right fucking here!"

They stared back at him in stony silence.

"Un-fucking believable." Throwing the last log into the circle, he sat on his haunches to start the fire.

Aiden patted Emma on the hand and got up to come over to help, adding more kindling under the logs.

"So where did you go anyway?" Nik asked after a moment.

"Oh! Yes, that. Well, I went outside to give you two some privacy. But then I thought as long as I was out there, I may as well look around a bit." He paused to blow on the small flames. "Someone else is in the area."

Nik left the fire to Aiden, who was much better at it than he was, and took a seat on one of the stones. "Who? Dante?"

Aiden didn't answer until the fire was licking merrily at the logs. "No, I don't think so." He sat next to Nik and watched the flames. "If it is, he's gathered more fighters. I found their tracks just a little ways north of here. Then they suddenly disappear after about two miles."

Nik thought a moment. "Wolves?"

Aiden shrugged.

"All right, I'll go check it out. See what I can find. I need to get out of here for a while." Nik grabbed his backpack.

Aiden carefully fanned the flames. "Nope. Can't let you do that. I'll go back out there and scope it out. I just wanted to check in with you. You stay here with Emma."

Taking out a couple of wicked-looking blades from the bag he'd brought, Nik strapped them around his thighs. "I'm going. I need the air. *You* stay here." He tore open a blood bag and chugged it down before he could taste it, then took a water bottle out to bring with him. Those things were getting nastier and nastier. With a sideways glance at Emma, he sauntered toward the tunnel, waving away Aiden's protests.

"I don't know why Luukas ever appointed me to you," Aiden said. "You completely ignore all of my endeavors to keep you safe."

Nik flipped him off and paused to tighten one of his knife straps.

He heard a quick exhale before Aiden finally gave it up. "Be careful. Don't get too close." He paused. "Although that *would* be the easiest way to find Luukas..."

"Aiden!" Emma didn't sound pleased with that plan.

Another pause. "No, you're right, Em. Leeha would love that. She'd have both brothers to torture, along with our missing Hunters, if that's where they are."

Nik resumed walking and tried his best to ignore the both of them.

"Although," Aiden continued, "I could follow to see where she took you, but I'm not sure how I would get you all out of there on my own."

Nik glanced over his shoulder to see Aiden waving a hand around in dismissal. "Eh, I'll figure something out."

He paused at the tunnel entrance, shooting an exasperated look at his friend. But he was already back on his radio, trying again to get a hold of the others.

Emma rose from her spot on the floor and brushed off her pants. "I want to come with you, Nik."

Nik barely glanced at her. "No. It's too dangerous, and you'll just slow me down." *And I need some space from your scent.*

A frustrated breath burst from her lungs. "It's my sister in there, too."

He turned to leave and heard her footsteps behind him.

"You're not going to just leave me here in this cave with this… this…unstable, womanizing, oversensitive, psychopath. No offense, Aiden."

Aiden grinned charmingly at her. "None taken, love." Then he looked pointedly at Nik. "See, Nik? Emma *understands* me."

Nik turned around and found the two of them watching him expectantly. "What? No. Absolutely not. Emma is too fragile. Too human." He ignored her sound of protest at that statement. "And too much of a distraction."

"Not disagreeing with you there, mate, she is quite the distraction," Aiden agreed. "Clear off and leave her here with me, I'm sure I can find her something to do." He winked at Emma, and the naughty grin on his face grew as Nik's simmering growl filled the silence.

That goddamn Brit was doing this on purpose. Nik knew it, but couldn't keep himself from getting sucked in anyway. In the space of a breath he appeared next to Emma, grabbed her hand and pulled her behind him. With a hiss of warning, he bared his fangs at Aiden. Then he grabbed her backpack and threw it over his shoulder with his.

Emma waved cheerfully at Aiden and he returned it as Nik stalked off, dragging her along behind him.

Once they got outside, Nik pinned her with his glare. "Fine. You can come. But you do exactly as I say. No arguments. No questions. If I say jump, you jump. If I say run, you run like the demons of hell are chasing you. Got it?"

"Got it."

"I'm serious, Emma. I am NOT fucking around here."

She glared right back at him. "I SAID I've got it. You forget, Nik. I know *exactly* what we could be running in to, and what they can do."

He hadn't forgotten. It was why he didn't want her to come with him. He contemplated sending her back in to stay with Aiden, but his possessive nature and the need to keep her close ultimately won out in the end.

"Here, take this." He handed her one of the knives. "And let's go. The night is wasting."

29

Shea checked the time again. Where the hell were they? She hadn't spoken to either Dante or Christian since they'd left last night.

Come to think of it, she'd never heard Christian come home. She always heard him come home.

Tired of waiting, she walked out of her apartment and down the hall to bang on his door. When there was no answer, she took the spare key she'd brought with her and let herself in.

"Christian?" she called. Closing the door behind her, she stuck her key back into her front pocket.

"Christian! Where the hell are you?" Her own voice echoed back to her from the empty apartment. He really needed to get some stuff for this place. Stuff like furniture, and throw rugs. Her boots were silent as she walked across the bare expanse of living area to his bedroom. The door was closed.

She rapped hard on the wood. "Hey, whoredog! Get your ass out of that bed! We need to go!" Cracking the door open, she peeked inside. The bed was unmade, blankets and pillows strewn about, some on the floor. Opening the door wide, she walked in and made her way over to the bathroom.

The door was wide open. He wasn't in there. She turned away from the doorway and looked around his room again. Where the hell was he? Pulling her phone out of her pocket, she checked it again.

Nothing. No messages from either of them. What the hell?

The hair rose up on the back of her neck. Something was wrong. She should call Nik and Aiden, but she wanted to check one more place before raising the alarm. Although she couldn't imagine Christian being there, it wouldn't hurt to look first.

Moving quickly now, she jogged out to the elevator. While she waited for it to take her down to Dante's quarters, she racked her brain, trying to come up with any reason that both of them wouldn't show up at the appointed time. She couldn't think of one.

The bell above the door chimed as the car finally arrived. Stepping inside, she hit the button repeatedly until the doors finally closed. The ride down to the underground was quick, and she bolted out as soon as the doors opened.

Shea ran full speed down the passageway. She turned left at the split, away from the area the tourists paid to see. She hated it down here. It was so wet and dark. A musty smell permeated the air and—

Wait, was that blood?

It *was* blood she scented. Some of it so faint it had obviously been here for quite a while. But some of it was fresh. Very fresh.

I don't even want to know.

She came to the wood and steel barricade that kept out any nosey thrill seekers and effortlessly leaped up to the top of it. Pulling at the top plank, it opened on unseen hinges to make a space just big enough for a body to get through. Crawling over, she dropped down to the other side and took off again.

Less than a minute or so later, she arrived at Dante's main hideout. The smell of blood was stronger here. Her fangs slid down in response, but she didn't see any evidence of it anywhere.

A damp mattress was thrown on the floor, nothing but a thin blanket on top of it. A few candles were scattered about the small space, unlit. The only other thing in the room was a thick book next to the bed.

Shea pushed on her temples. *Think, think.* Where would they be? She fought down her rising panic as she came to the conclusion that she just didn't know. She had no idea what Dante did in his free time, and Christian could be anywhere in the city.

Okay. Just calm down, Shea. Let's not panic until there's something to panic about. Maybe they're just running late.

But she didn't believe it. Neither one of them was ever late to leave on a mission like this. Something had to have happened.

She decided to go take a look around the building. Ask the security guards if they'd seen anything, see what she could find out. If nothing came out of that, then she'd give Aiden a call.

Back at the elevator, she hit the button that would take her to the underground garage. It was the only way either of them would have come in. The elevators in the lobby didn't go past the human floors.

Her heart pounded as she quickly rose up to the next floor. As the doors opened, she saw the guards standing at their station and hurried over to question them.

Unfortunately, neither of them remembered seeing either of the guys the night before. Shea thanked them and headed out to the street to have a look around.

She didn't make it past the first block before a van with black windows pulled up alongside her. Shea's scream of pain was muffled as a rag was shoved in her mouth and she was thrown in the back.

The doors shut, blocking out the lights of the city.

30

They'd walked in silence for about 25 minutes when Nik pulled up suddenly. He raised an arm to stop Emma and put his finger to his lips. Narrowing his eyes, he cocked his head and listened. It was quiet. Too quiet. No crickets. No nocturnal animals. He searched the area around them but didn't see anything other than the tree leaves twirling slightly in the breeze.

Nothing.

But something wasn't right. He could feel it. Closing his eyes, he sent his senses out farther, blending them into the night.

Yes. *There.* Something was coming.

Nik looked around again. They'd been following the rock face at the bottom of the mountain range that concealed their hideout, and he quietly steered Emma toward a narrow ravine in the stone large enough for her to squeeze into.

He kept his voice as low as he could. "Emma, I need you to stay here. Do not come out until I tell you. Do you understand?"

"What is it?" she whispered. Her eyes were wide and terrified as they travelled over his face.

"Just stay here. Do not make a sound. Do NOT move. No matter what happens." Removing her backpack, he pushed her toward the opening. "Got your knife out?"

She pulled it out and showed him.

He nodded with approval. "Anything sticks its face in here, stab it. It will slow them down enough for you to get away." *I hope.*

Once she was hidden out of sight, he turned around, dropped his bag, and paced a few feet away from her hiding place. Far enough to not draw attention to it, but close enough to help her if she needed him. Hopefully, they'd be too distracted by him to notice her in there.

Standing perfectly still in that disconcerting way vampires had, he waited. Every cell inside of him was focused on one purpose and one purpose only.

Protect his female.

He didn't have long to wait. They came at him out of nowhere and all at once, six of them.

What the fuck? What the hell *were* these things?

Exactly as Emma had described, these must be the "monsters" she'd told him about. They rushed him, and the shock of their appearance quickly wore off. Adrenaline rushed through him and Nik smiled, flashing his fangs. His body immediately prepared itself for the fight—and for revenge.

With a roar, he grabbed the closest one by the head with both hands. Its razor sharp teeth inches from his face, he twisted it sharply to the side until he felt the grey flesh tearing and the neck bones popping. Red eyes bugged out of its head right before they glazed over in death.

Launching the limp body into the creature coming at him from the front, Nik shot out a left elbow and grinned as he felt bones crack beneath it. He followed it up with a back kick, knocking two more away from him.

A low spin kick to the knee took the next one down. Yanking his knife out of his thigh sheath, he dropped on top of it, jerked the head up, and slit a gash in its throat so deep only a few tendons kept it attached.

As he shot to his feet, the remaining four came at him with supernatural speed. Fists, elbows and kicks flying, fangs tearing into putrid flesh, Nik blocked out everything but the exhilaration of the fight. His roars of rage mixed with their shrieks of agony as bones crunched and blood spattered. For a few heart-stopping minutes, it was hard to tell who was coming out on top.

And then, suddenly, it was over.

Nik swung around with fists up, prepared to kill anything else coming at him, but nothing moved. His chest heaved with his ragged breaths, his head throbbed from a particularly vicious blow he took, and his fangs ached to rip through more flesh. Blood dripped from his mouth and down his chest and arms, some of it his own, the rest of it belonging to the pieces of shit disintegrating all around him.

As the high of the fight dissipated and awareness slowly returned, he straightened up. "Emma? Emma!"

A small scraping sounded to his left. Nik swung around and dropped into a fighting crouch with a feral hiss, fangs bared.

Knife held shakily in front of her, Emma cautiously sidestepped from her hiding place in the stone. Wide-eyed, she took in the carnage on the ground, and then her gaze skipped up to Nik.

He raised his hands, palms out, and slowly straightened, spitting the blood out of his mouth and wiping his mouth on his sleeve. "Emma. Em, it's okay. I won't hurt you." He kept his feet planted where they were for fear she'd flee if he moved.

Her face remained white as a sheet, her freckles standing out in harsh relief. And her eyes had a glazed look to them as they darted from him, to the things on the ground, and back to him.

Then they locked on to his face and stayed there. His jaw dropped open in disbelief as she dropped the knife and ran, not away from him, but straight into his arms. She threw herself against him so hard he had a difficult time staying upright.

"Are you okay?" she cried. "Oh my God, you're bleeding!"

"I'm fine. I'm fine. Most of it isn't mine. Besides, vampire here, remember?" He hugged her close, surrounding her in the safe shelter of his arms and resting his cheek on the top of her head.

The feel of her subtle curves trembling against him wreaked havoc on his fragile self-control, but he couldn't bring himself to push her away. Instead, he rubbed comforting circles on her back to soothe her. The smell of her sweet blood and warm skin flooded his nose, and he inhaled deeply, unable to help himself.

Fresh from the fight, his senses were raw and exposed, and like a starving man, his body responded eagerly to the attack upon them. His mouth watered, and his fangs ached to pierce her flesh even as his cock swelled to a painful size. Nik wanted nothing more than to throw her down on the blood-soaked ground and sink his teeth into her flesh and his hardness into the slick softness between her legs.

Before he could stop it, he groaned aloud.

Emma pulled back just far enough to be able to look at him, her hands gripping his forearms. "Am I hurting you? You said you were okay!" she accused.

As she frantically checked him for injuries, Nik felt her brand him everywhere her eyes touched. Her hands touched him, and raging lust tore through his insides. Resisting the urge that came with it required an act of will he didn't possess at the moment. He needed more distance between them, needed her to back off a bit.

"You're not hurting me, not like that." Nik gently, but insistently, pulled away from her. He became aware that his head was still throbbing, and he actually felt almost...tired. How strange. "These are the monsters you were telling me about?" At her stiff nod, he looked around at what remained of them. "I've never seen creatures like this before, Em. I have no idea what they are."

Emma wouldn't, or couldn't, look at the things. He wasn't sure which. And he couldn't say that he blamed her. "Nik, are you sure you're okay? You look...not right."

"Yeah, I'm good. My head just hurts a little, is all." He nudged one of the creatures with his boot as it rapidly flaked away. "Maybe we should take one of these things back with us. Have Aiden check it out. We'd have to move quick, though."

She continued to study him like a bug under a microscope. "Are you sure you don't want to rest a minute?"

He was suddenly, irrationally, angry. Did she think him weak? "I'm fine, Emma. So get that fucking look off your face." No sooner had the words left his mouth than he was kicking himself in the ass. Where the hell had that come from?

He closed his eyes to avoid the hurt look he knew he would see, and tried to soften the blow he'd just dealt. "I'm sorry. I probably just need to feed, is all."

31

Emma could've face-palmed herself. Of course! He was bleeding. He needed to feed.

From *her*.

"Well, why don't you?" she coaxed.

"Why don't I what?" Nik straightened up from his examination of the body he'd been prodding.

"Why don't you feed?" she asked. Then quickly clarified, "From me."

He froze, but she could almost feel the tightly wound power in him simmering just beneath the surface. It was a palpable thing that both frightened and attracted her. His face was still cold, inhuman. And his blue eyes shone silver in the night with the unholy glow they took on when his emotions ran high.

"I'm not going to do that, Emma." Glancing around for their bags, he swung them both over one shoulder. "Come on. Let's get going."

But she stood her ground. He'd bitten her once already. It hadn't been that bad.

Ha! Who was she trying to kid? It had felt amazing. Much less traumatizing than being ripped apart like a piece of meat.

"You need to feed, Nik. What if we run into more of those things?" She grabbed his arm as he went to walk past her. "You need to be at full strength. You *need* to feed."

His eyes burned, the conflict he felt plain to see. "I *can't*, Emma."

"Can't? Or won't?" she retorted.

She felt the wall he threw up between them as he pressed his lips together and refused to answer her, and she had to stop herself from rubbing her arms against the sudden cold. Taking matters into her own hands, she stepped close enough to him so that the tips of her breasts brushed his ribs every time she inhaled.

He narrowed his eyes at her suspiciously, but didn't back away.

Emma reached up, pulled her hair away from her neck, and tilted her head to the side.

His eyes instantly darted from her face to the strong pulse in her neck. A low growl rumbled through his chest, and she shivered at the animalistic sound, desire unfurling low in her belly.

She didn't say anything else, just stood there quietly while the battle raged inside of him, and hoped he wouldn't be able to resist what she offered.

Nik sucked in a desperate breath, knowing he needed to stop this, but for the life of him unable to move away.

Bad idea, breathing.

His already swollen cock throbbed painfully against the confinement of his jeans as the scent of her desire rose in the air, enhancing her delicious smell even more. The memory of her wet, silky folds and the way she'd shuttered in his arms slammed through him.

He dropped the bags and clenched his fists tightly at his sides as he ground his teeth together. His vampire nature struggled to be given free rein, but somehow Nik held it back.

Quietly, he ordered, "Emma. Back off." His voice was low and rough, his words not quite convincing. Not even to himself.

In response, she leaned closer to him, pressing her soft breasts into his chest. Her heart pounded so hard, he could feel it thudding against him. In fear? Or anticipation?

Rising up on her tiptoes, she brought her exposed throat closer to his mouth. She let go of her hair, allowing the wavy mass to fall to the side as she slid her hands across his stomach to each side of his waist to steady herself.

Nik's muscles tightened and jumped everywhere she touched. He clenched his jaw, but he couldn't stop himself from lowering his head and skimming his lips over her pulsing artery. Her body molded perfectly to his. Smelled so good to him. He could pick out her unique scent over all the others covering their clothes, barely even noticed them. Her blood completely overpowered everything else.

As she leaned her soft length into his hardness, her faint moan of pleasure had him unclenching his fists. Grasping her hair with one hand, he pulled her head farther to the side, while his other arm came around her shoulders and squeezed her to him.

Another moan from her and he pulled his lips back, helplessly running the tip of one fang down her neck until it rested on that titillating pulse. He pressed against it, just enough, barely puncturing the surface of her skin.

He flicked his tongue over the drop of blood he'd drawn, and his eyes nearly rolled back in his head. He imagined he'd have the same reaction when he tasted her cunt. She'd be drenched with desire for him. He knew this for a fact. He could smell her. Could feel how much she wanted him.

His entire body shook with the effort it took to restrain himself, and as her blood coated his tongue and the scent of her lust filled his nose, Nik felt the last remnants of his waning willpower slip away. Every single fiber of his being was telling him to take what she was offering.

She was HIS, goddamn it.

Yet still, he tried one last effort to resist. "Emma," he pleaded. "Please...make me stop." Even as he choked out the words, his hand slid down her back to hold her hips still, and he ground his throbbing erection into her soft belly as he pressed a soft kiss to the wound he'd made. "Just...tell me to *stop*."

Her hands clenched his shirt as her body trembled against his. Her breasts swelled and her nipples throbbed against his hard chest. His arm was the only thing that kept her from sagging to the ground.

But instead of obeying him, she ordered him to take what he needed. "Nikulas. Take me. Do it." Whether she meant her blood, or her body, or both, he didn't know.

Her words were his undoing. With a shaky, "I'm so sorry," his head reared back and he struck hard, his fangs sliding seamlessly through her soft skin and piercing her artery. He vaguely heard her cry out as her hot blood raced into his mouth.

Nik lifted her off the ground as he drank. He strode forward to the stone and pressed her against it, caging her in with his body. Sucking hard, her blood flowed down his throat like the sweetest ambrosia, and began to heal him, body and soul.

Emma wrapped her legs around his waist as he fed, his soft moans in her ear the most erotic thing she'd ever heard. With every strong pull he took from her neck, an equally strong pulse of heat shot through her body from his bite straight to her core.

When he started rolling his hips, his erection hitting her swollen clitoris thick and hot even through their clothes, Emma couldn't hold back. Her orgasm hit her hard and fast, and she let it take her, clinging to his strong shoulders for dear life as she cried out her pleasure.

His arms were like steel bands, holding her tight as she came apart within them. The sounds he made ripped through her, altering her forever. He took one last, long draw, then licked at his bite, soothing the burning wound.

Without giving her a chance to recover, he covered her mouth with his, kissing her frantically while he continued to grind himself into her. He grabbed the neckline of her bloody shirt with one hand, tearing it open like it was made of little more than paper.

Emma's half-hearted protest went unheard as he palmed her aching breast, plucking at the nipple through her bra, before ripping that off of her also. The feel of his warm hand on her bare skin swiftly evaporated any fleeting concerns she had about him seeing her naked again.

Nik tore his mouth from hers, and Emma gasped as he lifted her until her breasts were at level with his hungry mouth, one arm under her ass and the other hand lifting her breast to his mouth. Sucking and nipping at her nipple, he drove all thought from her head except for the feel of his warm, wet mouth on her.

Holy shit. Emma felt like she was about to pass out, and at the same time, completely alive. She was lost. Lost completely to this male. Helpless to stop him from doing anything he wanted to her. Not that she *would* stop him, even if she could.

She cried out as he sucked hard on her nipple, flicking the tip with his tongue. Without warning, his fangs pierced her areola, drawing blood, and he groaned in delight as he sucked on her. She cried out again as pain mixed briefly with pleasure, her hips moving as she tried to ease the tension that was building within her again. Stabbing her hands into his hair, Emma held him to her breast.

"More," she demanded. "Nikulas, please…"

32

Out of his mind with lust for his female, Nik attacked her breasts. Her blood coursed through his body, stunning his senses. He'd never felt anything like it. It nourished him. Healed him. His muscles felt stronger, his eyesight sharper, his nerve endings electrified. And at the same time, he was completely drunk on the feel of her in his arms. In his blood.

He felt alive. More alive than he had since first becoming a vampire.

With a soft bite to her nipple, he leaned back slightly to admire her bare chest, and felt the breath still in his own. Her breasts were small, tipped with pale, pink nipples, but they were full and perfectly formed. Or they would have been if not for the small chunk missing from the lower part of her left breast.

Nik had a sudden urge to kill those things all over again.

"What's wrong?" Emma's breathless inquiry quickly diverted his attention back to her.

He met her worried gaze with his own. "You're beyond beautiful," he whispered hoarsely. And he meant it.

Kissing the hollow of missing flesh, he stepped away from the rock and lowered her down his body, licking and sucking his way up until her legs straddled his hips again. Her lips were soft and swollen under his as he kissed her, and he thrust his tongue into her sweet mouth over and over until she was kissing him back just as urgently. Her arms tightened around his neck, and her hands fisted in his hair to hold him to her. Like he was going anywhere. Dropping down to his knees, he lowered her down to the soft grass and settled his weight on top of her.

Stopping was not an option anymore.

Emma clung to him, her breathing ragged and her nails digging into his skin. He barely felt it, because just then she opened her legs and raised her hips up to meet him. She rubbed herself up and down his swollen member, and Nik responded in kind. Burying his face between her neck and shoulder, he gripped her hip with one hand to hold her where he wanted her.

He wanted to go slow, but he couldn't fight the drive to take her anymore. With lightning speed, he sat up and undid her jeans. Her shoes and pants were off of her before she realized what was happening, and as he gazed down at her, Nik felt his entire being go still.

She watched him worriedly as his vampire eyes traveled the length of her, taking in every detail—every curve, every scar—of her body. Before he was finished, she grabbed at the sides of what remained of her shirt, and tried to pull it together to cover herself.

But Nik would have none of it. He knelt over her, still fully dressed, and looked his fill, snarling at her and holding her wrists when she tried to hide the sight of her perfection from him. He would not be denied this. He wanted to see her. All of her. At his leisure. The darkness did not deter him in the least.

And...Ah...She was even lovelier than he'd imagined.

Her skin was creamy and smooth, with light freckles covering her nose and shoulders. The paleness contrasted deliciously with his natural tan as he laid his palm between her luscious breasts, directly over her heart. Her scars were discolored, ragged areas from the attack she'd survived. The ones on her front similar to the ones he'd already seen. But they only made her more beautiful to him.

His tiny warrior.

Her hips, though slight, were still full and feminine. Her legs and arms were toned and strong, her stomach subtly curving down to the soft, red curls that covered her sweet pussy. He wanted to bury his nose in those curls. Nuzzle down into them, spread her open with his tongue, and taste her until she came in his mouth.

But that would have to wait.

Yanking his shirt over his head, he threw it to the side, pausing a second to allow Emma the same time he'd demanded from her. Her eyes eagerly devoured his bare skin. When he moved to undo his jeans, her eyes flew to his waistband, and her tongue wet her bottom lip. He rose to his feet, and quickly divested himself of his boots and jeans. The entire time, he never took his eyes from her.

Then he was lowering himself back down to the female lying waiting in the grass. Nudging her legs open with his knee, he moved over her, sliding his throbbing cock up through her slick folds and back down again, spreading her moisture to prepare her for him.

Emma stopped breathing as his broad head nudged at her entrance. She hadn't had time to see much, but from the quick look he'd given her, he knew she was nervous. He felt the anxiety rear up inside of her, and he kissed her, thrusting his tongue into her mouth as he rolled his hips, sliding himself back and forth over her sensitive nub. In no time at all, she was raising her hips to meet him, hands squeezing his biceps as a different kind of tension rose between them.

He gathered her wrists in one hand and held them over her head. Sliding his other hand under her plump ass, he held her hips still as his cock slid through her slick heat. With one powerful thrust, he entered her, crying out against her mouth as her body tightly hugged his entire length. Nik heard her wince and he stopped. His muscles twitched as he allowed her time to adjust to the size of him. Kissing her softly, his entire body trembled with the effort it took not to pound into her, but he held himself still, waiting for her.

"You're so tight. Are you okay?" he rasped.

Emma lay completely still beneath him, breathing hard. "I think so." She moved her hips a bit, and Nik groaned as he slid in and out, just a little. Just enough to torture him. He fought to hold still, and a shudder ran through his entire body. He squeezed her ass as his head fell to her shoulder on a loud groan.

"I can't stay still much longer, sweetheart," he hissed in her ear. She moved again underneath him. "Emma! I *have* to fuck you, I...Ah!"

"Yes. It's okay. I'm okay." She moved her hips again, encouraging him with soft moans.

Nik pulled his arm out from under her and lowered her ass down to the grass. He slid his hand under her leg, lifting it onto his shoulder, and opened her up even more for him. Releasing her wrists, he propped himself up with a hand on each side of her shoulders, then slid himself nearly all the way out before slamming back into her with a hoarse cry. "You feel so good..." He slid out again slowly, and pushed back in. Lowering his head, he nipped at her nipples as she arched her back, then he could take it no more.

Nik braced himself on his forearms, holding her tightly beneath him as he gained speed. Taking her mouth with his, he swallowed her cries as he pounded into her. Everything else faded away except for her.

Emma clutched at Nik's shoulders as he took her further and further until each hard, fast thrust sent him so deep he could feel her womb. Everything she felt rose from her and directly into him, feeding his own lust as he fucked her mouth like he fucked her body, until she threw her head back, breaking off their kiss with a cry.

Taking her head between his hands, Nik held her still, and with an irrepressible snarl, he struck again. As his fangs pierced her skin, her body surged upward, then crashed over the edge.

Nik growled against her neck as her body bucked underneath him. The sounds of her cries and the feel of her wet warmth squeezing his cock as her blood ran down his throat was almost too much for him to bear.

Lifting his head from her throat, he slid his arms around her, holding her immobile as he took her almost violently. Until, with a hoarse cry, he shoved himself impossibly deeper and exploded inside of her, his entire body convulsing in time with his pulsing cock, filling her with his essence. He'd never come so hard before.

And as he slowly came down, he knew, he was never going to be the same again.

33

Emma lay limp as Nik continued to slide slowly in and out of her, catching his breath. *So that's really what all of the fuss is about.* She'd never quite understood the big deal about sex...until Nik had invaded her shower. And now this.

His tongue lapped at her neck and breasts, healing her wounds and cleaning off the last of the blood. Emma's head swam and her limbs felt limp and lifeless. She couldn't move if she wanted to. And she didn't want to.

"Emma?" She heard Nik's husky voice say her name, but couldn't get her throat to work to respond.

"Emma!" Louder this time.

She tried again to answer him. "Hmmm?"

"Open your mouth, sweetheart."

He was giving orders again, but she did as he told her. As soon as her lips parted, she felt the warmth of his skin, and the sweetest taste dripped onto her tongue. She swallowed automatically, and then began sucking in earnest. Raising her hands, she held his wrist to her mouth as she drank greedily.

When he tried to pull it away, she tightened her grip with a sound of protest.

"Enough, sweetheart." He licked the punctures to close them, and then dropped a kiss on her nose. "We need to go."

Emma felt a rush of cool air over her bare skin as he carefully pulled out of her and sat back on his heels. She licked her lips. *Whoa.* She'd just drank his blood. And it wasn't icky at all. It was more like an exquisite wine, only way better than the crap she bought at the grocery store.

It heated her blood, and she could feel it working its way through her system. She was suddenly wide-awake. Wide-awake, full of energy—

And horny as hell. Again.

Her hungry eyes locked on the perfect specimen kneeling so casually naked between her legs.

His cock hardened again as she bit her lip, drawing her eyes there, and she smiled with delight.

Nik tried, and failed, to suppress his own smile and told her in a stern voice. "Don't be eyeballing me like that, woman. We need to get out of here, before more of these things show up."

He chuckled softly as her eyes widened in comprehension and she looked around, suddenly remembering where they were. Clutching her shirt closed, she sat up so fast they almost knocked heads.

Nik took her by the shoulders to steady her. Leaning down, he whispered in her ear, "As soon as we're done here, though, I'm going to take you home and fuck you until there's not a single inch of you I haven't tasted and we're both too raw to move." He laughed again as her face heated at his words.

Emma smacked at his chest. "Stop it! Get off of me, you big oaf!"

"I will. Just let me do this..." He grabbed his shirt, wadding it up so the bloody part wasn't showing. Using the clean side, he cleaned her off, ignoring her embarrassed sputtering.

Emma gave up trying to get him to stop and took refuge behind her hands.

When she was as clean as he could get her, he pulled her hands away from her face and kissed her hard, then rose to his feet and stretched, completely unabashed by his nakedness.

Emma kept her head down and pulled her panties and jeans on. Sliding her feet into her shoes, she crossed her arms over her chest and squinted through the darkness for her bra. She found it about ten feet away, completely ripped in half.

She stared at the ruined undergarment, at a loss as to what she was going to wear. Taking the ripped ends of her bloody shirt, she tried to tie it together over her breasts, but they were too short and it wouldn't stay tied.

Right as she was about to resign herself to walking back holding her shirt together, and having to deal with Aiden when they got there, a clean piece of black cotton appeared in front of her face.

"Here you go."

With a mumbled "thank you", she gave him her back and yanked off her ruined clothes, using them to wipe off any lingering blood on her skin as best she could before pulling on his shirt. It nearly swallowed her whole, but it was clean and warm, and it covered her. Rolling the sleeves up and tying up the bottom to shorten it, she turned around to find Nik already dressed in a matching clean shirt, his jeans, and combat boots. She gave him a questioning look.

His eyes glowed as they traveled over her wearing his shirt. "I always carry extra clothes when I travel. Us vampires tend to get bloody."

An unexpected surge of jealousy rose in her before she remembered he only drank bagged blood. At least before she came around. He must be talking about fighting.

Right?

"I get into a lot of fights." He answered the questions running through her mind before she could ask them. She probably didn't need to. The connection between them from sharing blood was already growing. Even she could feel it.

"Of course," she answered blithely. Holding out her bloody, ruined clothes, she asked, "What should I do with these?"

Nik took them from her and shoved them in a pocket of his pack. "We'll burn them later." Scanning the area for anything they may have forgotten, he asked, "You ready to go, Em?"

She looked anywhere but at him. "Yeah. Let's go."

He cocked his head at her behavior, but didn't press the issue. With a last, longing look at her bare breasts filling out his shirt, he took her hand and led the way out of the carnage.

They walked through the darkness in a circular route that would take them back around to the cavern where Aiden waited, both lost in their own thoughts.

Emma took advantage of the lack of conversation to try to sort out her feelings. She knew she'd instigated it all, and she was glad Nik had finally given in. She was. And it wasn't that she wasn't attracted to him, or that she didn't want to be with him. She did.

But, forever? The implications boggled her mind. Forever was a very, very, long time for *regular* humans. For a vampire and his mate?

She was having a hard time wrapping her head around it.

True to her nature, she'd been more worried about him not feeding from her—and therefore causing his own death—that she hadn't thought much past that.

Well, she *had* thought about it...just not that seriously.

But now she wondered, did he even want to be with her? Really? He'd certainly fought hard enough to prevent it. She'd finally convinced him to feed, and the bond had been completed (and then some!), and she sort of expected him to be all, like, miserable and angry at her for goading him into it.

Sooo not the case.

In fact, his behavior was the complete opposite of what she'd expected. As she watched him swagger along amongst the trees in front of her, he appeared to be back to his old self. The cocky, carefree vampire she'd met at the bar a lifetime ago. Maybe, now that the pressure was off and the deed was done, he felt relieved because he didn't have to fight it anymore?

Or, had this all been his idea from the very start?

Was that it? Was she really so gullible? Sadly, she had to admit the answer was a most probable yes. She was. She was no match for the charm of an obscenely handsome vampire who'd had six hundred years of practice seducing women. After living that long, could she really blame him for finding ways to amuse himself?

Damn right, she could. She was not here for his amusement.

But, he wouldn't really have made all of that up, would he? And what about Aiden? He couldn't have been faking all of that concern for his friend. No one was that good of an actor. But, then again, Aiden *was* a little...off. Had it really all been nothing but a big act the two of them had conjured up to amuse themselves?

Emma glared at the broad, muscular width of his back in front of her. She didn't like this. She didn't like this at all.

Had he been tricking her this entire time just to get her to sleep with him? Making it seem like it was *her* idea? The more she thought about it, the more convinced she became that he'd been playing with her all along.

Bastard.

34

Nik found it impossible to keep walking with such pointy daggers stabbing him in the back. He'd felt the rollercoaster of Emma's emotions ever since they'd left the clearing, but thought it would be better to leave her to work out...whatever it was she was trying to work out.

He was going through quite a ride himself.

Nik had nearly wept with relief when her eyes had opened back by the stone face. When she'd lain there, so still and pale, his heart had stopped completely, memories of Eliana mixing with the present until they threatened to overtake his sanity. But then he'd felt her breathe, and noticed the small smile on her face.

Without hesitation, he'd done what he'd sworn he'd never do. He'd had no other choice. Or, so he told himself. Lifting his wrist to his mouth, he'd pierced the skin and opened his vein for her to drink.

Fascinated, he'd watched her accept his lifeblood, every swallow binding them irrevocably together forever. He should've freaked out. He should be running in the opposite direction as fast as his vampiric speed could take him.

But he'd done neither of those things.

Instead, he'd given her more, and reveled in the peace that came over him. Nothing had ever felt so right in all of his lifetimes. Even now, pride swelled in his chest whenever he looked at his female. She was so lovely, and fierce, and witty, and...stubborn.

A dark cloud weighed on his feeling of peace, his emotions leaping around as fast as his thoughts. He never should have let her coerce him into feeding from her. This wasn't what he wanted her life to be.

But it was done.

As fast as it came on, the dark cloud dissipated. He'd come to grips with what happened, and he'd give her the space to do the same. However, he couldn't ignore the downright hate he felt being levered at his back. He stopped walking.

"What's up, Em?" he asked casually as he turned around to face her, hands low on his narrow hips.

Even though she'd been glaring right at him, his abrupt halt must have taken her by surprise. Raising her hands in front of her as she crashed into him, she pushed off his chest with a "thump" and took a few steps back, crossing her arms in front of her defensively. "Why don't you tell me?"

He raised his eyebrows in a silent question.

She scoffed at his innocent look. "For someone who has spent the past few days 'fighting his attraction' to me, you seem awfully damned unconcerned now that you've fucked me. After getting me to practically beg you to do it!"

"Emma..." he began warningly. He didn't like her talking like that. He knew she was trying to adjust to their new situation, but he'd had no idea this crap was flying around in her head.

"Oh! And managing to convince me it was *my* idea for you to feed from me. Let's not forget that." Pushing on her temples with her fingertips, she closed her eyes tight. "You even managed to get me to drink your blood. Therefore completing this so-called bond that you—just thirty minutes ago—were supposedly so dead set against!" She dropped her arms back down to her sides and glared at him, her hands curling into tight fists.

Nik was trying really, really hard to concentrate on what she was saying. But she was so fucking hot when she was all riled up. Her eyes were bright green with anger, and her face was flushed with color. He could hear her heart pumping hard, hear her blood rushing through her veins. Her chest, braless beneath his shirt, rose and fell with each hard breath, her nipples begging for his touch. He wanted to throw her down and fuck the rage out of her until she was limp and sated and happy again.

With that thought in mind, he took a step toward her, automatically ducking when a branch flew past his head.

Emma jumped, startled, before giving him her attention again. She threw out a hand. "Don't even think about it," she growled, stopping him in his tracks.

Nik cocked his head to the side and studied her. Quickly reaffirming to himself he'd much rather be fucking her than arguing with her, he went to take that last step that would bring her within his reach, only to realize he couldn't. His little witch had—quite literally—stopped him. And he didn't think she even realized it.

His vampire mind immediately thought up and discarded various things he could use to get her to lose her focus, but the truth was, he needed to know. "Do you really think that about me?" he asked quietly.

Other than a barely discernible softening around her eyes, she held her ground.

"All right." Arms at his sides, he looked her straight in the eye and ripped open his soul a little bit more. Why the fuck not? "I've been alone for more than 600 years, Em." Shaking his head, he corrected himself. "No, not alone. Just lonely."

"Lonely? What about Eliana?" She rolled her eyes at him, trying to call him on his bullshit. "And the girls that came before her? And after? You can't tell me there weren't others. I mean, look at you. You have to be aware of how you affect women."

"Yes. I'm well aware." He wasn't egotistical about it. He was a vampire. Their lure was part of their makeup. An unattractive thought entered his head, sobering him. "What about you, Emma? Are you only attracted to the way I look?"

"It certainly doesn't hurt," she snipped at him. "It seems to be your main weapon, after all."

He wasn't sure he deserved that, but he decided to let it go for now. Hell, maybe he did deserve it. He scrubbed his face with his hands, trying to articulate what he was feeling in a way she would believe. But all of the thoughts and feelings sprinting through him ultimately came down to the same thing. "They weren't you, Em."

"What's that supposed to mean?"

Nik heaved a deep sigh. "What do you want to hear, Emma? You want me to tell you there were others before you? Fine. I've fucked other females before you. I've fed from other females before you. Hundreds of them. Maybe more. Over and over again. And I fucking liked it."

She flinched at his harsh honesty, jealousy and hurt flitting across her expressive features to fight with the angry draw of her brows.

He reigned in his temper, softening his tone. "But, they weren't *you*. You didn't even exist yet for most of that time. But from the moment I first saw you, before I ever got within twenty feet of you, I wanted you. Just you."

His eyes drilled into hers, willing her to believe him. "I've never felt that way about anyone else. Ever. Not in all of my years. And I hadn't even spoken to you yet!" A bittersweet ache filled his chest. "And then, when I kissed you that night at your house, and tasted you, and realized exactly what you were to me, all I could think about...ALL I could think about...was how I couldn't do this to you. Even if I *could* manage to complete the bond without killing you, I couldn't disrupt your life, force you to be with me. I couldn't tie you to me like this. I just wanted to protect you, and—" His gaze wandered off to the wilderness around them as he tried to vocalize everything he'd felt.

"Protect me from what?"

Unobtrusively, he tried to move and found he could, so he quickly closed the distance between them. "From me. From this never-ending life."

Lifting his hand, he took a soft, reddish blonde curl between his fingers. "I can stand here and make all kinds of excuses for what happened earlier. I can say I was messed up from the fight. Or I can admit I've been feeling more mortal every day since tasting you, and I don't want to die. But, the truth of it is," He let go of her hair and gently took her lovely face between his hands, so small and fragile in his grip. "I've been stupid. I've been so stupid. And I only realized it when I watched you drink from me. I really don't want to be alone anymore. I want to be with *you*. Only you, Em. Would you consider staying with me? Please?"

He felt her relax a bit. "I'm not *just* attracted to your looks, Nik. Although I would be lying if I said they weren't part of it."

Nik leaned down and kissed her on the head, before pulling back to dazzle her with his smile. Or try to, at least. "Well, you're not so bad yourself you know."

His smile faded as her cold anger fled and her warmth filled him again. "You make me happy. Just being with you makes me feel more at peace than I can remember being in a long, long time. I've never felt this way before with anyone else."

He memorized every feature on her lovely face. "I'm exhausted from trying to fight this thing with us. Give meaning to my ridiculously long life. Let me make you happy, Em. Let me love you. Let me protect you. I know this is all kind of strange. You've only known me for a few days, and I'm asking for a very long forever. And I know a relationship like this is way different than anything you've ever wanted or hoped for, but please, let me try."

"I'm sorry. I don't know why I'm being such a raging bitch," she apologized.

He cracked a grin at her description of herself. "It's a lot to adjust to in just a few days."

When long seconds went by without an answer from her, Nik began to squirm. He stepped back and ran his hands through his hair. "Look, just think about it. Okay? Please?"

For once he couldn't read her expression when she said, "Okay. I'll think about it."

35

Nik opened his mouth to say more, but then thought better of it. "Okay, then." He took her small hand gently in his. Turning it over, he placed a kiss on her palm. "Let's just head back to Aiden. I'm not sure what he thinks he found out here, but I'm not seeing any signs of anyone else other than your monsters." With obvious reluctance, he dropped her hand again and shrugged. "Their tracks must be what he saw."

As they started walking again, Emma asked, "Is Aiden okay by himself in that cave? I mean, nothing would find him in there, right? If the others still haven't showed?"

Nik looked back at her. He'd just been thinking the same thing. They'd been so distracted by everything that was happening between them, and he hadn't known those things were here, or that they even existed for that matter. Had they left Aiden in danger?

He picked up the pace as they continued on, breaking into a jog as they hurried back, Emma close on his heels.

Emma was sprinting to keep up as he rushed back down the tunnel toward the cavern, a small flashlight in his hand to help her see. About twenty feet from the entrance, he stopped and put his index finger to his mouth. Closing his eyes, he listened as Emma tried—unsuccessfully—to quiet her breathing. It didn't impede his ability in any way, but he appreciated her efforts.

After a few seconds, he gestured for her to stay behind him and stay quiet as they slowly moved into the cavern. After their last encounter, he wasn't taking any chances.

A quick glance around assured him they were alone, but just to be safe, he took Emma's hand and kept her near him. There was no movement. No sound. No one was there.

Aiden was nowhere in the room.

He let go of Emma and did a slow tour of the place, looking for signs of a scuffle. Nothing was disturbed. Aiden's bag was where he had left it. The fire in the pit had burned down and needed more wood, but the torches were still burning, so he couldn't have been gone very long.

Lifting his chin, Nik sniffed the air for any unfamiliar scents. Nothing.

He fought down the panic rising within him. Where the hell was Aiden?

Emma sat on one of the large stones near the fire.

"Do you see anything that looks strange?"

She shook her head with a shrug.

"Me either. So, where the hell is he?"

Emma just looked at him without answering. Her worried expression echoed his own concern.

"Maybe he went to feed." Even as he said it, Nik was unconvinced. Aiden had just fed a couple of nights ago. He shouldn't need to drink again already.

Not knowing what else to do, he glared into the fire, brow furrowed, hands low on his hips, trying to figure out where that damned Brit could be. He wanted to go look for him, but there was no fucking way he was leaving Emma alone. There was also no way in hell he was bringing her along into another potentially dangerous situation. Much as he loved his best friend, he would wait him out.

He had just stirred up the coals and was about to put a couple of logs on the fire when the sound of someone whistling *Rule Britannia* came down the tunnel.

Nik glanced over at Emma. She returned his bemused expression before they simultaneously swiveled toward the entrance as Aiden strolled in, not a care in the world.

Carrying a head.

A grey, bald, and quite mangled head.

What was left of the ragged neck dripped fresh blood. The wide-open eyes stared straight ahead, the shock of being killed so savagely still showing in their depths.

When Aiden noticed the two of them sitting there, a broad smile crossed his face.

"Finally! There you are. It's been bloody dull here since you two left. What've you been doing?" Casually dropping the disgusting head onto the floor, he plopped down on the rock next to it and put his blood-stained hands out toward the heat of the fire. "Why didn't you put some more wood on the fire, mate?" When no one answered him, he looked back and forth between their baffled expressions. "What?"

"Whatcha got there, Aid?"

"Hmm?" Aiden's face was the picture of innocence as he followed Nik's gaze to the head at his feet. "Oh! That. It's a head. I tore it off of a beastly thing...I don't even know what it bloody was. But it was creeping around our little hideaway here."

"Those are the same creatures that attacked Emma and took Keira a few years ago. Right around the time Luukas disappeared. We just ran into a few of them ourselves." Nik filled him in on their encounter in the meadow, but only the parts he needed to know.

Aiden's face lit up like it was Christmas morning. "Did you happen to keep the heads?"

Nik shook his head. "No, man. Sorry. They don't last very long." Pointing with his chin toward Aiden's trophy, they watched as it started to flake away.

"Bugger." Aiden nudged at it with the toe of his boot in disgust. "I wanted to add it to my collection."

"Your...collection?" Emma asked.

Nik put his hand on the back of her head, smoothing her soft hair. "Yeah. Aiden has quite the collection of his foe's heads."

"Um..." Emma turned to look up at him, and he pulled his hand away with an apologetic look. "And where exactly are these heads located?" she asked with a surprising measure of calm.

Aiden answered her before Nik could. "Don't worry, love. They're hidden away. It wouldn't be easy lugging them up to the apartment with all of those humans around. The smell and that, you know."

Emma blinked at him with a blank expression. Nik couldn't blame her. Aiden had a way of sounding so seemingly sane while talking about things so obviously insane—such as head collections—he often gave him the same look.

"Still no word from Dante?"

Aiden shook his head.

"From anyone?"

Another shake.

"Where the hell could they be?"

Resting his elbows on his knees, Nik contemplated the far wall for a moment before saying, "Emma and I did a wide loop around this place. I didn't see or scent anyone besides us, and those things."

"It wasn't these piss poor vamps I scented," Aiden told him. "It was someone else. Hard to tell who or what. The scent was kind of wonky."

"Wonky?" Nik asked.

"Mm hmm, the wily sods covered it up to confuse us. And they did a bang-up job, I tell you. Even I can't place it." Despondently kicking away his disintegrating head, Aiden got up and grabbed some water out of his pack to wash his hands.

"Well, I'm not going to waste my time worrying about it." Nik stood up. "Daylight is coming, and tonight we're going after

Luukas and Emma's sister, with or without the rest of the guys. I'm tired of waiting."

Aiden dried his hands on the tail of his shirt and came back to the fire, throwing on another log before joining them on the rocks. "And how do you propose we do that, Nik? Not that I'm complaining, mind you. You know I fancy a good fight."

Locking eyes with Emma, Nik answered, "I have no fucking idea."

36

Emma came back to consciousness as if in a fog. Disoriented, she lay still as she tried to place where she was—hard ground digging into her hip and shoulder, some kind of lumpy pillow under her head, the smell of smoke from a low-burning fire, and she was cold.

Except for her back. Her back was warm. She was laying on her side, fully dressed, knees pulled up in front of her, hands tucked under her cheek, facing the fire.

Why was her back warm when it was her front facing the fire?

Then she felt the warmth against her back move closer, and a large, male hand swept roughly up her leg, over her hip, and around her waist. The muscular arm it was attached to pulled her even closer to the warmth and snuggled her entire length.

Emma's eyes popped open wide, scenes from the last few days flashing through her mind. "Nikulas?" she whispered into the semi-darkness. Had he been here with her all day? The last she remembered before she'd drifted off, he'd been talking quietly with Aiden on the other side of the fire pit, ironing out their plans for tonight.

"Shhhh. We don't want to wake Aiden." His husky voice was right in her ear, his breath tickling the tiny hairs on the back of her neck. It sent chills down her spine and made her shiver. Nik tugged her in closer, pulling her blanket up around them.

Aiden? Her sleep-muddled brain belatedly noticed the soft snores coming from the other side of the fire. "What time is it?" she whispered.

"We have about two hours until nightfall. Sorry I woke you up, I just—" He paused. "I just needed to touch you." She felt cool air on her belly as his hand played with the bottom of her shirt. "Is that okay?"

Emma gave the fading embers of the fire a worried frown. He should be sleeping. They couldn't afford for him to not be at his best tonight. All of their lives depended on it. She crooked her head around to tell him so, only to swallow what she'd been about to say when he came into view. He looked so—

Vulnerable.

"Um, yeah. It's okay," she whispered. She laid her head back down and moved her arm so her hand covered his on her belly. Truth was, even if he wasn't nervous about tonight, she was. And having a strong, handsome vampire wanting to hold her didn't sound bad at all. She could use the reassurance.

But as he hugged her to him again, she squirmed, his hand pressing into her lower belly...and her bladder. "Nik?"

"Hmm?"

"I have to get up for a minute. I have to...um...I need a moment. A human moment. Outside." She could feel her face flaming as she tried to discreetly tell him she had to pee.

Nik's big body stilled behind her, but he didn't let go of her. Finally, he whispered, "It's still light outside."

She started to try to wiggle out from under his heavy arm. "I know," she whispered back. "I'll be quick."

"No, Emma." His arm was like a steel bar trapping her as she tried to shove it off. "No. You can't go out there by yourself."

She tried to roll over and slide out of his grasp, to no avail. "But I have to go to the bathroom." Oh no, she was about to pee her pants.

"Do it here," he ordered.

"No!" Her face flamed at the thought. "Jeez, I'm just stepping outside." Renewing her efforts, she managed to get about halfway out in spite of his determination to hold her there, when his hand fisted her shirt in his grip and his deep voice rang through the cavern.

"I can't fucking go with you!" They both froze at his outburst and slowly looked over at Aiden. He twitched in his sleep, giggled, mumbled something about marshmallows, and rolled over. His soft snores soon filled the cavern again.

Nik clenched his jaw and lowered his voice. "I can't let you go out there alone."

Emma temporarily gave up the struggle. His jaw was tense and his eyes frantically skipped over her face in the dim light. He was not just being a pain in the ass. He was worried.

"I'll just step right outside the entrance. I won't go far, I promise." She tried to reassure him she'd be ok for the few minutes she'd be out of his sight. "If I see or hear anything at all besides a bird or a deer, I'll call for you. You'll be able to just reach out and pull me in to safety."

Gritting his teeth, he looked away. She could tell he hated this. Despised this weakness that kept him from protecting her. A minute in the sun and she'd be toasting marshmallows over him.

With Aiden, apparently.

She tried again to reassure him. "I'll be fine. Really. Those things are vampires, right? They can't be out in the sun either."

"No. But what if something else happened? I wouldn't be able to get to you!" he whispered harshly. "Not in the sun." He looked around the room, and she followed his gaze, but there was nowhere private inside the cavern, not even a small alcove.

"The tunnel. You could stay—"

"No, I'm going outside," she whispered as she got up. "*You* stay in the tunnel." Grabbing up the little flashlight, she turned it on and quickly headed out of the cave.

Nik got up with her and followed her as far as he could. As they reached the entrance, he stayed far enough back so the suns' rays wouldn't hit him when she went out.

Looking back at him, she gave him a small, reassuring smile before lifting the branches just high enough to step outside into the late afternoon sunshine.

37

A minute went by. Then two. Then five. What the hell was she doing? Tanning? How long did it take her to piss for God's sake? Nik started pacing up and down the tunnel. When almost seven full minutes went by and she still hadn't come back in, he walked right up to the entry. Fuck the sun.

"Emma?"

Silence.

"Emma?" he yelled louder this time. Still no answer. She'd promised she wouldn't go far. That she would only be a minute. Fear hit him hard in the chest as his worst nightmare unfolded.

"Emma!" He pushed the branches back a bit, ignoring the smoke and sizzling skin on his hand and arm. "EMMA!!!"

The birds sang happily in the sunshine, mocking his fear. He looked as far as he could in either direction, but saw nothing but trees and sun-dappled grassy patches on the uneven ground. Invisible hands squeezed Nik's heart in terror as he jumped back from the light before it was too late.

A thunderous roar reverberated through the tunnel and into the cavern, dislodging debris from the ceiling, as Nik lowered his head and charged the branches disguising the entrance. Fighting his body's natural instinct to stay far away from sunlight, he bellowed for Emma at the top of his lungs, and retreated only after flames broke out on his skin. He slapped them out and did it again.

Aiden appeared at a dead run through the dusty air. "Nik? Nikulas! What's wrong, mate? What is it?"

As Nik jumped back inside, staggering into the wall and slapping out flames, Aiden tackled him before he managed to throw himself outside again.

Rolling around on the ground, Nik roared with frustration as he tried to rip Aiden off of him. But Aiden clung to him like a suction cup.

"Nikulas! Stop! You're not accomplishing anything by turning yourself into a barbecue."

Screaming with rage, Nik threw himself onto his back on top of Aiden, trying to break his captor's hold. "Let go of me, you fucking asshole!"

Nik slammed him into any surface he could find, trying to dislodge him, but the harder he tried, the tighter Aiden's grip became.

"Nikulas," Aiden yelled in his ear, "if you don't stop, I'm going to rip off both your bloody legs! Then how are you going to get to Emma while you're stuck here regenerating them?"

Nik ceased his struggle, knowing damn well that Aiden meant every word. The bastard. He *would* rip his legs off. He'd done it when Luukas disappeared to keep Nik from going off on a suicide mission to save his brother. It had only been one leg then, but growing it back fucking hurt like hell. And it took forever.

They lay there in the middle of the tunnel, Aiden wrapped around him like a parasite, catching their breath. When Nik's chest stopped heaving and his body relaxed a bit, Aiden finally spoke, "All right?"

"Yeah, I'm good," Nik gritted out.

Aiden loosened his hold, and Nik shoved him away and scooted back on his ass until he collapsed up against the wall. His face, chest and arms were black and blistered, but he barely felt it. He couldn't feel anything except the fear running through him. He wasn't sure if it was all his, or his fear and Emma's combined. Just the thought of her hurt and afraid...

"So what did you do to her this time?" Aiden asked between deep breaths.

Blinking his charred eyelids, Nik tried unsuccessfully to focus on his friend. "She's gone." His voice was hoarse from yelling. "She just stepped outside to piss. She said she'd only be a minute. That she'd stay right by the entrance. But she didn't come back."

His entire body shook with fear and the effort it was taking him to sit still.

"She didn't come back. She wouldn't have just left. She's not fucking stupid! She wouldn't have left me. She's hurt! Or something's taken her..."

He couldn't finish the sentence as the invisible hands squeezed his heart and he gasped, struggling to breathe.

Aiden gave a consoling squeeze to an unburned area on Nik's thigh. "Don't fret, mate. Emma's tougher than she looks. There's nothing to do for it now, but we'll find her. As soon as the sun sets, we'll head out, and you'll be able to find her."

As long as she wasn't too far away…and still alive.

Standing up, Aiden held out a hand. "Come on then, let's get you back together. You're in no condition to play the knight like this. Do you have any more of that bagged rubbish laying around?"

Nik staggered to his feet, pushing Aiden away when he tried to help.

"Yeah. It's in my pack."

Hands held out in front of him, he bounced off both walls before finally careening toward the cavern.

38

Emma sputtered with rage as she was unceremoniously dumped facedown out of the burlap sac she'd been thrust into. Spitting out dirt and leaves, she struggled to stand up and brushed off her clothes. "Who the hell do you think you are? You can't just...just..." Lifting her head and pushing her hair out of her face, her anger faded right along with any thread of coherent thought as she got her first good look at her captors. "You've got to be kidding me."

She blinked in the bright sunlight, not trusting what was right in front of her eyes—three of the most alluring males she'd ever laid her eyes on.

Or her anything on, for that matter, other than Nik.

With expressions that ranged from amused to downright hostile, they blatantly returned her scrutiny, eyeing her up and down as she returned the favor.

Dressed in jeans, T-shirts, and hiking boots, each one of them was at least 6'2", and built like they could toss cars around with ease.

The tallest one stood ramrod straight. His long, black hair was pulled back harshly from his chiseled face, with a strong, square jaw and broad cheekbones. His arms were crossed in front of his massive chest, muscles bulging, as he regarded her with bright eyes so pale they nearly looked white. They blazed at her from under the dark slashes of his brows, mesmerizing her with their intensity.

By his stance and his air of superiority, she deduced he was the leader of the group. She gave him her full attention. "Who are you? And why have you taken me?" she demanded.

He ran those unsettling eyes from her head to her toes and back again. There was no malice in his gaze, just a calm curiosity. "Feisty little lass, isna' she?" he said to the redheaded god closest to him. His deep voice rumbled up from his chest, sending sensual shivers across her skin.

"Aye." Red had blue eyes also, though the color was deeper. They reminded her of a stormy blue ocean, and just as intelligent and intense.

Emma bristled with irritation as they stood there looking at her like she was some sort of freak show attraction. She stiffened her spine. "I would appreciate it if you wouldn't talk about me as if I weren't here."

The dark one gave her a half smile, a slight dimple showing in his cheek. "My apologies. What's yer name, lassie?"

"You kidnap me and you don't even know my name?"

His smile widened slightly. "Not only are ye bonnie, but ye're smart too. However, you truly have me at a disadvantage, as I don't ken your name. But if you'll be a sweet lassie 'n' tell me, I will tell *ye* what we are."

His heavy Scottish brogue gave her a moment's pause, but she could get the gist of what he was saying. Not seeing any harm in telling him, especially if it would get her more information about whom she was dealing with, she said, "Emma. My name is Emma."

"Emma. That's a bonnie name for a bonnie lass." Uncrossing his arms, he bowed formally at the waist, the perfect gentleman.

She narrowed her eyes at him as her heart slowed to a more normal rhythm.

Straightening up again and giving his head a toss to throw his long ponytail back over his shoulder, he introduced himself. "They call me Cedric Kincaid. Leader o' the Kincaid pack." Indicating the males to either side of him, he introduced them. "This one with the red locks is Lucian. 'N' this handsome, green-eyed devil is Duncan."

Lucian gave her a stern nod, while Duncan gave her a lusty wink and a broad grin. He was obviously the friendlier of the two.

Wait a minute. "Pack?" Emma asked. "Don't you mean 'clan'?"

"No. I'm the leader o' the northwest *pack*. We're werewolves, you see." He smiled again, showing off strong, white teeth and long dimples in a smile that would make any girl swoon.

It took a second for his words sink in. Had she misunderstood him? "We...wer...Werewolves?"

"Aye. Werewolves," he confirmed with a firm nod.

Emma swayed on her feet, barely managing to step back out of his reach when he put a hand out to steady her. She'd half-thought Nikulas had just been messing with her when he'd told her about the "wolves". And maybe when she was younger, before she'd ever seen the things she'd seen, she would've laughed in their faces.

But now...well, now...

She blinked until she could focus again and took a closer look at them.

They stared at her as one, gazes steady and direct.

Holy shit. They weren't lying.

"Dinna look so worried, we won't hurt ye, lassie." Tall, dark, and yummy informed her nobly. "You came here with Nik 'n' the daft one? Aye?"

What had he just said? Something about Nik? "You know Nik and Aiden?"

"Aye, I do. Very well. We're old mukkers...uh, friends," he clarified. "We saw them pull up with ye' last night."

"Friends, huh?"

He gave her a reassuring nod.

"Then why did you kidnap me right out from under your 'friends' noses?"

Knowing Nik was right there in the tunnel, she had just stepped right around the corner, wanting a little privacy. No sooner had she finished her business and walked out from behind the tree she'd been using as a screen when a rough sac had been yanked down over her head from behind and she'd been scooped up and thrown over a burly shoulder. The owner of which had then taken off at a dead run. It had knocked the air out of her, and by the time she could breathe again, let alone scream, she'd been dumped back out again.

He rubbed the back of his neck with one hand, looking up at her sheepishly from under long, dark lashes. "Well now, that's a funny story." He gave her a shrug. "It seemed a good idea at th' time," he said a bit arrogantly.

"And what about now?" she asked, sarcasm dripping from her voice. "Does it still seem like a good idea now?"

"Well, ye dinna have to be like that about it," he said, obviously taken aback by her tone. Settling his weight on one powerful leg and his hands low on his narrow hips, he had the decency to look a bit guilty. "Although, I have to admit, we may have acted a wee bit rash. We didna really stop to think about it."

Emma took a step closer, about to give him a large piece of her mind. Immediately, the other two stepped up to flank their leader, and she rethought her decision. Pissing off a group of bona fide werewolves was probably not the smartest thing to do. A change of tactics might be a good idea.

She gave him her sweetest smile, "Well, it's not too late! You can just take me back."

His eyes widened and he glanced at his companions with a look that said he clearly thought she was completely off her rocker. "We canna do that! Are ye mad, lassie?"

So much for her attempt at womanly wiles. "Why the hell not?" She nearly stamped her foot with frustration. She was tired. And she was hungry. And, dammit, she wasn't in the mood for this shit.

"Just take me back! I won't even tell them it was you guys. I'll just say I went for a walk! Yeah. I just went for a walk! That's all. I *swear* I won't say anything about you, if you'll just take me back to Nik." She couldn't imagine what he must be going through after her little disappearing act.

And she had a sister to rescue.

Exchanging looks amongst themselves, they seemed to be considering her plea, and she dared to hope she may have gotten through to them. But as the minutes ticked by and no one made a move to honor her request, her small flame of hope was dashed.

Sighing heavily, she crossed her arms and gave them all a withering look. "What?" she snapped.

Cedric looked over at Red, but seeing he would get no help from that end, he finally turned back to Emma, who had started tapping her foot impatiently.

"What?" she demanded again. "What now?"

"Aren't ye worried he'll be pissed at ye for wandering off?" Cedric asked quietly. "I assume he told ye not to."

Shrugging nonchalantly, she assured him, "He will be. But he'll get over it."

Cedric gaped at her. "Ye do ken that he's a vampire?"

"Yes." She rolled her eyes with a heavy sigh. "I know he's a vampire." What the hell was he trying to get at? She wished he'd just spit it out already.

"'N' ye're no' scared o' him?" he asked in astonishment.

"No. Why would I be scared of him? He wouldn't hurt me," she assured him. "Look, I'll be fine. Just drop me off where you found me," she pleaded. "If you really are their friend, then you have to know he's probably sick with worry by now."

A dawning look of comprehension slowly came over his face. "Worry, ye say?"

"Yes!"

Exchanging a strange look with Lucian and Duncan, he mused, "A vampire only worries aboot his human mate. We've a' heard the stories. Is it really true, lassie?"

Emma gave him a stony look in reply, refusing to confirm or deny his assumption.

Cedric held up his index finger, indicating for her to excuse him a moment, then turned to the other guys. They huddled together, speaking rapidly but quietly, with only the occasional "och" or "aye" and one "Yer off yer head!" by Red, followed quickly by a "Haud yer wheesht!" by Cedric, loud enough for her to hear.

Watching them, she wondered if they'd notice if she just casually strolled away.

Taking a discreet glance around, she was almost positive they'd entered a small clearing from the way directly behind her. Maybe she'd be able to lose them amongst the trees until the sun went down and Nik could find her.

As quietly as she could, she started to back away from the arguing werewolves. She got about a hundred feet with no one paying her any mind whatsoever, so with a quick prayer, she slowly turned and started creeping forward as stealthily as she could, using the giant, mossy trees as cover. After another fifty feet, she silently thanked the gods and took off at a steady jog.

She didn't get ten more feet before she was gripped around the waist by a muscular arm and hoisted onto a hip.

"Damn it! Let me go, you stupid dog!"

Lucian, or "Red" as Emma liked to think of him, jostled her a little higher and trod back to the group with her tucked easily under his arm.

"Where do ye think ye're goin, lassie?" Cedric grinned at her as Lucian dropped her at his feet for the second time. Holding out his hand, Cedric offered to help her up, laughing heartily when she slapped his hand away and stood up on her own.

"Nikulas has got his hands full with this one." He chuckled in amusement as her eyes shot daggers at him.

She crossed her arms defensively and snapped, "Well, Nikulas doesn't have his anything right now, does he? Because you STOLE me from him."

Cedric boomed with laughter. "C'mon wee kitten, let's get going. We need to be there by nightfall." Turning his back to her, he swung his hand around in a circle. "Let's go!"

Herding her into the middle of the group, they set off, moving farther away from the cave. And farther away from Nik.

39

Nik and Aiden stood silent and motionless just inside the hidden entrance of the tunnel. Waiting.

The sun was finally setting.

Dressed to blend with the night, they were nearly invisible in the dim light of the tunnel. Black hoodies were zipped up with black zippers. Black hoods pulled up to conceal their faces and hair. Even the wicked-looking blades strapped to their thighs were black.

Nik's partially healed skin masked all but his fangs, which were displayed in a chilling snarl.

Aiden had only managed to get him to drink enough for his eyes to heal. Even with so little nourishment, his body fairly vibrated with the need to get to his mate.

The sun seemed to pause as it reached the horizon, hanging on to that last moment of daylight, before finally surrendering and dipping below the skyline.

The tunnel was empty before the final ray disappeared.

Emma shivered as the sun began its final descent. She was still wearing Nik's long-sleeved shirt, but hadn't grabbed her coat when she'd stepped outside.

Of course, she'd only planned on being outside for a few minutes. If she'd known she was going to be trekking through the Canadian wilderness against her will with three hulking werewolves, she maybe would have rethought that decision.

They'd been walking for miles without a word between them. But judging by the looks of approval she grudgingly received now and again, they were a bit surprised the "wee lass" was able to keep up.

She had a good idea where they were going, but not what her part in it would be. The one time Emma had dared to ask, Cedric had glanced back with a sympathetic smile. "Tis better if ye dinnae ken just yet, lassie."

That *so* did not make her feel any better.

With a weighted sigh, she took in the beauty of the scenery around her, trying to memorize any distinctive landmarks that would help her find her way back before the light faded.

Large Western Hemlocks dominated the landscape, covering the mountains that lined the valley they traversed through on foot. Here and there she would catch a glimpse of a snow-covered mountain peak. Jays screeched over the prettier songs of the chickadees, and small animals rustled in the vegetation around them as they passed. Somewhere in the distance, she could hear the trickling sound of water.

The whole place was breathtaking, really. She wished she were in a position to enjoy it more.

Her stomach growled loudly in protest at the lack of a recent meal, and she put a hand over it, trying to stifle the sound.

Duncan glanced over at her and reached into his pocket. He pulled something out and offered it to her.

Emma tried unsuccessfully to stifle her disgust at the piece of dehydrated meat. "Thank you, but I can't eat that," she managed to mumble.

He gave her a frown. "Ye dinna like jerky?"

She shook her head. "I don't eat meat."

His look of disbelief was almost comical. "Ye dinna eat meat? How do ye survive?" Running his eyes from her head to her toes, he nodded knowingly. "That's how come you're so wee. If ye ate meat, it would plump ye up some." He gave her another lusty wink.

Glancing over her shoulder at the sinking sun, she silently begged it to hurry up already, even as she wrapped her arms around herself against the dropping temperature.

"So what are you guys doing here anyway?" she asked him.

He cast a quick glance at Cedric, who shrugged his approval, before he deigned to answer her question. "We're 'ere to visit Leeha. Just like ye. She has my brother."

"How did you know she was back in the area?" she wondered, elaborating, "It's my understanding she went off grid for a few years."

He gave her a sly smile. "Ye're vampires aren't the only ones with eyes everywhere, lassie."

Emma gave the setting sun a nervous glance. Periodically, she ran her eyes over each of her captors carefully, ever watchful for any physical or behavioral changes. She prayed Nik would get to her before the moon fully rose. She knew what would happen if he didn't. She hadn't watched all of those werewolf movies for nothing.

They'd walked another couple of miles deeper into the ravine before Cedric finally called a halt to their little parade. As one, they all dropped down onto their haunches at the edge of the forest line.

With a yank on her arm from Red, Emma did the same.

In the space between two sets of broad shoulders, she could see the creek she'd heard earlier rambling along in front of her. It appeared to run right into the base of one of the larger mountains, where it disappeared into the deepening gloom.

"So here's the plan, lassie," Cedric told her quietly. "Leeha always has guards stationed just downstream a ways. We're aff to let them capture ye as soon as it's full dark."

"Excuse me?" she squeaked.

Duncan translated. "There are guards downstream. Leeha's guards. We're goin' to *pretend* to let them take you. We'll send ye out by yourself, staying upwind so they dinna ken we're here."

She felt the strong urge to protest this idea. "I don't agree with this plan. This is a *terrible* plan."

"It'll be fine," he assured her. "But we 'ave to wait for just the right moment. We canna let anything actually happen to ye, Nikulas would murder us all."

They all nodded gravely in agreement.

"By the time they show themselves 'n' start taking ye in, yer Nik will be here." Cedric smiled broadly. "'n' then he'll take care o' those guards, we'll take care o' any others that show, and we can take care o' this daft bitch together."

"Why not just wait for Nik and Aiden outside the cave? Let them know you're here and you want to help? Wouldn't that have been easier than going through all of this?" Emma hissed. *It would've been easier on me, that's for sure.*

"Well, now, where's the fun 'n' that?" The wolf leader chuckled softly. "Besides, then *they'd* ken that *we* ken where their 'secret' hideout is."

Duncan must've felt some sympathy for her, for he patted her gently on the back. "Dinna worry, lass. Nik 'n' Aiden will get here before anything happens tae ye. And they'll be so happy tae see us, they'll forgive us for stealing you away. Between us all, we'll be able tae handle them easy."

"You seem to be awfully confident of that. What if there are more than you expected?" she asked nervously. "What if they outnumber you? What then?"

Cedric smiled a knowing smile. "Nik is a vampire rescuing his mate. I will be surprised if he needs us at all!"

"It's time," Lucian announced.

"Aye." Cedric stood up, bringing Emma up with him. "A'right lassie. Off ye go. Just follow th' creek, 'n' act like ye're lost." Giving her a little push, he sent her in the right direction.

Emma managed about three steps before she dug in her heels, trying one last time to appeal to them. "Please! I don't want to do this!"

Her teeth started to chatter and her body to tremble. She couldn't do it. She couldn't willingly sacrifice herself like this for the amusement of these dogs.

Lucian bared his teeth at her. "Ye *will* do it. 'N' you'd better hurry, before th' moon rises." It was the first time he'd spoken. His voice was raw and gravelly, and the sound of it raked over her like hot coals. Emma felt chills run down her spine.

Her eyes widened at the sight of his long canines, and she turned her terrified stare to Duncan, who gave her a confident smile. "We need th' element o' surprise. We'll be right behind ye. Ye can do this, lassie."

Not seeing she had much of a choice, she walked jerkily toward the creek.

40

Tears streamed unnoticed down Emma's face as she followed the creek downstream, and her body shook so hard her teeth clattered. And not from the cold.

A quick peek over her shoulder didn't reveal anyone following her. Were the dogs even there? Or were they only pretending to be friends with Nik and Aiden and sending her off to her doom? She may have signed her own death wish by not denying she was Nik's mate.

Hurting—or killing—her would be the perfect way to destroy him. It would be a fatal blow. One that would make him suffer severely before he finally found his end.

Emma was getting closer to the mountain, and nothing and no one had leapt out to halt her progress. Where were these supposed guards?

She would kill those dogs. She really would.

If she made it out of here alive.

She thought about making a break for it. If the wolves were really following, she knew she wouldn't get far. But at least then she'd know they hadn't been lying.

And if they weren't following? Well, she'd know that, too.

Nik would be looking for her now. He'd said he'd be able to find her as long as she wasn't too far away. She tried to add up the number of miles they'd walked in her head. But she didn't know how far was "too far".

But, it didn't really matter, did it? There was no way she was just going to willingly get herself captured. She knew what the guards would be like. Abnormal things with grey, rotting skin and red eyes.

I'd rather die from exposure in the wilderness than be taken by those—

She couldn't even finish the thought. Mind made up, she took one last frantic glance over her shoulder, and took off running toward the thick trees.

She wasn't even halfway there when she heard the unsteady footfalls of something behind her. Terrified, she pumped her arms and stretched out her legs, her mind telling her to look, but her body rebelling against the thought. She didn't need to look. She knew what it was.

Emma never ran so hard in her life, but in spite of her best efforts, she could hear her pursuer gaining on her. The footfalls came closer and closer no matter how she pushed herself. Harsh, wheezing breaths sent chills down her spine, and she cut to the side.

Keeping her eyes on the trees, she hit her stride, giving it all she had. If she just made it to the cover of the forest, she could lose it, and she'd be safe.

She was only about twenty feet away when, from the cover of the trees, a pair of red eyes appeared straight from one of her nightmares, glowing eerily out of the darkness. Emma screamed as a loud hiss crawled over her skin, making every hair on her body stand up on end.

Running for her life, she didn't notice the anguished roar that came tearing through the trees in answer to her scream.

Emma veered off to the left, hoping against hope the werewolves were actually there and would help her. Tears ran down her face, making it hard for her to see. Something burst from the trees on her right, lurching toward her, long arms spread wide to catch her. With a shriek, she veered off again in the opposite direction.

Directly into the beast behind her.

It grabbed her up in a bear hug, hurtled her roughly to the ground, and fell on top of her.

For a brief moment, she froze as terror overwhelmed her. But only for a moment. Emma flipped onto her back as she hit the dirt. Pushing on its chest, she kicked her feet and threw her head back and forth. Long, yellow claws sliced into her skin through her clothes. Saliva mixed with blood dribbled from its open mouth as it screeched at her, landing in her hair, on her face—

No! No! No! Please no!! She repeated the mantra over and over as she tried to fight it off. This couldn't be happening to her again.

The urge to vomit was overwhelming as she felt the thing hump her, excited from her thrashing underneath it. But she couldn't let it get a good grip on her. It would rip her apart. And this time, she had no doubt, she wouldn't survive.

Pieces of its rotting flesh came off in her hands as she pushed and clawed at its chest and arms. Gripping her wrists, it tried to hold her arms down, its yellow claws slashing open her skin on the inside of her arms. But still, she fought. She didn't know where her strength came from, but didn't stop to think about it.

Frantically, she kicked and rocked her body from side to side, until she finally managed to get one of her legs between them. With all of her strength, she slammed her knee into its balls.

Throwing its head back, it shrieked in pain, but didn't roll off of her. Emma sobbed uncontrollably now, but somehow managed to pull one of her arms from its grip. She slammed her palm into its exposed throat, but she couldn't get her fingers far enough around the rotting flesh to cause any real pain.

Ignoring her weak attempts to strangle it, it lowered its head and pulled its lips back, tongue flicking out to lick her face. Gagging, she turned her face away only to see the other two had joined them and were eagerly waiting their turns.

Tongues flicked over sharp teeth as they palmed themselves disgustingly, grunting at the feel of their own hands and the sight of her wrestling with their companion.

She released a low, keening cry as hopelessness washed over her. It was over. She could feel her strength waning against its superior might with every second. Once one of them got its fangs into her, they'd fight over her like dogs.

A ragged sob escaped her as she thought of Nik finding what little would be left of her. He would blame himself for not protecting her. For not insisting she stay inside. The guilt would eat him alive. He didn't deserve that. It wasn't his fault she hadn't listened to him.

Emma floundered a bit as these thoughts flew through her head, but then she gritted her teeth and rallied herself. She couldn't let that happen.

With a yell, she bucked underneath the thing in one last ditch effort to get it off of her. Her muscles screamed in agony, yet she fought like a wild thing. She kept it up as long as she could, even when the only thing she seemed to accomplish was arousing the thing more. Until, finally, she could feel her muscles giving out on her. With one last feeble attempt to save herself, she curled her fingers on its throat and squeezed its trachea.

As its eyes bulged and it struggled to breath, she dared to hope...but she'd forgotten its two sidekicks.

Before she could cause any real harm, her hand was ripped away by one of the others. It pulled both of her arms up over her head and held them there.

The beast on top of her gave her a look of pure evil as it rasped and coughed. It pulled its lips back again, exposing those razor-sharp fangs.

Emma froze in terror as it reared its head back to strike.

A terrified scream tore from her throat, and a deafening roar joining it. Before she'd even processed the sound, the weight of the monster was ripped from her body. A second later, her wrists were released.

Emma lay there, unmoving, not yet fully comprehending she was free. She listened to the sickening noises around her in a daze. Unearthly screams blended with the sounds of crunching bone and the wet sucking noises of flesh being ripped from flesh, until she thought she *was* going to vomit after all.

Then all was silent.

Cautiously, Emma turned her head to the right. She blinked, not quite believing what she was seeing.

Nikulas stood with his back to her, sides heaving, fists clenched at his sides. Scattered around him were piles of rotting, grey flesh, ripped into pieces so small they were unrecognizable as any particular body part.

The wind picked up at that moment, and her stomach convulsed from the smell as the pieces started to flake away.

41

Pulling his hood back up over his singed hair, Nik swallowed hard. Slowly, fearfully, he turned around. But he kept his eyes closed, afraid of what he would see. Afraid he hadn't made it on time. She hadn't moved or made a sound since he'd torn the creature off of her.

Taking a deep breath, he opened them to see Emma's wide hazel eyes trained on him, shock reflected deep within the depths. Her body was deathly still. Her face was white. Blood trickled from slashes on her arms.

He stared at her lovely face, those invisible hands squeezing his heart harder and harder, and then...

She blinked.

Please, please tell me I'm not fucking hallucinating. Tell me I arrived in time.

He'd fled the cave before the sun had completely set, Aiden close on his heels. They'd stayed to the shadows, following the lure of Emma's blood to the creek.

He didn't hesitate as he was pulled to the scene of those things hunched over something on the ground. He knew it was Emma. A red haze had clouded his vision when he'd ripped the first one off of her, quickly annihilating the other two as well. He'd barely realized what he was doing.

However, he sure as hell was feeling it now.

Emma inhaled sharply. "What happened to your face?" Her voice was so hoarse from screaming, he barely understood her.

Falling hard onto his knees, Nik groped for Emma's hand and brought it to his burned mouth, kissing her palm and holding it there. His eyes burned with tears he couldn't shed, and a dry, heart-wrenching sob tore its way out of his scalded lungs.

"Nik? What the hell happened to your face?" Emma rasped. She lifted her other hand, but hesitated before touching the blackened skin.

But he couldn't answer her. He couldn't speak. He could only kneel there, her small hand engulfed within his larger ones, his eyes hidden behind their burned lids.

Aiden dropped down into her view, squatting on his haunches next to Nik. "Hey there, poppet. Brilliant idea you had here, luring them out this way. But you really should've waited for us to help you."

She redirected her question at him. "What the hell happened to his face?"

Nik opened his eyes to find Aiden grinning at him as he gave him a pat on the shoulder. "He looks a bit better now. You should've seen him when I found him."

Emma used her free hand to push herself up into a sitting position, as Nik had a death grip on the other one, and he wasn't going to be letting it go anytime soon. "That doesn't answer my question, Aiden."

"The arse tried to follow you into the sun. I finally had to tackle him before he managed to roast himself." Smiling reassuringly at Emma, he glanced over at Nik. Then went back for a second look.

"In spite of your recent one man destruction show, you're not looking so good, mate."

"I'm okay," Nik mumbled behind Emma's hand.

Aside to Emma, Aiden whispered, "Do you think you feel up to giving him a drink, love?"

Nik's big body swayed in the wind, but he managed to stutter, "I'm okay. I don't need any...she's been through enough...just need to rest." Pure stubbornness was the only thing keeping him upright. Now that he'd saved his beloved female, his body was giving in to all of the trauma it'd been dealt recently.

Gently pulling her hand from his, Emma pushed her sleeve back and offered him her wrist. "Here. Drink. And don't argue with me."

Aiden grinned at her with approval. "You know, love, I'm beginning to develop quite a crush on you."

Nik bared his teeth at his friend, but at her reproving look, he gently took her arm in his hands and sank his fangs into her sweet-smelling wrist. Closing his gritty eyes, he took a deep pull on her vein, groaning as her blood hit his tongue. A few swallows later, and he felt his burns start to heal.

Emma watched, fascinated, as the damaged areas began to fuse themselves together, new skin cells multiplying and creating fresh tissue at an amazing speed right before her eyes. Within a few heartbeats, he was nearly completely healed.

Holy shit. Her blood did that? If that's how it affected his outsides, she couldn't imagine how he felt on the inside.

No sooner had the thought drifted through her mind than Nik's bright eyes flashed open and locked onto hers, the hunger in them so intense, she was momentarily taken aback.

Emma had never experienced anything as erotic as those smoldering blue eyes burning right through to her core.

She watched him as he fed, each pull a direct tug on her desire for him. Every needy moan made her breath hitch and her heart beat faster. Her breasts swelled, her nipples tightening into hard, little buds that begged for his touch, his tongue, even his bite. Her lips parted, her tongue sneaking out to wet her bottom lip.

She moaned softly as a rush of wetness drenched her panties, her belly clenching with need for him as her body responded to him of its own accord.

42

Nik's focus narrowed in on Emma, and a low, deep growl rumbled through his chest. The scent of her desire heated his blood, made his body harden. His cock swelled painfully as he watched her little pink tongue wet her lip, her body leaning closer to him of its own accord. He wanted to bite that lip as he came inside of her.

The sound of Aiden noisily clearing his throat barely kept him from ripping the clothes from her body and pushing himself into her hot, little body. With a displeased snarl, he reluctantly removed his fangs from her inner wrist. Holding her wide eyes with his, he licked the soft skin, healing his bite and the slashes from the attack. Taking her other arm, he did the same.

Aiden stuck his face in front of Nik's, breaking the contact. "Hate to interrupt the moment, mate, but we have company."

Nik's head immediately whipped around, lips pulled back, fangs bared in warning, his body blocking Emma from this new danger.

Cedric, Lucian, and Duncan came jogging up to them, the shock on their faces explaining why they paid no mind of Nik's show of aggression.

"Whit th' fuck was that?" Cedric's deep voice thundered through the ravine. Blood covered the front of his shirt, as it did Duncan's and Lucian's.

Dropping down onto his haunches by Emma, Cedric looked at her beseechingly. "I'm so sorry, lass! I had no idea. I would've ne'er sent ye off on yer own had I known."

He looked from Emma to the vampires. "Whit th' fuckin' hell *were* those things?!"

Nik's nostrils flared and his mouth flattened into a thin line. "What do you mean, 'you wouldn't have sent her off on her own'?"

Rising to his full height, he took up a protective stance in front of Emma. Aiden stepped up to stand at his right. His blood, already heated by the contact with Emma, boiled now with rage. Nik stared down the wolves as one by one, they each dropped their gaze and hung their heads.

Lucian and Duncan kept their heads down and took a step back, letting Cedric answer that one.

As he *should*.

As their *leader*.

And, the whole thing being his idea and all.

Cedric also stood, slowly and cautiously, not making any sudden moves. Although he towered over Nik by a good five inches, he nevertheless visibly braced himself against the wrath emanating from the vampire as he lifted his hands, palms out.

"Now Nikulas, before ye go suckin' me dry, gimme a chance ta explain."

Nik gave his head a quick shake. He couldn't possibly be hearing this correctly. "Please, tell me that I misunderstood. Tell me my *friend* would never be stupid enough to purposefully put *my female* in danger." By the time he finished speaking, his entire body was shaking with rage.

"Nik, I didna ken those things existed. I swear it!" Cedric's steady gaze proclaimed he was telling the truth. "I thought a few normal vamps would be guarding th' walls. There would've been *no* danger tae Emma wi' us there. And I didna ken she was yers 'til we had already taken her!" he insisted. "I thought she was just a normal human, 'n' thought we'd have a bit o' fun."

"Well, that was just a horrible idea," Aiden piped in.

"That's exactly what *I* said," Emma agreed.

Cedric rolled his eyes at Aiden. "Yer one tae talk. Ye would've done th' same thing. If na' worse."

Aiden recoiled dramatically at the insult. "Are you daft, man? I wouldn't do something like that! That's just crazy!" He screwed his forehead up, deep in thought. "Or maybe it's completely brilliant. You did manage to flush out the guards and get us straight here at the same time. Hmm. Maybe I *would* do it." He shook his head. "No, no, I would never risk...well?" He slapped his hands onto each side of his head. "Ahhhh! I just can't decide."

Cedric turned back to Nik, who'd never taken his eyes from him throughout the entire exchange. "Once I figured it out, it was even better!" He gave Nik a knowing wink. "I knew ye'd come after her. Bonnie lass that she is."

Nik bared his fangs, a deep growl radiating out from deep inside him. He was *this* fucking close from taking out the alpha.

Cedric's wolf nature reacted instinctively to the threat. Bowing up, he ground out, "We were aff to surprise ye! That we were 'ere tae help." He slashed his hand through the air between them. "That's all! Nothin' happened tae her. She's braw. I would ne'er hurt a wee lassie! Ye ken that." His lips pulled back, exposing his own lengthening canines. "Now git out o' mah face afore I lose my temper."

Nik felt Emma's hand on his back, rubbing small circles over the tense muscles. "Nik, they didn't hurt me. And they treated me with the utmost respect. Well, other than throwing me into a bag and toting me around like a sack of grain."

As Nick leaned forward aggressively, she grabbed his fist before he could take a swing, and hurried to continue, "but they didn't hurt me! I promise!"

She stepped in front of him and finally managed to break up the pissing contest between him and Cedric as his focus redirected onto her. Locking eyes with him, she held his gaze until he calmed down. "Come on. They're here to help, even if they did go about letting you know in a rather strange way."

"Tha' bitch has one o' ours," Cedric said over her head.

That got Nik's attention. He noticed for the first time one of them was missing. They always traveled together in a pack. "Marc? She has Marc?"

Cedric nodded, his stance once again easy and relaxed. "Aye. She took him three weeks ago. She thinks we owe her a debt, 'n' took him as her pay."

Duncan smiled roguishly. "We've come tae take him back."

"What debt is that?" Aiden asked.

Giving Lucian a look Nik couldn't decipher, Cedric shrugged off the question with a derisive smirk. "Nothin' I'm wantin' tae get into right now."

No other information seemed to be forthcoming, and they didn't have time to try to pry it out of them, so Nik let it go. "All right. Well, as the rest of our guys seem to be MIA, we'd sure appreciate the extra manpower. Or wolf power, such as it is."

"Who does she have o' yours?" Duncan asked Nik.

"Luukas."

"Luukas??" Cedric breathed. His mouth hung open in shock, and Duncan and Lucian echoed his astonishment. "That's no' possible! How can that happen? He's a master vampire."

"Luukas took it upon himself to go and confront her. Alone. He refused to let me or anyone else come with him. He never came back."

"When did this happen??" Duncan asked.

"Seven years ago," Nik admitted.

"Seven *years*?" Cedric breathed. "How did we no' ken aboot this? I ken we've been busy, but seven years..."

"We may have had a bit to do with that," Aiden said.

Lucian glared at him. "Yer fookin' with my head, bloodsucker?"

Cedric restrained him with an arm across his chest as he looked between Aiden and Nik. "Is this true, then?"

Aiden pushed at the dirt with the toe of his boot. "It was Nik's idea."

"We didn't want to cause a panic," Nik told them. "We never thought he'd be gone this long. But one year led into another, and another, and another, and...you get the idea."

"Ye'r sure he's alive?" Cedric asked. "How has she managed tae hold him all this time?"

Nik glanced at Emma, but he didn't see any way to avoid disclosing her sister's involvement. "We think she has a witch helping her."

The werewolves stepped back as one, superstitiously making the sign of the cross. Witches creeped them out, and as a rule, they stayed far, far away from them.

Nik waited for them to wrap their minds around that before laying the rest of it on them. "We think the witch is Emma's sister, who went missing around the same time as Luukas."

Three heads whipped around to look at Emma with new eyes. They knew how witches worked. If one female in the family was a witch, they all were.

Cedric cocked his head to the side and stared at her like he'd never seen her before.

Duncan was brave enough to actually speak to her. "Ye're a witch, lass?"

Lucian snarled at her, and spoke low out of the side of his mouth to Cedric. "I told ye we coudna' trust them. They've taken up wi' a witch."

Nik speared Lucian with an exasperated look. "You *can* trust us. And that includes Emma. She hasn't hurt you yet, has she?" He squeezed Emma's arm lightly, hoping she'd take the hint and play along.

She gave them a sweet smile.

The Scots eyeballed her warily, restlessly shifting their weight from side to side, obviously not sure which way to go with this information.

Aiden looked between Emma and the wolves, thoroughly amused. "Really? The big, bad wolves are afraid of *you*, poppet?" He laughed out loud. "She couldn't even reach you to box your ears!"

Rolling his eyes, Nik supposed Aiden staying quiet for any amount of time was too much to ask.

Cedric puffed out his massive chest. "I'm no' scared o' a wee lassie." The other two followed his lead, if a little less enthusiastically.

With a deep breath and a last wary glance at Emma, the werewolf leader got his head back in the game. Nodding at the disintegrating bodies on the ground, he declared, "Well, th'... uh...*guards* are taken care o'. What do ye say we just waltz on in there 'n' find our kin?"

Nik shared a grin with Aiden. They'd been looking forward to this fight for a long time.

Emma turned to look up at Nik. "You're not serious. We're not just going to walk right in there, are we?"

"There is no 'we' when it comes to you," Nik informed her. "*You*, will be staying far, far out of the way."

Emma raised her eyebrows, but he gave her a warning look. Now was not the time to challenge him.

Lucian motioned Cedric and Duncan to the side and turned his back to the vampires.

It did no good, as Nik could hear him well enough anyway.

Lucian gritted out between clenched teeth, "How da we ken we can trust these two? They're fookin' vamps. 'N' they've taken up wi' a witch! They don't care aboot our brother. How da ye ken they won't use us tae get in, 'n' then leave us tae fight that bitch, while they escape?"

"Nikulas 'n' Aiden are my *friends*, Lucian. I trust them wi' my life."

"Yer choosing them over yer own kind."

"Haud yer wheesht!" Cedric told him. "No' another word aboot it."

Lucian clenched his jaw, his lips pressed into a thin line. In a deliberate move, he turned his back on his pack leader.

Cedric didn't pause before he grabbed him by the shoulder and spun him back around to face him. "If ye dinna like it, Lucian, ye'r welcome tae find a fresh pack. Unless ye think ye kin lead this one better than I kin?"

Shockwaves rippled through the males—vampire and wolf alike —as the gauntlet was thrown down and tension crackled in the air between them.

Nik surreptitiously took Emma by the hand and carefully pulled her behind him, as everyone backed away from the pair.

For a few insanely anxious seconds, it seemed there was going to be a fight for dominance. Lucian's face turned as red as his hair, his anger at being called out in mixed company plain for all to see.

But he must've decided it wasn't worth his life, for he took a deep breath and dropped his gaze in submission. After a moment, he lowered himself onto one knee before his pack leader.

Cedric visibly relaxed, laid a hand on Lucian's shoulder and gave it a quick squeeze. "A'right then?"

Lucian gave a terse nod. "Aye."

And just like that, the tension dispersed as quickly as it had appeared. Nik exchanged a look with Aiden as he took a deep breath. "Okay, then. Let's do this."

43

Emma's heart resumed its normal rhythm as Lucian rose to his feet and everyone relaxed. Nik wasn't kidding when he said they "run kind of hot". Their emotions were so up and down, she was mentally exhausted from spending just a few hours with them.

Aiden clapped his hands together loudly. "Alright then! Let's go see my girl!"

Cedric gave Nik a questioning look, but Nik just shook his head. "You really don't want to know."

With a sideways look at Aiden, Cedric motioned for everyone to huddle in, sticking Emma in the middle of the towering males.

Within minutes, they had their plan of attack.

"All right." Nik squatted down on his haunches, and drew a rough map in the dirt by the creek with a stick he'd snagged out of the water. The rest of the group hovered around him in a circle with their hands on their knees so they were able to see. Craning her neck, Emma tried not to fall on him as she peered over his shoulder.

"So, the main access to the hideout is still about a mile downstream. The creek flows directly into it, but we're not going to go in that way. Leeha's sure to have more guards stationed there." He pointed with the stick to an area around the right side. "There's another entrance here. It should be less guarded. Aiden and I will go in first. We'll take out whoever's there and make our way inside."

Standing up, he pulled Emma around in front of him and casually wrapped his arms around her shoulders from behind as she studied his drawing. Her skin felt hot and sensitive where he touched her, even through her clothes.

She stared at his rough drawing, not quite believing she'd be with her sister again before the night was out.

Nik kept her within the circle of his arms. Her eagerness rippled through him, and he felt his own adrenaline rise in response. He tamped it down with effort. He needed to stay calm and focused.

"When da ye want us tae join ye?" Cedric's face clearly showed what he thought about missing out on any of the fighting.

Duncan had a similar sour expression. "Or are we just here tae look bonnie?"

Nik understood how they felt. Still holding Emma with one arm, he gave Cedric a punch on the shoulder. "Don't worry, old friend, there'll be plenty of action for you three."

Hugging Emma to him again, he kissed her on the head. He didn't know what it was, but something was telling him to keep her close. "Once we get in, we'll get ourselves 'captured'—"

"That *was* a brilliant idea you had with Emma," Aiden told Cedric.

Nik grudgingly agreed. "I hate to admit it, but it was. We'll try the same tactic on the inside. We'll get ourselves 'captured', check out the layout, get a count of who's there. You four will wait out here, and when the opportunity presents itself—"

"Wait. Hold up a minute." Emma held up her hand. "You said four. You expect me to wait outside with these do...wolves?" she corrected. "No. I want to be inside with you. I want to help. And I need to see Keira for myself."

Nik crossed his arms and shook his head, not willing to give in on this one. "No. Absolutely not, Emma. Unlike some others standing here—"

Cedric eyebrows rose, his face the picture of innocence. "Whaa?"

"I'm not willing to risk your safety," he finished.

"*No-o?*" she repeated.

"Yeah. NO. I won't risk you. You'll stay out here until it's safe for you to come in. I'll find Keira personally, and make sure she's not harmed. Once I know it's safe, I'll bring her to you." He should've known it wouldn't be that easy.

"Oh, really? And who's going to protect me when the wolves run off, hmm? I'll be out here all alone. What if there are more of those?" She pointed where the last remaining pieces of the victims of Nik's temper were flaking away. "And they find me?"

She was playing dirty, and he knew it, but there was no way in hell he was bringing her.

Nik wasn't going to let her sway him. "Once Cedric and the guys get in there, it'll be over quickly. You will stay outside, hidden, where it's safe. This is not up for discussion."

She agreed. "You're right. This is not up for discussion. Because I'm coming with you."

"Let her come, Nikky-boy," Aiden told him. "It's all right. There won't be any fighting. She's expecting me."

Nik was confused. "She's expecting you? Who's expecting you?"

Aiden grinned. "Leeha."

Once again, Nik was struck speechless by the words coming out of his friend's mouth. "Leeha. *Leeha*—the bitch from hell—is *expecting* you."

"*Yes*. That's what I'm telling you."

Nik glanced around at the others, but everyone else looked as confused as he did. "And why, exactly, would she be expecting you, Aid?"

Hands on his narrow hips, Aiden rolled his grey eyes heavenward. He spoke slowly, enunciating each word carefully. "Because. She rang me. And invited me over."

Nik stared at Aiden blankly for a long moment. Opened his mouth, and then closed it again. Opened it again, and then shook his head.

He had nothing.

Duncan exchanged knowing grins with Aiden. "Aye. So ye've been keeping in touch wi' th' lassie." He gave a shrug of one brawny shoulder. "Canna say that I blame ye. Bonnie as she is."

"Wait a minute. Hold everything." Something had just occurred to Nik. And it didn't bode well for his buddy. "You mean to tell me you've been keeping in touch with the bitch who's been doing God knows what to my brother all this time? And you never told me?" He barely managed to get the words out between his gritted teeth.

Please, tell me Aiden is not so stupid as to let Luukas suffer all this time for nothing.

The smile slipped slowly from his face as Aiden held his hands up, palms out, in front of him. "Nikulas...mate...she didn't ring me all that often. And she never, ever, gave me any idea where she was. I tried to get it out of her, I did! I'm not a complete arse. But she never slipped. Not once." With an admiring tone, he admitted, "She's quite a crafty little twit, that one is."

Sometimes, Nik had to wonder if he really knew Aiden at all. "She's had your number, your secret cell number you're not supposed to give to anyone, all this time."

"Yes, and no," Aiden hedged. "She has a cell number, but only to my prepaid phone, not my super secret one. That's how I knew she was back here." He looked Nik directly in the eye, and his grey eyes pleaded with Nik to believe him. "I've really been trying, mate. She has a thing for me, you know, and I was hoping to get some info out of her about Luukas, but no dice. I would've told you, but I didn't want to get your hopes up unless I'd actually gotten something useful out of her. I didn't. I'm sorry." Pushing his hood off of his head in frustration, he scratched the top of his dark head until his short hair stood straight up.

Nik didn't know what to say.

Emma looked back and forth between the guys. "Good. Then it's settled. I'm coming with you." And with that, she turned on her heal and started following the creek downstream. Aiden smiled broadly and fell in behind her, leaving Nik little choice but to follow them.

Walking fast to catch up with them, Nik looked back over his shoulder at the three wolves. "Stay hidden. I'll give a whistle when it's time."

He broke into an easy jog to catch up with Emma before she tripped over something in the dark—she was really pretty quick for a human when she wanted to be. He didn't look back again as the wolves dispersed into the trees, completely trusting them to not fuck up the plan.

He hoped that trust wasn't misplaced.

Traveling at human speed to accommodate Emma, the vampires were silent as they approached the area Nik had drawn out in the dirt.

At Aiden's insistence that "truly, she's expecting me", they didn't sneak inside, but followed the creek, striding boldly up to the opening at the base of the snow-capped mountain. It loomed over them ominously.

Nik glanced around surreptitiously as the tunnel closed in around them. The creek narrowed once inside, the sound of the water picking up speed as it rushed over the smooth bed it had cut out of the rock over time. Something didn't feel right, but he didn't see or hear anything unusual.

Still, the hair rose on the back of his neck. They were being watched.

Indicating for Aiden to lead the way, he kept Emma close to his side and slightly in front of him, peering back over his shoulder every few feet or so.

Torches—similar to the ones in their own mountain hideout a few miles away—lit the tunnel as they descended deeper and deeper into the underground. But they did nothing to warm the air, and he felt Emma shiver in the damp cold.

Two hundred feet in, the tunnel split into two separate passages. Aiden left the creek and chose the smaller one to the left, Nik and Emma following close behind.

"Do you actually know where you're going, or are you just choosing at random and hoping for the best?" Nik asked him quietly. Although they normally kept an eye on Leeha's comings and goings when she was here, he'd never actually been inside her lair.

Pulling one of the torches off the wall at the division, Aiden gave him a wry look. "Have some faith, mate. This isn't my first rodeo here, as they say."

"That's what concerns me," Nik muttered under his breath.

44

Emma was equal parts nervous and excited as the tunnel narrowed, squeezing them in together until they had to walk single file. Excited that she might be seeing her sister again very soon, and nervous at the unknown prospect of what they'd have to face to get her and Luukas out of here.

Even the vampires were unusually subdued. And that couldn't be a good sign.

Falling in between the two taller males, she couldn't see very much, even with the torch Aiden had thought to grab. Because any nightmarish creatures that lived down here didn't need light to sniff out their prey?

Get a grip on yourself, Em. Yeah. Did she mention she was not a huge fan of the dark?

Nik stayed right behind her, one hand resting on her shoulder, his thumb occasionally rubbing small circles through her shirt. Her skin prickled where he touched her, and her breath came in shallow pants. From her claustrophobia or from his touch, she honestly couldn't say. But either way, she couldn't complain. She was the one who'd insisted on coming along, after all.

As they traversed deeper into the dark underground, Emma kept her eyes on Aiden's back. She continued to place one foot in front of the other, silently fighting the ongoing battle not to freak out in the enclosed space, when she suddenly felt a rush of air and got the feeling of more space around them.

Stepping from the passage, she heard a loud *whoosh* as a hundred torches lit simultaneously and without warning, temporarily blinding her. Shielding her eyes with her hands until she grew used to the sudden light, she squinted as she looked around.

Another immense cavern loomed before her like the vampire's hideout. But this one was not only larger, the stone was chiseled away to give the interior the appearance of a vast cathedral of old.

A vast, gothic, spooky as all hell, cathedral.

Illuminated by the fire that danced eerily along the dark stone walls, her eyes widened at the giant archways lining the wide, central aisle. Slender columns led up to a soaring ceiling of pointed arches a hundred feet or more above their heads.

When she could tear her eyes away from the majesty of the ceiling, she followed the columns back down to the floor, where mosaic tiles were laid out in a seemingly abstract order, but which created an overall pattern that directed the eyes forward to the other end of the room, and the main attraction.

Dropping her hands away from her eyes, Emma blinked hard as she stared down the endless aisle to the opposite end of the cathedral. Stone steps led up to a raised stone platform that took up the entire far end of the room. And alone in the center of the platform was a throne. An actual, honest-to-God throne, reminiscent of medieval days.

Made of the same kind of smooth, dark stone that lined the walls, it was interspersed with threads of shiny gold that glittered in the flickering firelight. Other than that, the starkness was only broken up by a blood red seat cushion along the seat and back. It contained no other ornamentation, the overall effect as sinister in appearance as the woman sitting upon it.

She was one of the most stunning creatures Emma had ever seen. So much so, she half wondered if she was a figment of her imagination.

Lowering his arm from his eyes, Nik immediately spotted the woman on the throne, and impaled her with his angry gaze. He reached for Emma's hand, and she let him take it as he pulled her along behind him.

"Enough with the party tricks, Leeha. Where is my brother?" he demanded.

But they weren't party tricks. There was magic in the room. Emma could feel it. It pulsed in the air like a living entity. Did he not feel it?

However, the magic did not come from the woman in the room. She wasn't sure how she knew, but Emma would bet her life on it.

Ignoring his question, their host sat forward, all of her attention on Emma.

Belatedly, Nik noticed Leeha zero in on Emma and stopped abruptly midway up the aisle, tucking her behind him.

"And who is *this*, Nikulas?" Leeha asked. Her richly accented voice pronounced each syllable in his name distinctly. "Have you *finally* found a new little human whore to warm your bed?" Undaunted by the warning growl aimed at her, she stood up and came toward them.

Emma stared, unable to look away as envy tore through her gut.

Leeha didn't so much walk, as leisurely seduce her way across the floor. Head high and arms confidently at her sides, she prowled over the stones with an erotic roll to her hips, designed to entice every male in the room into imagining it was *his* cock she wanted, and no one else's.

Her dark red hair was thick and soft and long, tumbling around her shoulders in artful disarray. Her deathly pale skin was unnaturally flawless and only made one startlingly aware of her full, red lips and hollowed cheekbones. A thin, sheer, white gown showed off her full, rounded breasts and each rose-darkened areola, the large nipples constantly tight from rubbing against the fabric.

As she walked, the gown slithered in and out around her legs, allowing only brief glimpses of her long, slender limbs and the shadowed area between them.

Emma's eyes widened, then narrowed as she realized the woman was completely bare underneath that gown. She was easily the most provocative creature Emma had ever seen.

And she hated her on sight. Not because she was beautiful, but because of how she used that beauty. Like males were creatures to be played with.

As she advanced on them, Emma's gaze was unwillingly compelled to her blood red eyes. She found she couldn't tear them away, hard as she tried. Locked into that hellish gaze, she saw nightmares beyond anything she'd ever experienced. The depths of despair—blood...horror...pain—they all swirled around in those depths. They drew Emma in, sucking her into the horridness she saw there, until she felt like her very soul would be forever lost if she couldn't look away.

Panic began to set in as she tried harder and harder to break the connection, but to no avail. She began to shake uncontrollably with the effort, sweat forming on her brow and trickling between her breasts.

Nikulas stepped between them, cutting off Emma's view and breaking the connection. "Back the fuck off, Leeha. Emma is *mine*," he snarled, his husky voice low and threatening.

Leeha didn't pause in her approach, or seem surprised by Nik's announcement, but only gave him a small, patronizing smile. She circled around the pair of them, getting a good look at her guest.

Emma's skin crawled everywhere her eyes touched her. She stood very still, and kept her eyes down so as not to look directly at her again. She was afraid to so much as breathe, even with Nik standing so protectively in front of her, warily watching Leeha's every move.

Leeha stopped just behind her, and Emma heard her inhale just behind her ear. The back of Emma's neck tingled like tiny spiders were crawling on her, and she had to resist the urge to smack at the nonexistent things. At least she hoped they were nonexistent.

"I smell you on her Nikulas. I smell you *in* her." She moved in front of him again. Her head tilted with a jerky motion, like a bird. "She's had your blood. And even more intriguing, you've had he*rs*. And yet, she's still alive."

An unpleasant smile spread across her face, and her attention returned to Emma with renewed interest, in spite of Nik's attempts to block her. "Emma. What a pretty name. Would your last name be Moss, by chance?"

"Yes." The word was forced from her mouth, try as she might not to answer.

Leeha gave her a small, indecipherable smile. "Tell me, Nikulas, does she fawn over you as Eliana did?" Her smile widened as Emma stiffened. "I don't think she does. Does that disappoint you?"

Her eyes roamed over Emma's face and form with appreciation. "She's quite pretty. A bit thin, but fuckable, I suppose. If you like that sort of thing."

Emma's breath caught at the insult, but she refused to give the bitch the reaction she was obviously hoping for.

Pouting a bit when neither Emma nor Nik rose to the bait, Leeha continued, "So, do tell, Nikulas. *Does* she fuck as well as Eliana? More importantly," she purred, "does she *taste* as good as Eliana?" She caught a strand of Emma's bright hair, rubbing it between her slender fingers as she wet her bottom lip with the tip of her tongue. "I'd love to find out."

Nik shoved Emma back behind him so fast, she had to grab his arm to keep from stumbling, and strands of her hair were left behind in Leeha's fingers. A menacing growl rumbled deep within his chest. Leaning forward, he bared his fangs and hissed in warning at the beautiful, evil creature in front of him, his eyes glowing with possession.

"You touch her again, you evil bitch, I'll rip your fucking head off," he promised.

She raised an amused eyebrow. "So protective, Nikulas. I don't remember you being so protective over Eliana."

"What the FUCK is it with you and Eliana!" he raged in her face.

Leeha pursed her lips, narrowing her eyes in warning at his outburst. Seconds ticked by with no sound other than Nik's harsh breathing.

Emma breathed a shaky sigh of relief when Aiden—who until now had been hovering silently by the entrance—took her attention.

He sauntered into the room, edging closer to Nik and Emma. Leeha jerked her head to the side again, blatantly devouring him with her eyes.

Puffing his chest out like a strutting cock, he winked at her and blew her a kiss. "Evenin' love." He gave her a slow, sexy smile.

Emma suddenly gasped out loud, interrupting their sick flirtation to blurt out, "It was you. *You* killed Eliana." As Leeha's haunting eyes skittered back her way, she sucked in a breath and immediately dropped her own again.

Aiden forgotten just as quickly as he was noticed, Leeha's lips turned up a bit at the corners. "She's smart, Nikulas. I would be careful with this one."

Retracting his fangs slightly, Nik frowned down at Emma even as he spoke to Leeha. "What are you talking about?"

"Why don't you ask *your mate* to explain it to you?" Aside to Emma, she murmured, "Isn't it a shame the pretty ones are always so slow?" Then she turned and slithered back to her throne.

"Yes! That's it!" Aiden smacked himself on the forehead. "You bloody bitch! *You* killed Eliana!"

"Flattery will get you *everywhere*, my love," Leeha murmured, adjusting the flowing material of her gown just so as she sat down.

"Would someone please tell me what the *fuck* you all are talking about?" Nik gritted out in frustration.

Emma moved in front of him, ignoring his frustration at her continued disregard of his attempts to protect her. "*Listen* to me," she beseeched him, placing her hands on his hard chest. "You didn't kill Eliana! It was *her*, Nik! *She* killed her!"

"What?" Grasping her hands in his, he held them where they were, his eyes bouncing around as he remembered that night. "No. No. Emma, I was...I was fucking *there*. It was me. She was alive when I came home to her. And dead five minutes after. No one else came in the room."

"How alive, Nik?" This from Aiden.

"I...What? I don't know. I was all riled up from the fight. She was asleep." But there was the slightest glimmer of hope in his blue eyes.

Emma smacked his chest excitedly as another thought popped into her head, one that had been eluding her since he'd told her this story. "Nik! Was it normal for the woman who supposedly loved you to be home, sleeping, while you were out fighting?" Looking at it from a woman's perspective, she'd finally realized what it was about his story that had been bothering her all this time. "Because I know if it were me, I wouldn't be able to sleep a wink until my man was home safe and sound."

45

Hope plucked at the guilt as Nik pondered Emma's question. He'd never questioned why she'd been in bed when he got home. Eliana always waited up for him. Always, without fail. Whether it was to welcome him home or fight with him was questionable, but Emma was right. Why had it never occurred to him before?

Because he'd been too entrenched in guilt and self-loathing, that's why.

Aiden whacked him hard on the back as Emma gave him one of her mind-numbing smiles. He memorized her glowing face, a face that had become more beloved to him in these few days than anything or anyone in his life.

Slow applause came from the front of room, and Leeha heaved a sigh. "Finally! I thought I was going to have to spell it out for you, like, literally. I-k-i-l-l-e-d-h-e-r." Admiring her manicure, she added, "This is why I went after Luukas, and not you,

Nikulas. You are but a weak replica of your brother. You could never rule."

Emma whipped around at the insult, her small form vibrating with fury. "Don't you *dare* talk about him like that! You're not worthy of licking the mud from his boots."

Nik pulled back in surprise. His little Emma was standing up to a crazed female vampire, because she'd insulted him? He felt a pulse of magic reverberate through the room. Keira was here, too. Her magic felt similar to Emma's, but stronger. A lot stronger. It was *her* spell that caused the torches to come alive as they entered.

"Easy there, killer." With one eye on Leeha, he grabbed Emma by the shoulders and pulled her back against his chest. "It's not worth it." He kissed the top of her head and whispered, "But, thank you."

He rubbed her shoulders until he felt her calming down. Though he understood her desire to lob rocks at the bitch, they needed to keep their heads about them if they wanted to get to their siblings.

"Ick." Leeha made a face. "You two are disgusting." She narrowed her gaze at Emma. "And I should kill you where you stand for how you just spoke to me." She crossed her legs and contemplated the three of them. "But, I'm feeling generous today, so I'll spare you. This time. However, I would strongly suggest you watch your tongue from now on, or I may change my mind. I still need a replacement human for Eliana."

Aiden slapped a hand on Nik's shoulder just in time, physically holding him in place and repeating his own words to him, "It's not worth it, mate."

As Nik struggled to take his own advice and get his hair trigger emotions under control, Aiden stuck his hands in his pockets and strolled closer to Leeha.

"So, tell me love. Why did you kill Eliana? What ever did she do to you?"

"I didn't like her." Her red lips pouted. "She was too close to Luukas."

"But she didn't belong to Luukas," Nik pointed out.

"She didn't belong to you, either."

Nik waited for the pain of Eliana's loss to hit him, but surprisingly, there was nothing more than a lingering need to know the truth. His gaze fell to Emma's bright hair.

Maybe not so surprising.

Leeha's chin rose as she turned those blood red eyes back on Nikulas. "She was mine. We were lovers, you know. *I* sent her to you. To get close to you, and therefore close to Luukas. Learn his secrets. His habits." She sighed with disappointment. "She was supposed to help me win him over, but she was jealous, and became rebellious. She wouldn't cooperate. She stopped reporting in to me. And then everything changed. She became too enamored with *you*, Nikulas. Why? I don't know. But, she did."

Standing up, she paced back and forth along the platform. "She stopped sneaking out to see me. Didn't want to be with me anymore. She just. Wanted. YOU." Leeha looked back and forth between Aiden and Nik with her horror-filled eyes, her expression open and beseeching. Nik felt her need pulling at him, willing him to understand. "I couldn't just let her leave, you understand. She was mine. And she betrayed me." With a sigh, she turned and sat down again.

"Luukas is meant to be with me. And Eliana wouldn't help me anymore. So, I killed her. I coaxed her into coming to see me by promising to release her. And then I drained her to the point of barely being alive and had her returned to your bed. It didn't take much for you to finish the job. And then, since he still refused to see what was right in front of his eyes, I had to resort to taking Luukas forcibly." Satisfaction dripped from her tone. "With a little help, of course." A secret smile played about her mouth. "And you don't even know the best part."

"I'll bet." Aiden put a hand dramatically over his heart. "But, you're ripping my heart out, love." Flopping down on the steps leading up to her throne disconsolately, he was the picture of a broken heart.

Leeha stared at the back of his hanging head, an internal struggle written all over her face, before rising and coming down the stairs to sit next to him. Pulling his hood down, she stroked his dark hair. "Don't be jealous, my sweet. I'm so very happy you've finally come to see me. My relationship with Luukas doesn't have to affect what we have between us."

She lowered her voice. "Why don't you stay with me for a while?" "We can stick these two in the dungeon for a fortnight or two—separate cells, of course—and let them wallow in their self-righteousness, while you and I wallow in other earthly pleasures."

Sniffling, Aiden played it up a bit before finally raising his head to look at her with watery eyes. Lifting his hands to her face, he blocked her view while he placed a sweet kiss on her forehead, and then her nose. Pulling her to him and wrapping his arms around her, he winked at Nik.

Nik smiled, then put two fingers in his mouth. A piercing whistle ripped through the cavern.

Leeha tore herself from Aiden's embrace, pushing him aside and jumping to her feet to stare at Nik.

He just shrugged at her. "Sorry. The sight of you two was making my stomach turn."

Narrowing her eyes, she didn't get the chance to form a rebuttal before a hair-raising howl rent the air.

Whipping her head around, her glowing eyes pierced through Aiden. "You brought *wolves* to my door? WOLVES?" she shrieked at him.

Scratching his head, his features twisted up in a grimace. "I had no choice, love." He sounded sincerely sorry. "They just showed up, and you know how stubborn those bloody Scots are." Placing his hands low on his narrow hips, he gave her an admonishing look. "Besides, if you would just stop *stealing* people—"

With an ear-piercing screech, the back of her hand lit across his face. Stumbling from the strength of the impact, he nearly toppled down the stairs.

Charging down after him, she got right up in his face, fangs bared. "You have no idea what you've just done!"

Smiling broadly, he spit out a mouth full of blood and sneered at her. "Oh, I know *exactly* what I've just done, love."

She drew herself up to her full height. "You all think you're so smart, don't you." It wasn't a question.

Another spine-tingling howl sounded, closer than before.

"This isn't how I planned for this meeting to go." Leeha sighed. "I was hoping to make you *all* disappear, like your Hunters. But I can adapt...TAKE HIM!"

Before anyone could move, dozens of rotting, grey bodies filed out of a hidden door to the left of the throne. The horrid stench of them flooded the space as their angry snarls vibrating throughout the room.

A group surrounded Aiden, and though he gleefully managed to take a couple of them out, they dragged him back up the stairs and out of the room.

With a last, angry glare at Nik, Leeha followed, appearing to disappear right through the wall behind them.

Nik watched them go, a feeling of sick helplessness washing over him. Torn between keeping Emma safe and saving his best friend, he fisted his hands at his sides, and threw back his head with an anguished roar.

46

Terror flooded through Emma as the monster's shrieks drowned out Nikulas's roar. They were completely surrounded.

"Nik?" Her voice shook so much she didn't think he could hear her over all the noise.

But he did.

Emma gasped as he turned toward her, and for a brief instant, she recoiled in fear at the sight of him. He seemed larger, his muscles straining against the fabric of his clothes. Like in the midst of this overwhelming danger, his physical form couldn't hold all of what he now was. His lips were drawn back from his dagger-like fangs as he snarled rabidly at the creatures surrounding them. The skin pulled so tight across his features, his cheekbones and eye sockets were stark slashes across his face. Bright eyes glowed so blue they were near colorless as they darted around the room, tallying his prey like the killer he was.

Scooping Emma up in his arms as she shrieked, another roar thundered from his chest, daring any one of them to try and take her. Emma knew this. She could feel everything he felt, more so with him in this heightened stage than ever before.

Slowly backing away, Nik threatened them with bared fangs as they prowled around him. They seemed hesitant to attack, as if they sensed he wouldn't be an ordinary opponent.

Eventually, though, they would.

Emma's clung to Nikulas as her eyes skittered around, trying to watch everywhere he couldn't. Glancing over Nik's shoulder, she saw they were almost to the wall behind them. "Nik. Put me down."

He growled softly in response.

"Nik. You can't fight them while you're holding me. Put me down!"

The creatures were close now. One of them made a half-hearted swipe at them even as she spoke. Nik stiffened, snarling back in response.

"Nik!"

Suddenly, complete and utter chaos erupted around them as the wolves, in full-blown wolf form, arrived on the scene. Their guttural howls echoed off the walls as they tore into the creatures. Going for their throats, they ripped out jugulars, their long jaws snapping spines and nearly beheading them in the process.

Emma was happy Nik was still holding onto her, for she was momentarily stunned by the utter violence of the werewolves as he took full advantage of the commotion to get Emma the hell out of there.

Keeping a close eye on the battle around them, he tucked Emma up against his chest, hunching over her to protect her with his body as well as he could. Sprinting across the room at full speed right through the thick of it, he roared as the creatures slashed at his back and arms.

Knocked to the side by a flying corpse, Emma flung out her arms, but he quickly regained his footing, and deposited her in the hidden doorway just off the platform. The same doorway Aiden had disappeared through.

Nik planted himself in front of her and whipped around with a bellowing roar. As Emma huddled behind him, he swiftly annihilated any of the creatures who were unlucky enough to stumble near them.

Looking around for a weapon—a loose rock, anything—but failing to find so much as a piece of gravel, Emma quickly decided her best move would be to crouch down into the corner and try to stay out of Nik's way. Magic sure would come in handy right about now, but unfortunately, it only seemed to make an appearance when she was angry. Not terrified.

Here and there, she'd catch a closer look at the wolves between his legs.

Twice as large as their human forms, a perfect wolf/human hybrid, they were fearsome to behold. Sparse hair covered their powerful physiques, more muscular than normal wolves. Long snouts were lifted in a snarl, encasing rows of dagger-like teeth capable of ripping through both flesh and bone with ease.

Running at the creatures on all fours at supernatural speeds, their eyes glowed with an unholy light as they tore into their victims with a ferocity Emma had never seen before from any other animal.

How much of their human side was left when they were changed? Would they even recognize them as friends?

Wait a minute. She peered around Nik's blood-covered legs as she searched the room. There were only two of them. Where was the other wolf? Was he hurt? She looked again. No, he wasn't in the room. She only saw the one with the reddish fur and the larger, black one.

It scanned the room with glowing eyes, but when nothing moved, the largest one—Cedric?—raised up on to his rear legs, lifted his snout to the sky, and let loose another hair-raising howl.

An answering howl came from below, joined by a second one, and followed by a tormented roar that shook the walls so forcefully, Emma stumbled and would have fallen if she hadn't caught herself against the door.

Then silence.

"Luukas!" Nik bellowed, as both the wolves howled again.

All motion stopped as everyone held their collective breath, listening.

Emma quietly rose from her crouched position, afraid to bring attention to herself in the deafening silence, and listened with the rest of them. Was her sister down there somewhere?

One breath.

Two breaths.

Three...

The ground rumbled under their feet, gradually gaining power, the floor vibrating like a train was passing underneath them.

Nik backed up, shielding Emma from the rock particles raining down from the ceiling as the rumbling grew stronger.

The wolves prowled nervously back and forth on all fours, occasionally glancing toward the passageway out.

Emma wondered why they didn't leave. Were they waiting for the missing wolf?

The smaller one looked at the large, black wolf and whined softly, then shook the dust from his fur.

Emma shivered as the temperature suddenly dropped. The sound below them grew louder and louder still, until she had to shout to be heard above it. "What *is* that?" she finally yelled.

Nik glanced over his shoulder, one side of his mouth turned up in a relieved smile. "My brother."

47

Suddenly, a blast of ice cold air shot across the room as a large portion of the wall exploded out from within, sending pieces of rock flying, and causing the wolves to scamper frantically toward the protection of the tunnel.

Nik spun around and hunkered down over Emma, protecting her as well as he could from the flying debris.

When the dust settled, Luukas stood in the opening, feet spread wide, one hand clenched into a fist at his side.

The other hand was wrapped around the wrist of a curvy, dark-haired female.

Eyes on his brother, Nik stepped out from the doorway, and Emma stumbled out from behind him. Pushing him out of the way, she ran toward the stairs before he could stop her. "Keira!" Her voice caught on a sob.

"Emma," her sister breathed. Her hazel eyes, so similar to Emma's, were wide with disbelief.

Luukas's dark head whipped around at the sound of Emma's voice, his eyes wild as they focused in on the tiny human running toward them. Nik watched as he pulled his lips back in a snarl, and hissed at her in warning.

But Emma couldn't know the danger she was in, and so she ran, ignoring the warning.

Nik's heart stopped, and he was suddenly on the step below her. Grabbing her up mid-air, he forcibly held her against his hard chest.

"Let me go!" She struggled hard against him, kicking his shins and pounding his shoulders with her small fists. Tears ran unchecked down her face.

But Nik held her tight, keeping his back to his brother, not wanting to entice him further by staring directly at him. He took the pounding she gave him, repeating softly in her ear, "Sweetheart, just wait. Something isn't right with him. Emma, something isn't right with him."

Nik halfway turned with Emma still struggling in his arms and studied his older brother. His dark hair was long and lank, his T-shirt so riddled with blood and dirt, you couldn't tell its original color. His jeans were also stiff with dirt. And he was barefoot. The girl he held onto wasn't in much better shape.

But the thing that stood out the most to him were his eyes. Luukas's grey eyes had gone completely black. They skittered about the room, not focusing on anyone or anything in particular. He bared his fangs at all of them.

Even Nikulas.

Nik set Emma down. "Emma, look at me. Look at me!" He gave her a little shake until she looked at him. "You can't go down there. I honestly don't know what he'll do." He shook his head when she started to protest. "Give me a minute to talk to him, Em."

She wasn't happy, but with a longing look at her sister, she finally agreed. Once he made sure she was going to stay put, he glanced over uneasily at the wolves before he slowly eased down another step. "Luukas? Hey, big brother. It's just me. It's Nik."

He eased down another step.

A snarl ripped from Luukas's throat as his eyes swung from the pacing wolves to his brother. Cocking his head, he watched Nik ease toward him, recognition finally flickering across his face. Sheathing his fangs a bit, he yanked Keira partly behind him with the death grip he maintained on her wrist.

Nikulas noticed she wasn't fighting him. Interesting.

"The witch is *mine*." His deep voice was raspy and broken. From lack of use? From screaming?

Nik tampered down his rising anger at the sound of it. Right now, he just needed to get his brother calm.

"Okay, man, you can have her." Ignoring Emma's sound of protest, he eased down a few more steps. "No one is going to take your witch. I just want to say hello to my brother."

He'd reached the bottom of the steps, and was now less than twenty feet from the hole in the wall where his brother stood. Checking the urge to run over and grab him up in a bear hug, he left Luukas some space and waited to see what he would do.

Luukas took a halting step into the room, scanning the area in that twitchy way he now had.

"*Where is she?*" he ground out between gritted teeth.

Nik knew whom he was referring to without having to ask. "She's gone. She took Aiden." His voice broke slightly as he briefly filled Luukas in on what had happened after they'd arrived.

Luukas growled low in his throat as his lips twitched back off his fangs in anger. "I'm going to rip her apart. Slowly. *Painfully.*"

Keira's mouth twisted in pain as her arm was twisted. "Luukas. You're hurting me!"

He immediately loosened his hold, releasing her wrist but pinning her where she was with his eyes. He stared at her for a long moment as Nik watched the exchange with interest.

Never taking his gaze from Keira, Luukas told his brother, "Leave us."

The wolves took full advantage of his distraction to slink past them, quickly disappearing through the edges of the hole to go find the rest of their pack.

Emma ran down the remaining steps to Nik. Grabbing his hand, she silently begged him to do something.

Nik looked from her to his brother. "Luuk, man. Let's just get out of here."

Emma shivered beside him, the cloud of her breath forming icicles as Luukas's anger permeated the room.

"LEAVE! US!" he roared.

Nik chewed his bottom lip as he contemplated the back of his brother's head for a minute, and then he turned and took

Emma by the arm, knowing Luukas would brook no argument when he was like this. "Come on. Let's go." Over his shoulder, he told his brother, "We'll be at the hideout."

Emma struggled futilely against him as he dragged her across the room. "What? No. Nik! NO!! Dammit, that's my SISTER over there!"

Ignoring her pleas, he pulled her with him toward the door.

"Nikulas! Stop! I'm not leaving without her!"

Her heart pounding, Emma looked back toward Keira, who was staring at Luukas in alarm.

Now they were just *pissing* her off. She abruptly dug in her heels and ripped her arm from Nik's grasp, turning her focus to Luukas.

"I will *not* leave without my sister," she ground out.

Gathering energy within herself, she focused all of her anger and hatred on the vampire holding her sister. The air hummed with magic as the stone he'd knocked loose from the wall began to hover off the floor.

Nik moved in front of her, his eyes swimming with alarm. "Emma, NO!" Softening his tone, he told her, "I don't know what he will do if he sees you as a threat. He's not the same as he was. Please," He paused. "*Please*, don't make me fight him to protect you now that I've finally found him."

Emma felt for him, she did. But, this was her sister. Her only family. She wasn't leaving her here with his crazy brother who was looking at her like he wanted to eat her.

She had a purpose for her magic for the first time. Though the feel of it was something she was only beginning to recognize, it flowed through her, gathering strength, and Emma concentrated on that feeling. She felt high, lightheaded but grounded at the same time. And if she weren't so upset she would have laughed aloud from the power of it.

Lifting her right hand, she swung it through the air, aiming a particularly large boulder just to the left of Luukas. A direct hit would risk her sister. She hoped it would distract him and Keira would be able to get away.

Without moving his eyes away from Keira, Luukas flicked his left hand, easily deflecting her attack with nothing but the power of his will.

"Nikulas. You *really* need to remove her," he warned. "NOW. I'm not in the mood to play."

Emma gritted her teeth in response and prepared to send another large stone flying. This time at his head.

Keira found her sister across the room. "Emma, it's okay. Luukas and I have some things we need to discuss."

Nik stepped in front of her. "Sweetheart, that's enough. We're leaving."

She looked up at him as her vision blurred with angry tears. "He's going to kill her, Nik!"

"No, he won't. He's very angry right now, but he won't hurt her. You need to trust me here."

She stared defiantly up into his stubborn blue eyes. "You don't *know* that."

"Actually, I kinda do."

"It's okay, honey. Go with Nik. I'll be out in a bit," Keira told her.

Emma stepped around Nik and stared at her sister in disbelief.

"Keira?" She couldn't believe her sister was telling her to leave her with that maniac.

"Emma, just GO. I'll be fine," her sister insisted.

"Come on." Nik put his hand on the small of her back to lead her out of the room.

She flinched away from him. "Don't touch me," She hissed. With a last look at Keira to confirm she really wanted her to leave, she turned around and marched from the room, Nik close on her heals.

Emma stomped down the passageway until she had to stop and wait for Nik and the torch he'd snagged off of the wall. As soon as he'd caught up to her, she turned on him. "I'm only going as far as the end of the tunnel. And then I'm waiting for my sister."

She began walking again, and didn't give him a chance to reply.

What the hell was Keira doing? She couldn't really want to stay there with that...that...monster that was Nik's brother. Could she?

Angry tears ran down her face. She should have fought harder to bring her sister with her. Nik should have fought harder. It was *his* brother, after all.

Her mind spinning and her heart breaking in too many tiny pieces, Emma shook with anger as she trekked through the passageway, swiping at the tears that wouldn't stop.

She couldn't decide if she was angrier with Nik, with Keira, with Luukas, or with herself.

Nik let her go, not blaming her in the slightest for the way she was feeling, but not knowing what to say to fix it. His own mind was spinning, worrying about Aiden, and worrying about his brother.

The one thing he *wasn't* worried about was his brother hurting that female. He'd seen the possessive way he'd looked at her. The way he'd immediately let her go as soon as he'd realized he was hurting her.

No, he wasn't worried about him harming her.

His brother's mind, on the other hand—yeah, that was another story. He'd never seen him this disoriented before. Guilt wracked Nik until he could barely breathe. He should have searched every inch of the earth for him. Instead, he'd given up and waited for something to happen.

That wasn't exactly true, but still, there was no excuse for it. Luukas had obviously suffered severely over the years—more than Nik could ever have guessed—to the point his mind may never be right again. He'd never be able to make it up to him.

And Nik wouldn't blame him if his brother never forgave him.

They traversed the length of the tunnel, each lost in their own thoughts, until they hit the creek again. Emma picked up speed as the passageway widened and the moonlight lit up the night outside. Bursting out into the fresh air, she followed the shoreline until, with a loud sob, she broke into a run.

With a curse, Nik tossed the torch he carried into the flowing water and picked up his pace. His chest ached with her pain. And his own too.

But he was going to fix it. He was going to fix everything. He knew how to keep her safe, and how to take away her pain. And he would send her sister home to her as soon as he could get her away from Luukas.

He caught up to her just as she stumbled to a halt, but when he reached out to steady her, she slapped his hand away.

"Don't touch me! Don't you ever touch me again!"

Though he'd expected it, the force of her anger hit him full in the chest. "Emma..." he pleaded.

Whipping around, she raised her hands and threw all of her weight into shoving him away. "Don't 'Emma' me! You son of a bitch!"

She covered her face with her hands, and Nik gave her a minute to collect herself. He was glad this was happening sooner rather than later. No matter his feelings for her, she would come to resent him for binding her life to his so selfishly. For making her give up her life to keep her captive in his. He knew this, and he couldn't in good conscience allow her to throw away her life. Not for him. If he did, he would be no better than Leeha.

He was going to break his promise to her.

With a shuddering breath, she dropped her arms down to her sides and stared up at him, her hazel eyes bright with tears. "You left her there. Just left her there with *him*. What if he hurts her? He's your brother! Why didn't you do something! If not for her, then for me!" she accused.

Nik felt helpless. "No, Emma. No. How could you think—"

"YOU LEFT HER!!" she screamed her anger and frustration at him.

Nik bared his fangs at her, his own emotions getting the best of him. "I did leave her there! I didn't know what he was going to do! And you wouldn't STOP, Emma! You wouldn't fucking STOP! He could have killed you with a fucking *thought*. You don't know what he's capable of! I probably saved your fucking LIFE!"

She reared back like he'd slapped her.

Stabbing his hands through his hair, he backed off. But when he looked at her again, he knew things would never be the same between them. She was never going to forgive him.

An icy-cold tranquility came over him. Let her hate him. He was good with that.

Nik stepped closer and took her chin in his hand, forcing her to look up at him. When her eyes met his, he caught and held them with his own. Ignoring the voice in his head raging against what he was about to do, he burrowed into her mind with his own.

Emma became complacent as all of the tension drained from her body. Her pupils dilated until there was no color left, only black.

Nik probed her mind, and found it open to him completely. "I'm going to give you directions and send you home in the SUV. Everything you need to get a flight home is in the center console. You'll remember meeting me, will remember our time together, and you'll remember coming here with me, but that's all. We didn't find your sister. No one was here when we arrived. It was a dead end."

He took a deep breath. "You're going to go home, and go back to your life. You'll go on as you did before you met me. You won't remember the intimacy between us. You won't remember how I drank from you, or our bond. You won't remember my feelings for you." His voice broke, and he had to pause. "You'll be happy, Emma."

If he cared for her at all, he would make her forget him entirely. But he was too damn selfish. He wanted her to remember him. If only a little.

He broke the contact, and stepped back, wiping at the moisture in his eyes with the heel of his hand.

Emma came out of her daze, blinking up at him. She glanced around at the trees. "Well, I guess this was all for nothing."

"Not for nothing." He cleared his throat. "At least we know they're not here. And we'll keep looking."

She glanced up at him. "Thank you for trying. And you'll call me if you find anything? Anything at all?"

"I promise." The words were sour on his tongue. Taking her by the elbow, he said, "Come on, let's get back to the car. It's time for you to go so you don't miss your flight."

She looked around and frowned, like she was trying to remember something. But in the end, she just sighed and allowed him to lead her away.

His heart chipped away more with every step she took until he didn't think there was anything left by the time they reached the hideout.

But as she started the car and pulled away, he knew he was wrong as it shattered all over again.

48

Emma pulled into her driveway in the deepening twilight. Grabbing her gym bag, she got out and locked her car. Two long weeks had passed since the long flight home from Seattle, and she'd heard nothing more from Nikulas. Not a phone call. Not an email. Nothing.

Apparently, the attraction she felt was one-sided. But what did she expect? He's a vampire. A predator, made to be attractive to humans. It wasn't his fault he'd crawled under her skin during the time they'd spent together.

Emma swallowed the pain of his rejection. She could've sworn he'd felt something for her, too. But, apparently, she'd been wrong. He was handsome, and charming, and masculine, and there were probably a few dozen women out there who felt the same way she did about him.

But it was more than disappointment he hadn't pursued their relationship. For some reason, she worried about him, though she couldn't quite put her finger on the reason why. Something was wrong, though. Her intuition never steered her wrong. She couldn't sleep, couldn't concentrate, and when she could bring herself to eat, she had to force the food past the anxiety in her stomach.

At work, her co-workers watched her with concern. They still didn't know everything that had happened while she was gone. Emma had only told them she'd followed up a lead on her sister, but it had turned out to be nothing. She didn't tell them about Nik and Aiden. And she most certainly didn't tell anyone they were vampires.

Or that she and her sister were witches.

Exhausted, she climbed the front steps, trudged across the porch and pulled open her screen door, holding it with her foot while she unlocked her storm door.

Once inside, she flicked on the lights and went into the kitchen, dropping her purse and her gym bag on the counter. Her lunchtime runs on the treadmill were the only thing helping her to keep her sanity, although she had no idea where she was finding the energy to do it every day.

Grabbing a clean glass from the dishwasher, she filled it with water and gulped it down. She was so thirsty all the time, and the more water she drank, the worse the thirst became. It must be dehydration from the trip.

She was very careful not to look around too much. Whenever she did, she would end up standing in the middle of her kitchen, staring around the room with the feeling she'd come in there for something and now couldn't remember what it was. Like she was forgetting something.

Or maybe someone.

Setting the empty glass on the counter, she left her stuff in the kitchen and went to shower. Upstairs, she stripped off her work attire and padded barefoot into the bathroom.

She paused as she passed the mirror. Slowly, she turned until she faced her reflection. Lifting her heavy eyelids, she gazed fully upon her nude form for the first time in seven years. Her fingertips traced the scars that marred her skin, following the path of her eyes. Her body was far from beautiful, covered as it was by the remnants of the attack, yet the repulsion she normally felt wasn't there.

Something teased at the edge of her mind—Nik's voice telling her...something. A memory, perhaps. But it was there and gone before she could grasp it.

With a sigh, she turned away and yanked on the shower, getting in before the water had a chance to heat up. Perhaps she was only imagining it.

I won't think about him. I won't. I'm fine. He doesn't deserve my concern, and I don't need him.

She'd been repeating that mantra to herself every day since she'd gotten home. But as the days passed, it became harder and harder to believe it.

She did need him. He just didn't need her.

Viscously, she scrubbed her hair and body, trying to scour away thoughts of him. But instead of distracting herself, she only managed to sensitize her skin until every drop of water that hit her only fed her yearning to feel his hands on her.

Emma ran her hands over her breasts and belly, and lower still. Her eyes slid closed on a moan as she imagined it was Nik touching her. She missed him so much. How was it possible to miss his touch when she'd never felt it before?

Dropping her hands, she finished her shower and got out. Emma towel-dried her hair, foregoing a comb to run her fingers through it, and grabbed her nightshirt off the end of her bed and pulled it over her head. Tossing her wet towel into the hamper, she grabbed her comfortable, blue robe and headed downstairs to get something to eat, her appetite suddenly returned.

She would try to call Nik, she decided. He'd given her his cell number. He wouldn't have done that if he didn't want to hear from her. And maybe if she spoke to him, the anxiety would go away.

Eager now, she stepped off of the bottom stair and turned the corner to go into the kitchen. Lifting her eyes from the floor, she gasped out loud, coming to an abrupt halt just inside the doorway.

Nikulas sat at her kitchen table.

Nik smiled as he saw her round the corner in that ratty, blue robe, her bare feet peeking out from its uneven hemline. But as his eyes hungrily roved over her features, his smile quickly dissipated. She was pale and gaunt looking, even after her shower. Her eyes looked bruised from the dark circles under them.

His heart skipped in his chest. Was she sick? Could she be sick? She'd had his blood, but only that one time. And it had been weeks ago.

Emma stared at him like she was seeing a ghost.

He rose to his full height, shifting uncomfortably as he remembered she might not be happy to see him. He could have called her first, he supposed, and he'd meant to. He really had. But then, somehow, he'd found himself standing outside her house, with barely any recollection of how he'd gotten there.

He ran his hands through his hair, pushing it back off of his face, then cleared his throat. "You're door wasn't locked, and I guess you never rescinded my invite," he said in way of an explanation for his sudden appearance in her kitchen.

Smooth, man. Real smooth.

Emma glanced over at her front door in surprise, confusion spreading across her features. "I didn't lock it?"

He shook his head. "No, you must've forgot."

She lifted a hand toward him, but then lowered it again.

"Why are you here, Nik?" Her expression remained neutral, gave nothing away.

He cleared his throat again, shifting his weight. "Um. Yeah. About that. I should've just called you instead of barging in like this, I know. I meant to. I really did. But, then, I just found myself here, outside your house. I was going to leave, and I did. The last time. But then I came back today. And I was about to leave again. But I saw you pull up and walk inside, and I just... didn't." He was rambling, but couldn't seem to stop himself.

"How long have you been here?" she asked him quietly.

"A while." His voice was husky with emotion. He'd been here every night for the last week.

Watching her leave him had been the hardest thing he'd ever done. And not just because of his vampire instincts to protect his mate.

He missed her. More than he ever imagined he would.

They faced off across the small space between them, until Emma broke the tense silence. "Have you heard anything about Keira? Or your brother?"

"Oh, yeah! Keira!" Nik snapped his fingers as he suddenly remembered the reason he was there.

Emma took a hesitant step forward. "What about Keira?"

Nik held up his hands, fending off her questions. "We found her, and she's fine. That's what I wanted to tell you. She and my brother are…ah…working things out," he finished lamely.

He heard her heart stutter, right before it began to pound.

"You found my sister?"

He smiled at the cautious joy on her face. "Yes. She's okay. She's with Luukas."

"What does that mean, exactly? Where is she?" Emma asked with a frown.

"She's back at the apartments. Luuk is in really bad shape, Em. Something seems to have snapped in there." He tapped the side of his head with his finger.

As her eyes creased with worry, he quickly tried to reassure her. "But, Keira…she seems to help him. She calms him, somehow. I don't know." He shrugged.

Emma searched behind her blindly for a chair as she started to sit down, and Nik shoved one beneath her just in time. He also sat. When she looked at him again, her eyes were large and shiny with unshed tears. "Are you all right?"

He couldn't quite hold back his smile at her concern. "I'm good."

"How did you find them?"

"They showed up in the same place we took you. Our sources were correct about them coming back there. We just showed up a few days early. It all went as planned, but Aiden got taken. I need to find him."

"Leeha?"

He nodded. "She ran when we found her, and took Aiden with her."

"The wolves?"

"They were there, also. They're fine. They found Marc, their friend they were looking for."

"Oh, good."

Then she frowned. "Why hasn't Keira called me?"

Nik scratched his head while he thought of how to word his answer. "She was a little...tied up for a while with Luukas. And he destroyed all of the phones in the apartment, which is why she asked me to let you know she was okay. She wanted me to tell you she'd be in touch as soon as she could, but for you not to worry. And she can't wait to see you."

"Oh, okay. Thank you." She pulled her robe tighter.

With everything having been said, the tension in the air gradually thickened. Nik fidgeted, glancing up at her, but didn't know what to say or do to bridge the gap between them.

367

His blood hummed through his veins, every cell in his body aching for her. For her smile. For her touch. Even just the sound of her voice or the feel of her eyes on him.

It's better this way. I should just go, Nik thought. Picking up his hoodie from the back of the chair where he'd dropped it, he stood and prepared to leave.

Emma stood also. "Are you thirsty?" she blurted.

Nik paused with his arm midway through the sleeve, his fangs punching down and his mouth salivating at her words. Clenching his jaw, he resumed his movements. She didn't know what she was saying. She didn't remember anything that happened between them, thanks to him.

"I'm good. Thank you."

He zipped up his coat, but when he went to move past her, she stopped him with a hand on his chest.

"Nikulas. Are you thirsty?" she persisted. "You don't look well."

His body hardened immediately at her touch. Her hand was like a branding iron, scorching his skin even through his clothing, as her sweet scent seared his lungs.

His fangs, and his heart, ached at her offer. "I'll be fine, Em," he managed to get out. "Thank you."

He tried to go, but her small hand was like a wall, holding him there.

She searched his face. "Nik, please talk to me. Is something wrong? Are you sick?"

"I don't need your pity, Emma."

"It's not pity!" she threw back at him, dropping her hand. "I care about you! I want you to be happy, and healthy! I want you to—" Her mouth snapped shut with an audible 'click'.

"Nik, please. Is there anything I can do?"

His eyes flew to the pulse at her throat. He could smell her blood, just beneath the surface. Grinding his teeth, he drew his will power around him like a shield. "Take care, Emma." Squeezing past her, he pulled the door open and let the screen slam behind him.

"Nikulas!" Emma ran out after him into the cool night air. "Please don't vamp off into the night on me." Her voice was thick with unshed tears. "Please, stay."

He stopped walking, but didn't turn around. "It's better this way, Em. Please don't torture yourself worrying about me. It's okay. Really. It is." He started walking again. "Take care of yourself."

He heard her footsteps behind him. "I love you!" she yelled.

Nik pulled up short halfway across the yard. He couldn't have heard her correctly. He'd erased any intimate memories of him.

His back still to her, he turned his head to the side so she could hear him. "What did you just say?"

49

Emma stood barefoot in the soft grass of her front yard, shocked at what had just come out of her mouth, but unable to take it back. She wished he'd turn around so she could see his face. Was he laughing at her? Angry at her? Or was he hurting too?

Oh, what the hell. Just tell him. What have I got to lose? She let her hand fall back down to her side. "I said, I love you. I don't want you to leave. I want you to stay. Here. With me." She wished she could think of something more eloquent, but that was about the gist of it.

She held her breath as she waited to see what he would do.

Nik spun around on his heel to face her, and Emma had to take a step back as she was hit full force with a desperate wanting. The sensation slammed into her, feeding her own need, and she realized, somehow, it had come from Nik. Steeling her spine, she stepped forward again. Twisting her hands in front of him, she searched his face.

His expression was open, honest...nervous.

She wished he would take her back inside and straight up her bedroom, where she could properly show him how much she'd missed him.

When he didn't respond, Emma felt a single tear roll down her cheek. She wasn't imagining this...thing between them. She knew him. Somehow, she knew him. "Nikulas?"

Nik struggled to hold himself in check as his emotions, too many emotions, washed through him. Happiness. Doubt. Guilt. Hope. Hunger.

"Nikulas?"

Haltingly, he took a step toward her. Then another. And another. Picking up speed until he was so close she had to crane her neck back to see him.

His hands shook with barely controlled restraint as he raised them to cup her face, his eyes roving lovingly over her features. "Do you mean it, Em? Don't say it if you don't. Please, don't... don't say it if you don't really mean it."

Emma wrapped her hands around his wrists, holding his hands to her face as another tear slid down her cheek to disappear under his palm. "I've been so miserable since I left. I told myself it was because I was worried about my sister, but it wasn't just that. I've missed you so much, Nik." Her face crumpled as she began to cry in earnest. "Please, stay with me. Tell me I'm not imagining this. Tell me you feel it, too. Tell me..." She dwindled off, her eyes telling him everything she couldn't say.

"Shhhh." Nik wiped her tears away with his thumbs. He felt the truth of her words flow through him, her emotions twisting and twining with his own. Not as strong as before since it had been so long since they'd been together, but still there.

He pressed a soft kiss to her nose, her soft cheeks, and finally her mouth. His entire body shuddered at the feel of her beneath his lips, and he felt her own body tremble in response.

There was no fucking way he could put into words the extent his body—and his soul—had craved her these last two weeks. She was his entire world now. Being away from her for so long had thrown him into a place worse than hell. He couldn't feed, couldn't sleep, couldn't even concentrate on what he needed to do to get Aiden back. All he'd thought about was Emma.

Breaking off the kiss, he pressed his forehead to hers. "I've missed you, too. So much, Em. You're not imagining things. Of course, I'll stay with you. Where else would I go?"

Fresh tears welled in her eyes. Happy tears this time, he hoped. Her smile widened to match his as he wrapped his arms around her, lifting her feet off of the ground. Squeezing her so hard she gasped for breath, he planted a sound kiss right on her mouth. Her laughter was the sweetest thing he'd ever heard.

Sliding one hand under her pert ass, Nik lifted her up until she wrapped her legs around his waist. Sliding his other hand to the back of her neck, he tucked her face into the curve of his neck and shoulder as she wrapped her arms tightly around his neck. He needed to get them inside, and quickly, before he took her outside on the ground like an animal.

A low growl rumbled deep in his throat as he felt her soft lips kiss the skin on his neck, and he strode determinedly back to the house as quickly as he could.

He would tell her what he'd done. He would bring her memories back, and hope and pray she didn't hate him for it.

Later.

"You feel so cold," she murmured against his skin.

"'Cold' is the exact opposite of what I'm feeling right now, sweetheart."

Taking the stairs two at a time at supernatural speed, he took her straight up to her bedroom and carefully laid her down on the quilt, then lowered himself between her legs. Her robe fell open and he tugged at her nightshirt until she was bare to him. He rolled his hips, hoping his jeans weren't too rough on her. But damn if he could tear himself away long enough to take them off.

Emma welcomed his weight with open arms. She wrapped her limbs around him and slid her fingers into his hair as he dropped his head down and took her mouth with all of the hunger he was feeling.

She gasped, and he took the opportunity to thrust his tongue inside, beginning a rhythm that matched the rolling of his hips. Emma allowed him take control, opening to him completely.

Nik moaned as the scent of her desire wafted through the air to mingle with the sweetness of her blood. She arched into him, pressing as close as she could. His cock throbbed, fighting the confinement of his jeans as he pushed his swollen member into her softness, over and over, until he thought he lose his fucking shit if he wasn't inside of her.

Emma moaned, and worked her hands between them to fumble at his clothes, but he grabbed her wrists and held them on either side of her head as his mouth wandered across her jaw and down her neck.

If he allowed her to touch him, he would lose control.

Nik paused at her throat and inhaled deeply, breathing in the scent of her skin, her blood, the very essence of her.

To his surprise, she tilted her head to give him better access. But he just kissed the tender skin softly and kept going, kissing his way across her collarbone and down her chest until her shirt got in the way.

He couldn't feed from her. Not until she remembered.

Releasing one wrist, he lifted himself just enough to get his hand between them, took a fistful of the offensive material and yanked. It tore down the middle, exposing her to his heated gaze, but it wasn't enough. So, he reared up and sat on his heels, put a hand behind her neck and sat her up with him, then removed the ruined nightshirt and her old, ratty robe out from under her.

He lowered her back to the bed, but remained sitting, watching her beautiful breasts rise and fall with her heavy breaths, her pink nipples puckering for him prettily.

Her skin was flushed, causing her scars to stand out in stark relief. At the sight, his mouth pulled back in a snarl, exposing his long fangs. He wished he could kill those things all over again.

Emma's hands gripped the quilt, no doubt wanting to cover herself, and hide her scars, but he slowly shook his head at her in warning. He would not be denied the right to look his fill after so long apart from her.

He pulled his shirt and hoodie up and off in one smooth movement. The ropes of muscle across his stomach tightened and released with need as he ran his eyes from her breasts, down her soft belly, to her slick folds spread wide and glistening before him.

Nik ran his tongue over his bottom lip, imagining the taste of her, then reached out with one hand and laid it flat between her hip bones as his thumb slid down, dipped into her moisture, then found her hard nub and rubbed it slowly. His eyes never left the erotic view of her spread out before him as he slid his other hand down the front of jeans, cupping the hard bulge there and squeezing slightly, before undoing the button on his waistline and slowly pulling the zipper down.

Emma stopped breathing as she watched him take his thick length in his own hand, her attention torn between what he was doing to her and the sight of him sliding his hand up and down his cock. He watched her watch him, and a bead of moisture appearing at the tip. Nik groaned, squeezing the base tight until he gained control again.

He rubbed her faster with his thumb, and under his hand he felt the muscles low in her belly tightening, surging, and easing again. She strained against him as he worked her body, and his eyes flew to her face to watch her as she came.

"Nikulas!" Her eyes flew up to his as she came fast and hard, her back arching with the power of it, her hands clenching the comforter like a lifeline.

Nik's lips pulled away from his aching fangs as he watched her, his cock throbbing for release in his hand.

He wasn't done with her yet. But before he would let himself go any further, she needed to know the truth.

"Emma, sweetheart."

Her eyes slowly flickered open, and she smiled.

Nik's heart fluttered in his chest. If he lost her now, it would be the end of him, and not because he needed her blood to survive. But he couldn't go on deceiving her. Not now. Not like this.

"Emma, I need to tell you something."

The smile faltered, became confused, before it fell from her face completely. "What is it? Tell me," she insisted.

"I'm scared," he whispered.

She sat up until they were nearly face to face, and touched his cheek as her eyes traveled over his face. "Nik, you're scaring *me*."

"I don't want to lose you." He could barely say the words.

"Just tell me." Her small hand gripped the back of his neck, allowing him no escape.

His body shuttered with need, but he had to tell her. She deserved to know. "I did something to you. Before you left. Something I promised I would never do."

To her credit, she didn't pull away. "What did you do?"

Gathering his courage, he forced the confession from his soul. "I fucked with your head. I changed your memories. Not all of them, but...some. Enough."

She studied him a moment. "Why?"

"Because I needed you safe, and I wanted to give you a chance."

"A chance at what?"

"A chance to live your life."

She looked away, and her hand fell to the bed between them. "A life without you, you mean."

"Yes," he whispered.

When she looked at him again, her mouth was set in a hard line. "Don't you think that should've been my choice?"

He gave her a small smile. "Perhaps."

She fiddled with a loose thread on the quilt. "Can you give them back?"

Nik frowned. "Your memories?"

"Yes. I want them back."

And that's what he was afraid of. His heart sank to his stomach. "Yes."

"Then do it. Now."

"Okay." Nik tenderly brushed her bright hair away from her eyes. Taking her face between his palms, he held her gaze with his and sank into the depths of her mind.

"Remember everything I told you to forget."

50

Emma cried out as her memories, and the emotions they held, came crashing back. For a few seconds, it was all too much.

Fear, shame, sorrow, lust, anger, happiness...love.

The kitchen. His shower. The RV. The clearing after the fight, when he took her like a man possessed. And where they shared blood.

Her sister.

My sister!

Screaming as she tightened her fingers around the monster's throat.

The witch is MINE.

It's okay, honey. Go with Nik. I'll be out in a bit.

I probably saved your fucking LIFE!

Nikulas watched her. His jaw was clenched and his blue eyes were darker than she'd ever seen them. But beneath it all, she saw his fear. Fear of losing her.

"Oh, my God. Nikulas." Emma gripped his shoulders, recollections of their time together jumbling together in her head. She felt like she was losing her mind, but eventually, they sorted themselves out and fell into a kind of order.

She remembered. She remembered everything. A sob escaped her as she felt everything they'd experienced all at once.

Her eyes flew to his. "My sister. She's really okay?"

He nodded. "She is. She's with Luukas. He won't hurt her. I wasn't wrong about that."

She blinked away tears and stared at the male before her, and really saw him this time. "Nik! You need to feed! You need to feed from me."

He frowned. "You're not angry at me?"

"I am. A little." She paused before admitting, "But I understand why you did what you did."

He took her hand in his, and kissed her knuckles before pressing her palm to his chest. His eyes pleaded with her to believe him. "Luukas was unpredictable. He still is, a bit, although he's improving. But sweetheart, if you'd tried to come between him and Keira—"

"He would've torn me apart like you did to the creatures that attacked me," she finished for him.

"Yes," he breathed.

She edged closer to him. "Nikulas, *I love you*. I want to be with you. There's nothing I want more. Even without my memories of us, I knew that."

"I'm so sorry," he told her.

"I know." She sniffed, and her eyes dropped to his cock, still thick and hard between them. Desire for him rushed through her anew. "You might just have to make it up to me, though."

He grinned and moved in to kiss her.

Emma stopped him with a hand over his mouth. "And if you ever do that to me again, Nikulas, I won't forgive you next time."

He mumbled something behind her hand, and kissed her palm.

Emma smiled and removed her hand.

Hopping off the bed, he quickly shed his pants and shoes, returning before she'd had a chance to miss him. He lay down and pulled her down alongside him.

Emma felt every inch of him as he took her wrists in one hand, kissed the pulse there, and lifted them above her head, pressing them down into the mattress. With his other hand, he held her jaw, turning her face to him for a kiss.

She moaned as he took her mouth. She could feel his throbbing length against her hip, but when she tried to turn toward him, he moved his hand from her jaw to her hip, holding her in place.

She whimpered in protest, but he just smiled against her mouth.

Then suddenly, he released her wrists and rolled onto his back, pulling her on top of him. One hand on the back of her head and one on her lower back, he pressed the hard length of him into her belly, growling low in her ear.

Emma pulled her legs up to either side until she was straddling his lean hips. Lifting up, she ran his length through the slick folds of her pussy. The ropes of muscle in his stomach clenched, and his cock jerked beneath her, weeping drops of semen. As she did it again, he shuddered underneath her.

"Stop. Before I come too soon."

He pulled her to him until they were nose to nose. She watched his eyes glow bright with desire as he told her, "When I come, I'm going to be deep inside of you, Em. I want to feel your tight warmth gripping me, pulsing around me, when I do. But I want to taste you first."

Emma moaned as she felt a flood of moisture between her legs. She caught a flash of his fangs as he lowered his head to her neck, and a small sound escaped her as he pressed his mouth to the skin over her artery. But still, he didn't bite her.

Instead, he worked his way down to her aching breasts, his hands lifting her as he fastened his mouth over one throbbing nipple. Sucking it into his mouth, he teased it with his tongue before sucking hard. Then he released it to do the same to the other side.

Lifting her higher, he kissed his way down her belly, hitting each and every ragged piece of skin, until he reached the soft, red curls at the apex of her thighs.

Emma gripped the top her headboard as Nik lifted her above his mouth. At his urging, she spread her legs, placing a knee on each side of his head. She looked down and gasped as his fiery blue eyes met hers. Nose in her curls, he inhaled deeply, growling low in his throat.

Emma's belly clenched as she felt another rush of wetness in response.

Nik reached up and ran his hands up over her breasts, kneading them in his large palms, before gripping her hips and placing her over his mouth. She lurched uncontrollably when she felt his warm tongue, but his grip tightened on her hips to hold her still as he ran his tongue over her, his eyes closing as he settled in.

Emma's head fell back as he found her clitoris, and flicked it with his tongue. Moving her hips in unison with his movements, the tension in her belly returned. Desire flooded through her where he manipulated her with his mouth, spreading through her body before centering in her core.

Emma began to tremble uncontrollably, her muscles straining toward her orgasm. She hovered on the brink, until with a growl, Nik sucked her throbbing nub into his mouth and bit down, piercing her with his fangs. She cried out as the pain mixed with pleasure and sent her crashing over the edge.

His fingers dug into her hips to hold her to his mouth as her body convulsed above him.

51

Nik's eyes rolled back in his head as the sweetness of her blood mixed with the muskiness of her sex to flood his mouth and throat. He continued to suck her off as she bucked above him, his cock jerking with every cry.

Unable to wait any longer, he lifted her away from his mouth and moved her down the length of him. Bending his knees to meet her, he was deep inside of her with one strong thrust, his own cry of pleasure joining hers at the feel of her tight grip around him.

One hand on her hip, he used the other one to grip the back of her neck, and pulled her down to his throbbing fangs. Sliding out of her, he thrust back in at the same time his fangs sank deep into her nape. With a deep pull, he growled as her blood rushed down his throat, healing him and exciting him, filling him with her lifeblood as he filled her.

With strength flooding through him, he sat up and flipped her over, and sank his fangs into her again.

Then Nik allowed the hunger to overtake him.

There was no gentleness as he took her, just an overwhelming need to consume her, body and soul.

Emma cried out beneath him as another orgasm hit her, pulling him over the edge with her. Releasing her neck, he threw his head back with a roar as he exploded inside of her, her pulsing sheath squeezing every last drop from him.

Head thrown back, fangs bared, muscle straining, Nik gave himself over completely to her.

Her hands roamed limply over his chest and arms as he lowered his head and closed the wound in her neck, and he thought he'd never get enough of the feel of her touching him.

Collapsing on top of her, he rolled to the side, pulled her with him and held her close. For a long time, the only sound was their ragged breathing as they lay curled around each other.

Running his hand over her bright hair and down her soft back, Nik asked, "Did I hurt you?"

Emma pulled back a bit and looked up at him with heavy lids, her lips curving up happily. "No. I'm fine. Truly. Just a bit sleepy."

Nik took in her tired features. She looked even paler than before, if that was possible, even after all their exertion just now. "Here. Drink from me, Em. It'll make you feel better." He paused. "And, because I'd like you to. I want you to be with me. Completely. And for a long, long time."

"Okay." She smiled a little. "But only if you promise to do *that* again."

Chuckling, he lifted his wrist to his mouth, efficiently opening a vein. He offered it to her, and watched her drink from him. A strong feeling of contentment washed over him as she raised her hand and held him to her mouth.

This was right. This was how it should be.

He let her drink a little more than she should have, enjoying the sound of her soft moans, watching the color come back into her face. Her eyes popped open as he started to pull his arm away, her brows lowering in a frown of displeasure. "That's enough, Em. You need to leave me some, ya know." He smiled as her eyes widened and she immediately let go of him.

"Sorry," she mumbled, licking her lips.

He could practically see his blood rushing through her system, chasing away the fatigue, tickling her nerve endings, heating her blood.

She reached down and wrapped her small hand around him, licking her lips again as he grew in her hand. He rolled his hips toward her as she ran her hand up and down his length, and she gasped as he swelled to his full size, her fingers unable to reach completely around him.

Desire and deep need shone from her eyes when she looked up at him, and he knew the same reflected back to her from his.

"Nikulas," she pleaded.

Nik ran his hand up the outside of her thigh and over her rounded ass, dipping his hand between her legs from behind. She was wet and ready for him. With a helpless moan, he rolled her beneath him. Sliding an arm under her leg, he entered her with one long, smooth thrust.

L.E. WILSON

His Emma didn't need to ask twice.

52

Nik cracked his eyes open and squinted at the clock next to the bed. It was almost dawn. He groaned and pulled Emma in closer to him.

"We're never going to leave this bed again, are we?" she teased. Her voice was husky from the cries he'd wrung from her throughout the night. They'd spent the night re-learning each other, until Emma was so exhausted, even his blood couldn't keep her eyes from sliding closed.

Nik sighed against her back. "Unfortunately, we're going to have to. Well, at least I am. The sun will be up soon, and you don't have any shades over your windows."

Emma frowned as she squinted at the windows. "I'm going to have to order some."

He dropped a kiss on her shoulder, then Nik rolled over and flicked on the bedside lamp. He needed a shower, and he planned on sharing it.

Gazing over his shoulder at his lovely mate, he caught her pulling the quilt up to cover herself. She'd dragged it with her every time she'd gotten up during the night, and he was losing his patience.

"Don't do that," he commanded harshly.

Emma's eyes flew up . "Nik...I..."

He stood and stalked over to her side of the bed, pulling her up with him. He took the comforter from her, leaving her as naked as he was. Gently pushing her along in front of him, he ignored her protests and walked her into the bathroom.

Flicking on the light, he turned her so she faced the mirror and he was standing behind her. The top of her head barely came up to his shoulder.

Emma kept her eyes down. "Nik, please don't do this," she whispered.

When she tried to leave, he wrapped his hands carefully around her upper arms and held her in front of him. "First of all, don't *ever* hide yourself from me again. I love looking at you."

Still refusing to look up, Emma scoffed. "You can't mean that."

"That's where you're wrong, sweetheart. I've never meant anything more. Look in the mirror, Em." When she refused, he shook her slightly. "Look in the mirror, Emma."

Sighing heavily, she raised her eyes and visibly cringed.

Nik gave her a second to take a good look. "Do you know what I see in that mirror? I don't see a woman who is flawed, or imperfect. I see a strong woman. A woman who defended herself. A woman who fought for her survival against all the odds and won. A woman who never gave up on finding her sister. A woman who didn't crumble under pressure. A woman who took meeting *me*, a vampire, in stride." He caught her eyes with his in the mirror. "That woman makes me proud. That woman is a warrior. That woman is amazing. That woman is sexy as all hell. That woman is the most beautiful and precious thing I've ever laid eyes on. *That* woman, Em, is YOU."

"Don't ever hide yourself from me," he said softly. "I couldn't stand it. I love you. All of you. I only wish I'd been there to protect you." Lowering his head, he wrapped his arms around her and whispered in her ear, "I'll never let anything like that happen to you again. I swear it."

Emma turned in his arms, and this time he let her. Wrapping her arms around his lean waist, she told him, "I love you, too. And I'm going to hold you to that."

He hugged her to him, letting himself enjoy the moment, then ran his hands up and down her back. "Come on, woman, we need to get a shower. Then I need to find a place to hole up for the day. After I call to secure our flight back to Seattle."

"I have a cellar, you can stay down there—" she began. "Wait. Seattle?"

With one last hug and a kiss on her adorable nose, he reached over to start the shower. "Yeah. I have to get back. And you're coming with me."

Joy lit up her face. "Okay."

When the water was warm enough, Nik turned back to her with a grin. "So, we still have about an hour before the sun comes up," he said, running his eyes up and down her lithe body.

Emma turned to walk away. "I'd better get packing then. Is it cold in Seattle?"

She squealed as Nik grabbed her with one arm from behind, dragging her under the hot water with him. Bending down, he nibbled on the side of her neck before breathing in her scent. "Oh no, you don't. You're not running away from me again."

"Never."

With a groan, he pierced the supple skin of her throat. And as her sweet blood filled him and she wrapped her slender arms around his neck on a sigh, Nik sank into his female.

And knew his life was only beginning.

Thank you for reading! I hope you loved meeting Nik and Emma. The next book in the Deathless Night series is
<u>A Vampire's Vengeance</u>
Find out if Luukas's instinct to love and protect Keira is stronger than his urge to kill the witch who broke him.

ABOUT THE AUTHOR

L.E. Wilson writes romance starring intense alpha males and the women who are fearless enough to love them just as they are. In her novels you'll find smoking hot scenes, a touch of suspense, some humor, a bit of gore, and multifaceted characters, all working together to combine her lifelong obsession with the paranormal and her love of romance.

Her writing career came about the usual way: on a dare from her loving husband. Little did she know just one casual suggestion would open a box of worms (or words as the case may be) that would forever change her life.

On a Personal Note:

"I love to hear from my readers! Contact me anytime at le@lewilsonauthor.com."